The
Last
Runaway

The Last Runaway

TRACY CHEVALIER

DUTTON

10/13
gift

Che

DUTTON
Published by Penguin Group (USA) Inc.
375 Hudson Street, New York, New York 10014, USA

Penguin Group (Canada), 90 Eglinton Avenue East, Suite 700, Toronto, Ontario M4P 2Y3, Canada (a division of Pearson Penguin Canada Inc.); Penguin Books Ltd, 80 Strand, London WC2R 0RL, England; Penguin Ireland, 25 St Stephen's Green, Dublin 2, Ireland (a division of Penguin Books Ltd); Penguin Group (Australia), 707 Collins St., Melbourne, Victoria 3008, Australia (a division of Pearson Australia Group Pty Ltd); Penguin Books India Pvt Ltd, 11 Community Centre, Panchsheel Park, New Delhi–110 017, India; Penguin Group (NZ), 67 Apollo Drive, Rosedale, Auckland 0632, New Zealand (a division of Pearson New Zealand Ltd); Penguin Books, Rosebank Office Park, 181 Jan Smuts Avenue, Parktown North 2193, South Africa; Penguin China, B7 Jiaming Center, 27 East Third Ring Road North, Chaoyang District, Beijing 100020, China

Penguin Books Ltd, Registered Offices: 80 Strand, London WC2R 0RL, England

Published by Dutton, a member of Penguin Group (USA) Inc.

First printing, January 2013
2 4 6 8 10 9 7 5 3 1

REGISTERED TRADEMARK—MARCA REGISTRADA

LIBRARY OF CONGRESS CATALOGING-IN-PUBLICATION DATA
has been applied for.

ISBN 978-0-525-95299-2

ISBN 978-0-525-95393-7 (export edition)

Printed in the United States of America
Designed by Nancy Resnick
Poster image on page 43 by Terence Caven

PUBLISHER'S NOTE
This book is a work of fiction. Names, characters, places, and incidents either are the product of the author's imagination or are used fictitiously, and any resemblance to actual persons, living or dead, business establishments, events, or locales is entirely coincidental.

This book is dedicated to Catoctin Quaker Camp and Oberlin College: two places that shaped and guided my younger self

The
Last
Runaway

Horizon

 SHE COULD NOT go back. When Honor Bright abruptly announced to her family that she would accompany her sister Grace to America—when she sorted through her belongings, keeping only the most necessary, when she gave away all of her quilts, when she said good-bye to her uncles and aunts, and kissed her cousins and nieces and nephews, when she got into the coach that would take them from Bridport, when she and Grace linked arms and walked up the gangplank at Bristol—she did all of these things with the unspoken thought: I can always come back. Layered beneath those words, however, was the suspicion that the moment her feet left English soil, Honor's life would be permanently altered.

At least the idea of returning drew the sting from her actions in the weeks leading up to their departure, like the pinch of sugar secretly added to a sauce to tame its acid. It allowed her to remain calm, and not cry as her friend Biddy did when Honor gave her the quilt she had just finished: a patchwork of brown, yellow and cream diamonds pieced into an eight-point Star of Bethlehem, then quilted with harps and the running feather border she was known for. The community had given her a signature quilt—each square made and signed by a different friend or family member—and there was not room for both quilts in her trunk. The signature quilt was not so well made as her own, but of course she must take it. "'Tis best left with thee, to remember me by," she insisted as her weeping friend tried to push the Star of Bethlehem quilt back at her. "I will make more quilts in Ohio."

Jumping over thoughts of the journey itself, Honor tried to fix her mind instead on its end at the clapboard house her future brother-in-law had sketched for Grace in his letters from Ohio. "It is a solid house, even if not of the stone thee is accustomed to," Adam Cox had written. "Most houses here are made of wood. Only when a family is established and unlikely to move do they build a brick house.

"It is situated at the end of Main Street on the edge of the town," he had continued. "Faithwell is still small, with fifteen families of Friends. But it will grow, by the grace of God. My brother's shop is in Oberlin, a larger town three miles away. He and I hope to move it when Faithwell has grown large enough to support a draper's. Here we call it 'dry goods.' There are many new words to learn in America."

Honor could not imagine living in a house made of wood, that burned so quickly, warped easily, creaked and groaned and gave no feeling of permanence the way brick or stone did.

Though she tried to keep her worries confined to the notion of living in a wooden house, she could not stop her mind straying to thoughts of the voyage on the *Adventurer*, the ship that would take them across the Atlantic. Honor was familiar with ships, as any Bridport resident would be. She sometimes accompanied her father to the harbor when a shipment of hemp arrived. She had even gone on board, and watched the sailors furling sails and coiling ropes and mopping decks. But she had never set sail in one. Once when she was ten her father took them to nearby Eype for the day, and Honor and Grace and her brothers had gone out in a rowboat. Grace had loved being on the water, and had shrieked and laughed and pretended to fall in. Honor, however, had gripped the side of the boat while her brothers rowed and tried not to appear alarmed at the rocking, and the curious and unpleasant sensation of no longer having stable footing. She had watched her mother walking up and down the beach in her dark dress and white bonnet, waiting for her children to come back safely. Honor avoided going out in a boat again.

She had heard stories of bad crossings but hoped she would cope with such a thing as she did any other hardship, with steady patience. But she did not have sea legs. That was what the sailors said. Perhaps she should have realized this from her encounter with water under her feet in the rowboat. After leaving Bristol she stood on deck with Grace and others, watching the Somerset and north Devon coast unfold alongside them. For the other passengers the unsteadiness was an amusing novelty, but Honor grew more and more unsettled, responding to the ship's movement with a wrinkled brow, tightening shoulders and a heaviness deep in her gut, as if she had swallowed an iron pound weight. She held out as long as she could, but as the *Adventurer* was passing Lundy Island, Honor's stomach finally convulsed and she vomited onto the deck. A passing sailor laughed. "Sick and we're barely out of Bristol Channel!" he crowed. "Wait till we reach the ocean. *Then* you'll know sickness!"

Honor was sick down Grace's shoulder, onto her blankets, onto the floor of their tiny cabin, into an enamel basin. She threw up when there was nothing left to bring up, her body like a magician managing to conjure something from nothing. She did not feel better after each bout. When they reached the Atlantic and the ship began its long roll up and down the swell of the waves, she continued to be sick. Only now Grace was ill too, as well as many of the other passengers, though only for a time, until they got used to the new rhythm of the boat. Honor never got used to it; the nausea did not leave her for the whole month-long voyage.

When not seasick herself, Grace nursed Honor, rinsing her sheets, emptying the basin, bringing broth and hard sea biscuit, reading to her from the Bible or the few books they had brought: *Mansfield Park*, *The Old Curiosity Shop*, *Martin Chuzzlewit*. To distract Honor she chattered on about America, trying to get her to think about what lay ahead rather than the grimness of the present moment. "What would thee rather see, a bear or a wolf?" she asked, then answered her own question. "A bear, I think, for wolves are like overgrown dogs, but a bear is only like itself. What would thee rather travel on: a steamboat or a train?"

Honor groaned at the thought of another boat. "Yes, a train," Grace agreed. "I wish there were a train we could take from New York to Ohio. There will be one day. Oh, Honor, imagine: soon we will be in New York!"

Honor grimaced, wishing that she too could see this move as the great adventure Grace clearly did. Her sister had always been the restless Bright, the one most ready to accompany their father when he had to travel to Bristol or Portsmouth or London. She had even agreed to marry an older, duller man because of the promise he held out of a life away from Bridport. Grace had known the Coxes, a family of five brothers, since they had moved from Exeter several years before to open a draper's shop, but she only showed interest in Adam when he decided to emigrate to Ohio. A brother—Matthew—had already gone there but had become infirm, and his wife had written to ask a spare brother to come and help with the business. Once

Adam had moved to America, he and Grace corresponded regularly, and with gentle hints she led him to ask her to join him in Ohio as his wife, where they would run the shop with Matthew and Abigail.

The Brights were surprised by Grace's choice; Honor had thought she would marry someone livelier. But Grace was so thrilled by the prospect of living in America that she did not seem to mind her prospective husband's reserve.

Though patient, and perhaps feeling guilty for subjecting her sister to weeks of seasickness, even Grace grew irritated by Honor's persistent illness. After a few days she stopped urging her to eat, as Honor never kept anything down for more than a few minutes. She began to leave her sister alone in their cabin to walk on deck and sit and sew and chat with the other women on board.

Honor tried to accompany Grace to a Meeting for Divine Worship organized by the handful of other Friends on board, but as she sat in silence with them in a small cabin, she could not let go of her thoughts enough to empty her mind, worrying that if she did so, she might lose what little self-control she had and vomit in front of them. Soon the rocking of the ship and the upheaval in her stomach forced her to leave the cabin.

Sometimes on the fraught voyage between Bristol and New York, when she was curled like a shrimp in her cramped berth or doubled over a chamber pot, Honor thought of her mother standing on the pebbles at Eype beach in her white bonnet, and wondered why she had left the safety of her parents' house.

She knew why: Grace had asked her, hoping a new life would quell her sister's heartache. Honor had been jilted and, though her spirit was less adventurous, the prospect of remaining in a community that pitied her propelled her into following Grace. She had never been dissatisfied in Bridport, but once Samuel had released her from their engagement, she was as eager as Grace to leave.

All of her clothes stank with a sour meatiness no washing could remove. Honor avoided the other passengers, and even her sister: she couldn't bear the disgust mixed with pity in their faces. Instead she found a space between two barrels on the leeward deck where she tucked herself out of the way of busy sailors and curious passengers, but close enough to the railing that she could run across and heave into the water without drawing attention. She remained on deck even in the rain and the cold, preferring it to the tiny cabin with its hard board for a bed and the close stench of her blankets. She was, however, indifferent to the seascape—the huge sky and sea that were such a contrast to the neat green hills and hedgerows of Dorset. While others were amazed and entertained by the storm clouds and rainbows and sunlight turning the water to silver, by schools of dolphins following the ship, by the sight of the tail of a whale, for Honor monotony and nausea struck dead any wonder she might have felt for such feats of nature.

When not leaning over the railing, she tried to take her mind off her sore, churning stomach by bringing out her patchwork. As a gift for the journey her mother had cut out hundreds of yellow and cream cloth hexagons and paper templates for Honor to sew into rosettes. She had hoped she might complete a whole grandmother's garden quilt during the voyage, but the swaying of the deck made it impossible for her to establish a steady rhythm in which to make the neat, tiny stitches that were her trademark. Even the simplest task of tacking the hexagons onto the templates with loose stitches—the first sewing Honor had learned as a young girl— required more concentration than the movement of the ocean allowed. It soon became clear that whatever cloth she worked with would be forever tainted with nausea, or the idea of it, which was much the same thing. After a few days of trying to sew the rosettes, Honor waited until no one was about, then dropped the hexagons overboard—they would make her sick if she ever saw that fabric again. It was a shocking waste of precious cloth, and she knew she should have given them to Grace or other women on board, but she was ashamed of the smell that lingered on them, and of her weakness. Watching the bits of cloth flutter down to the water and disappear, Honor felt her stomach grow calm for just a moment.

"Look at the horizon," a sailor commanded one day after witnessing her dry heaves. "Get up the bow and keep your eyes on where we headed. Pay no mind to the humping and bumping, the rocking and the rolling. Watch what don't move. Then your stomach'll settle."

Honor nodded, though she knew it would not work, as she had already tried it. She had tried everything anyone suggested: ginger, a hot water bottle on her feet, a bag of ice on her neck. Now she studied the sailor out of the corner of her eye, for she had never seen a black man up close before. None lived in Bridport, and when she visited Bristol once, she'd seen a black coachman drive past, but he was gone before she could take him in properly. Honor eyed the man's skin: it was the color of a conker from a horse chestnut tree, though rough and wind-burned rather than smooth and shiny. He made her think of an apple that has ripened to a deep, rich red on the tree while its neighbors remain pale green. His accent was untraceable, from everywhere and nowhere.

The sailor was studying her too. Perhaps he had not seen many Quakers before, or he was curious what she looked like when her face was not ragged with nausea. Normally Honor's forehead was smooth, punctuated with eyebrows like wings over wide gray eyes. Her seasickness, however, etched lines where there had been none, and pinched the calm beauty from her face.

"The sky is so big it frightens me," she said, surprising herself by speaking.

"Better get used to that. Everything's big where you headed.

Why you going to America, then? Going to find you a husband? Englishmen not good enough for you?"

No, she thought. They are not. "I am accompanying my sister," she answered. "She is marrying a man in Ohio."

"Ohio!" The sailor snorted. "Stick to the coast, love. Don't go nowhere you can't smell the sea, that's what I say. You'll get trapped out there in all them woods. Oh, there she goes." He stepped back as Honor leaned over the railing once again.

The captain of the *Adventurer* said it was the smoothest, quickest crossing the ship had ever made across the Atlantic. This knowledge only tormented Honor. After thirty days at sea she stumbled, skeletal, onto the docks at New York, feeling she had vomited out every bit of her insides so that only a shell of her remained. To her horror, the ground heaved and bucked as much as the ship's deck had, and she threw up one last time.

She knew then that if she couldn't cope with the easiest crossing God could give her, she would never be able to go back to England. While Grace knelt on the docks and thanked God for reaching America, Honor began to cry, for England and her old life. An impossible ocean now lay between her and home. She could not go back.

My dear Mother and Father, William and George,

It is with the heaviest heart that I must tell you of the passing today of our beloved Grace. God has taken her so young, and when she was so close to reaching her new life in America.

I am writing from a hotel in Hudson, Ohio, where Grace remained during the final stage of her illness. The doctor said it was yellow fever, which is apparently more common in America than in England. I can only accept his diagnosis, since I am unfamiliar with the disease and its symptoms. Having witnessed my sister's painful demise, I can say that Dorset is lucky to be spared such a horror.

I have already written of our journey across to New York. I hope you received my letters from New York and Philadelphia. I do not always feel confident when I hand letters over here that they will reach their destination. In New York we changed our original travel plans, and decided to go by stage to Philadelphia and across Pennsylvania to Ohio, rather than take boats along the rivers and canals of New York to Lake Erie and down to Cleveland. Though many told me that such boats are very different from ships on seas, still I could not face being on the water again. I fear now that my lack of courage proved fatal to Grace, for perhaps she would not have caught the fever if we had gone by boat. With your forgiveness and God's understanding, I must live with this guilt.

Apart from a mild bout of seasickness, Grace remained very well on the crossing, and down to Philadelphia, where we stayed with Friends for a week to recover from our journey. While there we were able to attend the Arch Street Meeting. I have never imagined one could be so large—there must have been five hundred Friends in the room, twenty *times the size of Bridport. I am glad that Grace was able to witness such a Meeting in her life.*

When travelling to Ohio, there is an established network of Friends one may stay with in Pennsylvania. All along the way—in large cities like Harrisburg and Pittsburgh and smaller settlements too—we were welcomed, even when Grace showed the first signs of the yellow fever, two days out from Harrisburg. It begins with a fever and chills and nausea, which could be any number of illnesses, so at first there was little concern except for Grace's discomfort in the various coaches in which we crossed Pennsylvania.

We stayed for a few days in Pittsburgh, where she seemed to rally enough to insist that we press on. I am sorry that I listened to her and did not follow my own instinct, which told me she needed more rest, but we were both anxious to reach Faithwell. Unfortunately within a day her fever had returned, this time accompanied by the black vomit and yellow tinge to her skin that I now know confirms yellow fever. It was only with great difficulty that I managed to convince the coachmen not to leave us by the side of the road, but to continue on to Hudson. I am sorry to say that I had to shout at them, though it is not in a Friend's nature to do so. The other passengers would not allow us to sit inside for fear of contagion, and the coachmen made us perch on the luggage on top of the coach. It was very precarious, but I propped Grace against me and held tight to her so that she would not fall off.

In Hudson she lasted just a night before God called her home. For much of that time she was delirious, but a few hours before she died she became lucid for a little while, and was able to call out her love to each of you. I would have preferred to take her on to be laid to rest in Faithwell amongst Friends, but she has already been buried today in Hudson, for everyone is fearful of the infection spreading.

Since I am so close to Faithwell, I am determined to go on. It is only forty miles west of Hudson, which is no distance after the five hundred miles we came from New York and the thousands more across the ocean. It grieves me that Grace was so near to her new home, and now will never see it. I do not know what I will do when I get there. Adam Cox is not yet aware of this sorrowful news.

Grace suffered much and bore it bravely, but she is at peace now with God. I do know that one day we shall see her again, and that is some comfort.

Your loving daughter and sister,

Honor Bright

Quilt

 IT STILL SURPRISED Honor that she had to rely so completely on strangers to shelter her, feed her, bring her from place to place, even bury her dead. She had not traveled much in England: apart from short trips to neighboring villages, she had been only to Exeter for a Yearly Meeting of Friends, and once to Bristol when her father had business there. She was used to knowing most people she came in contact with, and not having to introduce and explain herself. She was not a great talker, preferring silence, as it gave her the opportunity to notice things, and to think. Grace had been the lively, chattering member of the family, often speaking for her sister so that Honor did not have to herself. Now without her sister Honor was forced to talk more—to describe her circumstances over and over to the various strangers who took charge of her when the coach first dumped the Brights at the hotel in Hudson.

Once Grace was buried, Honor did not know if she should send word to Adam Cox and wait for him, or find another way to Faithwell herself. She discovered, however, that Americans were practical, resourceful people, and the innkeeper had already found her a lift. An elderly man called Thomas was visiting Hudson, but lived near Wellington, a town seven miles south of Faithwell. He offered to take Honor with him on his way back. From Wellington she could find someone to drive her on to Adam Cox's, or contact Adam to collect her. "Only we must start early," Thomas told her, "for I want to get home in one day."

They set out for Wellington when it was still dark, her trunk stowed behind them in the wagon. It was heavy with Grace's clothes, for Honor had left behind her sister's trunk to keep Thomas's load lighter. She had also been forced to leave behind the quilt she'd made especially for her sister's marriage: whole-cloth in white, quilted with a delicate rose medallion in the center and surrounded by intricate geometric borders, the space between filled in with double diamonds. Honor had done all the quilting herself and was pleased with the result. However, the innkeeper at the hotel had insisted they use their own bedding, and afterwards the doctor told her the quilt, along with any clothes Grace had worn, must be burned so they wouldn't spread the fever.

Before bundling up the clothes for burning, Honor defied the doctor: she got out her scissors and cut a piece of material from Grace's chestnut-brown dress. One day she would use the cloth for part of a quilt. And if it was infected with fever and killed her, then that was God's will.

Though she had not cried when her sister passed—Grace was in such a state at the end that Honor prayed for God to release her— once she'd handed over the clothes and the quilt, she hid in her room and wept.

Thomas seemed to prefer silence as much as Honor did; he asked no questions, and for the first time since reaching land in America she was able to sit and look about without other passengers or the worry over her sister to distract her. Though they drove into darkness, soon the sun rose behind them, tinting the surrounding woods in a soft light. Birdsong intensified until it became a frenetic chatter, most of the sounds unfamiliar to her. She was startled too by the vivid plumage, in particular a tufted scarlet bird with a black face and a blue bird with black and white striped wings, their raucous screams scattering smaller, duller birds. She wanted to ask what they were, but did not like to disturb Thomas. Her companion sat so still that she would have thought he was asleep except that every few miles he stamped his foot twice and shook the reins, seeming to remind the fat gray mare pulling them that he was there. The horse was not fast but she was steady.

They were on a much smaller road than any Honor had ridden along in the stagecoaches through New Jersey and Pennsylvania. There she and her sister had followed well-traveled routes, where the roads were wide and sprinkled with houses and towns as well as inns for changing horses and eating and sleeping. Here it was more a track of dry, rutted mud cutting through dense trees. There were few houses, or clearings, or anything other than woods. After several miles driving through the same forest without any sign of people nearby, Honor began to wonder why such a road existed. Most roads where she was from had a clear destination. Here the destination was much farther away and less obvious.

But she mustn't compare Ohio to Dorset. It did not help.

Occasionally they passed a house carved out of the woods alongside the road, and Honor found herself letting out a breath, then taking in another and holding it as the woods closed in on them once more. Not that the houses were much in themselves: hardly more than log cabins, many of them, surrounded by stumps. Sometimes a boy was outside chopping wood, or a woman was hanging out a quilt to air it, or a girl was hoeing a vegetable patch. They stared as Thomas and Honor passed and did not respond to Thomas's raised hand. He did not seem to mind.

An hour into the journey they descended a shallow valley to a
bridge crossing a river. "The Cuyahoga," Thomas murmured. "In-
dian name." Honor was not listening, however, nor looking into the
river. Instead she was staring above her, for the straight wooden
bridge they rumbled across had a roof. Thomas must have noticed
her bewilderment. "Covered bridge," he said. "You've not seen one
before?"

Honor shook her head.

"Keeps the snow off, and the bridge from freezing."

The bridges crossing streams and rivers from her childhood were
stone and humped. Honor had not thought that something as fun-
damental as a bridge would be so different in America.

They stopped after a few hours to give the horse water and oats,
and to eat the cold corn mush Ohioans liked for breakfast. Afterwards Thomas disappeared into the woods. While he was gone
Honor stood by the wagon and studied the trees on the other side
of the track. They too were unfamiliar. Even trees like oaks and
chestnuts she knew from before seemed different, the oak leaves
more pointed and less curly, the chestnut leaves not in the fanned
cluster she was accustomed to. The undergrowth looked foreign,
dense and primitive, designed to keep people out.

On his return Thomas nodded at the woods. "You'll want relief."

"I—" Honor had been about to protest, but something in his
manner made it clear she should obey him, the way one does a
grandfather. Besides, she could not admit she was frightened of
Ohio woods. She would have to get used to them at some point.

She stepped off the track and into the trees, placing each foot
with care onto dead leaves, mossy rocks and fallen branches. All
around there was a raw, earthy smell of ferns and decay; rustling
too, which Honor tried to ignore, reasoning that the noises must be
made by mice or gray squirrels or the small brown rodents with

furry tails and black and white stripes down their backs she had learned were called chipmunks. She had heard that the woods were home to wolves, panthers, porcupines, skunks, possums, raccoons and other animals that did not exist in England. Most she would not even recognize if she saw them—which in a way made them even more frightening. Apparently there were many snakes as well. She could only hope that none was in this patch of forest on this particular morning. When she was thirty feet or so from the road, Honor took a deep breath and forced herself to turn around so that she was facing the wagon, her back to the endless ranks of trees potentially hiding animals. Finding a place where she was shielded from Thomas, she lifted her skirts and squatted.

Apart from the wind rustling the leaves and the birds singing, it was quiet. Honor heard Thomas open the hinged seat they had been sitting on, where there must be storage space. She heard his low voice, probably talking to the horse, reassuring it as Honor herself needed reassurance that wolves and panthers were not hovering. The horse replied in a low nicker.

Honor stood up and rearranged her skirts. She could not relieve herself: being so exposed in the woods made her too tense. She looked around. This is as far from home as I can be, she thought, and I am alone. She shuddered, and ran back to the safety of the wagon.

When she had climbed onto her seat, Thomas stamped his foot twice and they started again. Breakfast seemed to have awakened him. Though he did not speak, he began to hum a tune Honor did not recognize, probably a hymn of some sort. After a while the humming, the rattle of the wagon and jangling of the horse's bridle, the wind, the birds—this ensemble of sounds lulled her, as did the track extending straight out of sight ahead of them, and the trees rippling by. She did not fall asleep, but settled into the familiar meditative state she knew from Meeting. It was as if she were having a two-person Meeting with Thomas right on the wagon—though Friends did not normally hum during it. Honor closed her eyes and allowed her body to sway naturally, harnessed to the rhythm of the wagon's movement. Steady and comfortable at last, she sank down inside herself to wait for the Inner Light.

It was all too easy to be distracted during Meeting for Worship. Sometimes her mind would be crowded with thoughts about a cramp in her leg, or remembering that she had forgotten to run an errand for her mother, or noticing a mark on a neighbor's white bonnet. It took discipline to quieten the mind. Honor often found a kind of peace, but the true depth of the Inner Light, that feeling that God accompanied her, was harder to reach. She would not expect to find it in the middle of Ohio woods with an old man humming hymns beside her.

Now, as she sat in the wagon that was taking her west, Honor began to feel a presence, as if she were not alone. Of course Thomas was with her, but it was more than that: there was almost a buzz in the air, a knowledge that she was being accompanied on her journey into the depths of Ohio. Honor had never felt this so tangibly before, and for the first time in a lifetime of Meetings, she was moved to speak.

She opened her mouth, and then she heard it. From far behind them there came a kind of scratching sound. After a moment it separated into a rhythm of hoofbeats, pounding fast.

"Someone's coming," Honor said—the first words she had spoken to Thomas all day. It was not what she had intended to say.

Thomas turned his head and listened, his eyes expressionless until he too picked up the sound. Then his gaze seemed to intensify, revealing some meaning Honor could not decode. He looked at her as if wanting to acknowledge something without saying it, but she did not know what it was.

She pulled her eyes from his and looked back. A dot had appeared on the road.

Thomas stamped his foot three times. "Tell me about your sister," he said.

"Pardon?"

"Tell me about your sister—the one who died. What was her name?"

Honor frowned. She did not want to talk about her sister now, with someone else appearing and a new tension in the air. But Thomas had not asked her many questions on the trip, and so she obliged. "Grace. She was two years older than me."

"She was to marry a man from Faithwell?"

The sound was clearer now: one horse, ridden at a gallop, with a thick shoe that made a distinctive thud. It was hard not to be distracted. "He—he is English. Adam Cox. From our village. He emigrated to Ohio to help his brother run a shop in Oberlin."

"What kind of shop?"

"A draper's."

When Thomas looked puzzled, Honor thought back to Adam's letter. "Dry goods."

Thomas brightened. "Cox's Dry Goods? I know it. On Main Street, south of College. One of them's been poorly." He stamped his foot three times again.

Honor glanced back again. The rider was visible now: a man riding a bay stallion.

"Why did you come with your sister?"

"I—" Honor could not answer. She did not want to explain to a stranger about Samuel.

"What are you going to do now you're here without her?"

"I—I don't know." Thomas's questions were direct and cutting, and the last was like a needle pricking a boil. It burst, and Honor began to cry.

Thomas nodded. "I beg your pardon, miss," he whispered. "We may need those tears."

Then the rider was upon them. He pulled up next to the wagon, and Thomas stopped the gray mare. The stallion whinnied at her, but she stood solidly, with no apparent interest in this new companion.

Honor wiped her eyes and glanced at the man before folding her hands in her lap and fixing her gaze on them. Even sitting on a horse it was clear that he was very tall, with the leathery tanned skin of a man who spends his life outside. Light brown eyes stood out of his square, weathered face. He would have been handsome if there were any warmth to his expression, but his eyes were flat in a way that sent a chill through her. She was suddenly very aware of their isolation on this road. She doubted too that Thomas carried a gun like the one prominent on the man's hip.

If Thomas had similar thoughts he did not reveal them. "Afternoon, Donovan," he said to the newcomer.

The man smiled, a gesture that did not affect his face. "Old Thomas, and a Quaker girl, is it?" He reached over and pulled at the rim of Honor's bonnet. As she jerked her head away he laughed. "Just checkin'. You can tell the other Quakers you know not to bother dressin' niggers up in Quaker clothes. I'm on to that one. That trick's old."

He removed his battered hat and nodded at Honor, who stared at him, bewildered by his words, for they made no sense to her.

"You don't have to take your hat off to Quakers," Thomas said. "They don't believe in it."

The man snorted. "I ain't gonna change my good manners just 'cause a Quaker girl thinks different. You don't mind if I take off my hat to you, do you, miss?"

Honor ducked her head.

"See? She don't mind." The man stretched. Under a brown waistcoat his collarless white shirt was stained with sweat.

"Can we help you with something?" Thomas said. "If not, we have to get along—we've a long road ahead."

"You in a rush, are you? Where you headed?"

"I'm taking this young woman with me back to Wellington," Thomas said. "She has come to Ohio from England, but lost her sister in Hudson to yellow fever. You can see from her tears that she is in mourning."

"You from England?" the man said.

Honor nodded.

"Say something, then. I always liked the accent."

When Honor hesitated, the man said, "Go on, say something. What, you too proud to talk to me? Say, 'How do you do, Donovan.'"

Rather than remain silent and risk his insistence turning to anger, Honor looked into his amused eyes and said, "How does thee, Mr. Donovan?"

Donovan snorted. "How *does* I? I *does* just fine, thankee. Nobody's called me Mr. Donovan in years. You Quakers make me laugh. What's your name, girl?"

"Honor Bright."

"You gonna live up to your name, Honor Bright?"

"A little kindness to a girl who has just buried her sister in a strange land," Thomas intervened.

"What's in that?" Donovan switched his tone suddenly, gesturing to Honor's trunk in the wagon bed.

"Miss Bright's things."

"I'll just have a look in it. That trunk's the perfect size for a hidden nigger."

Thomas frowned. "It's not right for a man to look in a young lady's trunk. Miss Bright will tell you herself what's in it. Don't you know that Quakers don't lie?"

Donovan looked expectantly at her. Honor shook her head, puzzled. She was still recovering from Donovan pulling at her bonnet and could barely keep up with their conversation.

Then, faster than she could have imagined, Donovan jumped from his horse and onto the wagon. Honor felt a dart of fear in her gut, for he was so much bigger, faster and stronger than her and Thomas. When Donovan discovered the trunk was locked, that fear made her pass over the key, which she'd kept on a thin green ribbon around her neck during the long journey.

Donovan opened the lid and lifted out the quilt Honor had brought to America. She expected him to set it aside, but instead he shook it out and draped it over the wagon bed. "What's this?" he asked, squinting at it. "I never seen writing on a quilt."

"It is a signature quilt," Honor explained. "Friends and family made squares and signed them. It was a gift to mark my move to America. To say good-bye."

Each square consisted of brown and green and cream squares and triangles, with a white patch in the middle signed by the maker. Originally begun for Grace, when Honor decided at the last minute to go to America as well, the makers rearranged the configuration of names so that hers was in the central square, with family members in the squares around it, and friends beyond those. Quilted in a simple diamond pattern, it was not especially beautiful, for the work varied according to the skill of each maker, and it was not designed the way Honor would have chosen. But she could never give it to anyone else: it had been made for her to remember her community by.

Donovan squatted in the wagon bed and studied the quilt for so long that Honor began to wonder if she had said something wrong. She glanced at Thomas: he remained impassive.

"My mother made comforts," Donovan said at last, running his fingers over a name—Rachel Bright, an aunt of Honor's. "Nothin' like this, though. Hers had a big star in the center made out of lots of little diamonds."

"That pattern is called a Star of Bethlehem."

"Is it, now?" Donovan looked at her; his brown eyes had thawed a little.

"I have made that pattern myself," she added, thinking of the quilt she had left behind with Biddy. "They are not easy, because it is difficult to fit together the points of the diamonds. The sewing must be very accurate. Thy mother must have been skilled with her needle."

Donovan nodded, then grabbed the quilt and stuffed it back in the trunk. Locking it, he jumped down from the wagon. "You can go."

Without a word, Thomas flicked the reins and the gray mare sprang into life. A minute later Donovan rode up alongside them. "You settlin' in Wellington?"

"No," Honor answered. "Faithwell, near Oberlin. My late sister's fiancé is there."

"Oberlin!" Donovan spat, then pressed his heels into the stallion's belly and flew past them. Honor was relieved, for she had wondered how she would tolerate him riding alongside them all the way to Wellington.

His horse's hoofbeats remained in the air, quieter and quieter, for many minutes, until at last they faded away. "All right, now," Thomas said softly. Stamping twice, he flicked the reins over the mare's back again. He did not hum, however, for the rest of the journey.

It was only miles later that Honor realized Donovan had not given her back the key to her trunk.

Belle Mills's Millinery
Main St.
Wellington, Ohio
May 30, 1850

Dear Mr. Cox,

I got your fiancée's sister, Honor Bright, here with me. Sorry to tell you your intended passed. Yellow fever.

Honor needs to rest up here a few days, so could you come pick her up this Sunday afternoon, please.

Yours ever faithful,

Belle Mills

Bonnets

 HONOR HAD SLEPT in so many beds by the time she got to Wellington that when she woke she did not remember where she was. Her dress and shawl were hanging over a chair, but she could not recall undressing or putting them there. She sat up, certain that it was not early morning, when she usually rose. She was wearing an unfamiliar cotton nightgown that was too long for her, and covered with a light quilt.

Wherever she was, there was no doubt that this was America. The quality of the sunlight was different—yellower and fiercer, biting through the air to warm her. Indeed, it was going to be a hot day, though at the moment it was fresh enough for her to be grateful for the quilt. She ran her hand over it: unlike most American quilts she had seen so far, this one was not appliquéd or pieced squares, but proper English patchwork, well made, so that while the cloth was faded, there were no tears or loose seams. The design was of orange and yellow and red diamonds that made up a star in the center of the quilt—a Star of Bethlehem like Biddy's quilt, and what Donovan had described his mother making. Recalling her encounter with him the day before, Honor shuddered.

Though of a good size, and containing the bed she had slept in, the room was not a bedroom so much as a storeroom. Bolts of cloth leaned against the walls, many of them white but also solid colors, plaids and floral prints. Spilling out of open chests of drawers were gloves, ribbons, wire, lace and feathers dyed in bright colors. In one corner, dominating the room, smooth blocks of wood in oval and cylindrical shapes were precariously stacked, as well as peculiar oval and circular bands like wheels or doughnuts, some of wood, others made of a hard white material Honor did not recognize. She leaned forward to study them more closely. The blocks reminded her of heads. When Thomas had left her off late the evening before, she'd entered a shop of some kind. While at the time she had been too tired to take note of it, now she understood: she was in a milliner's storeroom.

Quaker women did not wear hats, but plain caps and bonnets, and usually made their own. Honor had only been into the milliner's in Bridport a few times to buy ribbon. She had often peeked in the window, however, to admire the latest creations displayed on their stands. It had been a tidy, feminine space, with floorboards painted duck-egg blue and long shelves along the walls filled with hats.

On top of the dresser full of trimmings was a china jug decorated with pink roses sitting in a matching basin, the same Honor had seen in homes all across Pennsylvania. She used them now to wash, then dressed and smoothed her dark hair, noting as she put on her cap that her bonnet was missing. Before she went down, she glanced out of the window, which overlooked a street busy with pedestrians and horses and wagons. It was a relief to see people again after a day on the empty road through the woods.

Honor crept down the stairs and entered a small kitchen with a fire and range, a table and chairs, and a sideboard sparse with dishes. The room felt underused, as if little food were prepared there. The back door was open, bringing in a breeze that passed through the kitchen and into the front room. Honor followed it to the heart of the house.

In many respects the shop was like the Bridport milliner's: hats on shelves lining the walls, hats and bonnets on stands on tables around the room, glass cases along the sides displaying gloves and combs and hat pins. A large mirror hung on one wall, and two front windows made the room light and airy. The floorboards were not painted but worn smooth and shiny from customers' feet. In one corner on a work table were hats in various stages of construction: layers of straw molded around carved wood hat blocks, drying into shape; brims sewn into ovals and awaiting their crowns; hats banded with ribbon, a pile of silk flowers waiting to be attached among a tangle of ribbons and wire. There was little order on the table; the order lay in the finished hats.

In another way the room was completely different, as so many things about America felt to Honor. Where the Bridport shop was orderly by design, the Wellington milliner's felt as if it had come about its order by accident. Some of the shelves were crammed with hats while others were bare. The room was bright but the windows dusty. Though the floor looked as if it had been swept clean, Honor suspected the corners housed dustballs. It felt as if the shop had sprung up suddenly, whereas Honor knew that her great-grandmother would have bought plain ribbons from the Bridport milliner's.

The hats and bonnets too were peculiar. Though no expert in trimmings since she wore none herself, Honor was startled by some of the things she saw. A straw hat with a shallow crown pinned with a huge bunch of plaid roses. Another flat hat rimmed with a cascade of colored ribbons bound together with lace. A cottage bonnet with a deep crown much like Honor's own, but with white feathers lining the inside rim rather than the usual white ruffles. Honor could wear none of them, for Quakers followed rules of simplicity in dress as well as in conduct. Even if she could she was not sure she would want to.

Yet these hats must sell, as the shop was full of women and girls, gathered around the tables, sorting through frilly caps and sun bonnets, plucking at baskets of pre-cut ribbons and cloth flowers, laughing and chattering and calling out.

After a moment she noticed a woman standing behind the back counter, surveying the room with an experienced air. This was the proprietress, whom Honor had met briefly the night before. She caught Honor's eye and nodded. She was not at all what you would expect of a milliner. Tall and thin, she had a bony face and a skeptical air. Her hazel eyes bulged slightly, the whites tinged with yellow. For a milliner she wore a surprisingly simple white cap, with a burst of scrubby fair hair hanging on her forehead. Her tan dress hung from her shoulders and exposed a ridge of collarbone. She reminded Honor of the scarecrows hanging on wooden frames in Dorset gardens. The contrast between her angular plainness and the frilly wares she sold made Honor want to smile.

"What you grinnin' at, Honor Bright?"

Honor started. Donovan had entered the shop, his heavy tread among the customers causing them to fall silent and take a collective step back.

Honor remained still. She did not want to cause a fuss, so she simply said, "I wish thee good day, Mr. Donovan."

Donovan rested his eyes on her. "I was passing and saw you in here. And I thought to myself, 'Why in hell did Old Thomas leave a Quaker girl at Belle Mills's when she can't wear none of the hats?'"

"Donovan, don't be so rude to our guest, or she'll go right back to England and tell everyone what bad manners American men have." Belle Mills had come out from behind the counter, and turned her attention to Honor. "You're English, ain't you, Miss Bright? I could tell from the stitching 'round your neckline. Looks like something only an Englishwoman would think up. I never seen such a striking detail, certainly not on a Quaker woman's dress. Very fine, that. Simple. Effective. Did you design it or copy it from something?"

"I made it up myself." Honor glanced down at the white V of cloth edging the neckline of her dark green dress. It was not the crisp white it had been when she left England. But then, nothing was quite as clean in America as it had been back home.

"Hey, you bring any English magazines with you? *Ladies' Cabinet of Fashion* or *Illustrated London News*?"

Honor shook her head.

"Shame. I like to copy hats from 'em. By the way, if you're wonderin' where your bonnet is, I got it here." Belle Mills pointed to a shelf behind her. Honor's bonnet—pale green, with the crown and brim merged into one horizontal line—had been pulled over one of the hat blocks. "It needed a little attention. I just gave it a brush and a sprinkle of starchy water. Give it an hour and it'll get its shape back. You got it new for your trip?"

"My mother made it."

Belle nodded. "Good hand. Can you sew like that?"

Better than that, Honor thought but did not say. "She taught me."

"Maybe while you're here you can help me out. Usually I'm not so busy once the Easter-bonnet rush is over, but it's heated up all of a sudden and everybody's decided they want a new bonnet, or new trim on their hats."

Honor nodded in confusion. She was not expecting to remain in

Wellington, but to go immediately on to Faithwell. It was only seven miles away, and she hoped to find another farmer with a wagon to take her, or get a boy to ride there with a message for Adam Cox to come and fetch her. The thought of seeing him so soon filled her with dread, though; she did not know if he would welcome her as warmly without Grace at her side.

Donovan interrupted her thoughts. "Jesus Christ, is this what you gals talk about all day? Dresses and bonnets?"

The customers had been soothed enough by Belle's chat to go back to browsing the merchandise. Hearing Donovan's tone, however— so alien to a millinery shop—they froze once again.

"Nobody asked you to come here and listen to us," Belle countered. "Get out of here—you're scaring my customers."

"Honor Bright, are you stayin' *here*?" Donovan demanded. "You didn't tell me that before. Thought you said you was headed to Faithwell."

"You keep out of her business," Belle said. "Old Thomas told me you was botherin' her on the road. Poor Honor has had to meet the lowest of Ohio society before she's even had a chance to catch her breath."

Donovan was ignoring Belle, his eyes still on Honor. "Well, now, guess I'll see you round Wellington, Honor Bright."

"Mr. Donovan, may I have my key back, please?"

"Only if you call me Donovan. Can't stand Mister."

"All right—Donovan. I would like my key back, please."

"Sure, darlin'." Donovan moved his hand, but then stopped. "Aw, sorry, Honor Bright, I lost it on the road." He held her eyes so that she would know he was lying but could not accuse him. His expression was no longer guarded, but intent, and interested. Her stomach twisted with a mixture of fear and something else: excitement. It was such an unsuitable sensation that she flushed.

Donovan smiled. Then he lifted his hat to the room and turned to go. As he reached the door Honor saw around the back of his neck a thin line of dark green ribbon.

The second he was gone the women began chattering like chickens riled by the sight of a fox.

"Well, Honor Bright, looks like you've already made a conquest," Belle remarked. "Not one you'd ever want to take up with, though, I can guarantee that. Now, you must be starved. You didn't eat nothin' last night, and little on the road, I bet. Ladies"—she raised her voice—"you all go on home and get dinner on the table. I got to feed this weary traveler. You want to buy something, come back in an hour or two. Mrs. Bradley, I'll have your bonnet ready tomorrow. Yours too, Miss Adams. Now I got a good sewer with me I can catch up."

Honor watched the women obediently filing out, and confusion threatened to overwhelm her. Her life seemed to be in the hands of strangers—where she was going and where she stayed and for how long, what she ate and even what she sewed. It seemed now she was to make bonnets for a woman she had just met. Her eyes pricked with tears.

Belle Mills must have seen them, but said nothing, simply hung a CLOSED sign on the door and went back to the kitchen, where she heaped a ham steak and several eggs into a skillet. "Come and eat," she commanded a few minutes later, setting two plates on the table. Clearly cooking was not something she spent much time on. "Look, there's corn bread there, and butter. Help yourself."

Honor gazed at the greasy ham, the eggs flecked with fat, the stodgy corn bread she'd had at every meal in America. She did not think she could face eating any of it, but since Belle was watching her, she cut a tiny triangle of ham and popped it in her mouth. The sweet and salt together surprised her, and opened a door in her belly. She began to eat steadily, even the corn bread she was so tired of.

Belle nodded. "Thought so. You were looking mighty pale. When did you leave England?"

"Eight weeks ago."

"When did your sister die?"

Honor had to think. "Four days ago." Already it felt like months and miles away. Those forty miles between Hudson and Wellington had taken her deeper into a different world than any of the rest of the journey.

"Honey, no wonder you're peaky. Thomas told me you're going on to Faithwell, to your sister's fiancé."

Honor nodded.

"Well, I sent him word you're here. Told him to come Sunday afternoon to pick you up. I figured you need a few days to recover. You can help me with some sewing if you want. Earn your keep."

Honor could not remember what day it was. "All right," she agreed blindly, relieved to let Belle take charge.

"Now, let's see what you can do with a needle. You got your own sewing things or you want to use some of mine?"

"I have a sewing box. But it is locked in the trunk."

"Damn that Donovan. Well, I can probably get it open with a hammer and chisel as long as you don't mind me breakin' the lock. All right? We don't have much choice."

Honor nodded.

"You do the dishes and I'll work on the trunk." Belle surveyed the table, Honor's clean plate and her own, almost untouched. Picking up the latter, she set it on the sideboard with a napkin over it. Then she disappeared upstairs. A few minutes later, as Honor was scrubbing the pan, she heard banging and then a triumphant shout.

"English locks ain't any better'n American," Belle announced as she came downstairs. "It's broken now. Go and get your sewing things. I'll finish up here."

When Honor brought her box down, Belle was dragging a rocking chair through the back door. "Let's set on the back porch, catch the breeze. You want this rocker, or a straight chair?"

"I will bring out a straight chair." Honor had seen rocking chairs everywhere she went in America; they were much more common than in England. The sensation reminded her too much of the ship. Besides, she needed solid stillness for sewing.

As she picked up a chair in the kitchen, she noticed Belle's plate of food on the sideboard was gone.

The milliner's was on the end of a row of buildings that included a grocery, a harness shop, a confectionary and a drugstore. The backyards of these establishments were underused, though one had a vegetable garden, and in another there was laundry hanging out. Belle's yard had nothing in it but a pile of planed wood and a goat tethered in the weeds. "Don't go near the wood," Belle warned. "Snakes there. And leave that goat be. It belongs to the neighbors, and it's evil." There was also an outhouse, and a lean-to along the side of the house for storing wood, but clearly Belle's energy went into her shop.

Honor sat and opened her sewing box to lay out her things. This ritual, at least, was familiar. The sewing box had belonged to her grandmother, who, when her sight began to fail, handed it on to the best stitcher among her granddaughters. Made of walnut wood, it had a padded needlepoint cover of lilies of the valley in green and yellow and white. This was an image Honor had known from an early age; eyes shut, she could perfectly re-create it in her mind, as she had often done to distract herself during her seasickness. The upper tray contained a needlecase Grace had made, embroidered with lilies of the valley similar to the box lid; a wire needle threader; a porcelain thimble her mother had given her, decorated with yellow roses; a beaded pin cushion her friend Biddy had made for her; packets of pins wrapped in green paper; a small tin holding a lump of beeswax she used on her quilting thread; and her grandmother's pair of small sewing scissors with green and yellow enameled handles, sheathed in a soft leather case.

Belle Mills leaned forward to inspect. "Nice. What are these?" She picked up pieces of metal cut into different shapes: hexagons, diamonds, squares, triangles.

"Templates for cutting patchwork. My father had them made for me."

"Quilter, eh?"

Honor nodded.

"What's underneath?"

Honor lifted the tray to reveal spools of different colored thread, each slotted into its place.

Belle nodded her approval, then reached between the spools to pick out a small silver thimble. "Don't you want this in the top section with the other things?"

"No." Samuel had given her the thimble when their feelings for each other were ripe. She would not use it now, but could not quite give it up.

Belle raised her eyebrows. When Honor did not elaborate, she dropped the thimble back into the spools to ruin their perfect order. "All right, Honor Bright," she chuckled, "everybody's entitled to their secrets. Now, let's get you started. You sewed much on straw before?"

Honor shook her head. "I have not made hats, only bonnets."

"Bet you only got two bonnets—winter and summer. You Quakers don't go in for fancy clothes, do you? Well, then, let's start you on cloth. I got a sun bonnet for Mrs. Bradley needs finishing. That's easy—no straw structure, just corded. Most women make their own, but Mrs. Bradley's got a fancy notion she don't ever need to pick up a needle. Think you can manage this? Here's the thread. I been using a size six needle." She handed Honor a soft bonnet that had been cut and tacked together with loose stitches, and only needed sewing; it was a simple enough design, with a long, wide bavolet of cloth to cover the neck from the sun. The fabric was a light blue plaid crisscrossed with thin yellow and white stripes. It was not a style Honor was familiar with—no English woman would be willing to let so much fabric flap around her neck—but the sun was stronger here, so perhaps such covering was needed. At any rate, it would be easy to sew.

Honor reached for a spool and her needle threader and quickly threaded six needles, poking them into the pincushion in readiness. Though Belle's scrutiny made her self-conscious, in the sewing realm at least she was confident of what she was doing. She began to sew the crown onto the brim using a back stitch for strength, and gathering the crown cloth into little pleats as she made her way around. Honor was a fast, accurate seamstress, though she went more slowly on this bonnet, to make sure she was doing what Belle wanted.

Belle sat in the rocker next to her and sewed cream silk over the top of the straw, oval-shaped brim of a bonnet. Every so often she glanced over at Honor's work. "I can see I don't have to look after you," she remarked when Honor had finished the sun bonnet. "Now, watch the pleats I'm makin' to get this cloth to lay flat around the brim. See, like this. Think you can do that? Here, try it. Use this—it's a milliner's needle—better for straw."

When Honor had sewn enough to Belle's satisfaction, the milliner stood and stretched. "Guess I got lucky with you comin'. When you finish that, you can work on these." She patted a pile of bonnets in various stages of construction that she had placed on a table between them. "I'll trim 'em later. You got any questions I'll be in the shop. Got to open for the afternoon."

It had grown warm, with the sun high in the sky and the porch less shaded. Honor had not been alone much since landing in America, and was glad to sit still on a bright spring afternoon with familiar work to do but nothing more expected of her. She would have liked a cottage garden to look at, with drifting borders of flowers such as her mother grew—lupins and delphiniums and columbine and love-in-a-mist and forget-me-nots. She didn't know if any of these flowers even grew in America, or if Americans cultivated that sort of garden. She suspected not—it was not practical, especially here, where society was still being hewn from the wilderness and energy was directed toward survival rather than decoration. Mind you—she surveyed the pile of bonnets Belle had left her— Ohio women did allow themselves some frivolity in their headwear: the bonnets were in brightly colored ginghams and chintz.

She finished the cream bonnet and picked up another, of pale green fabric dotted with tiny daisies, and a brim that could be folded back to reveal another color—tan in this case. Honor would have expected pink, but she was not about to suggest so. As she worked on the second bonnet, the steady, familiar rhythm of sewing took over, its repetition meditative, freeing her to her thoughts rather as Meeting for Worship did. She felt her shoulders begin to sink, the tension she had been carrying with her since leaving England easing a little. Reaching the end of the thread, she let her hands rest on the bonnet in her lap and closed her eyes. That calm, and her solitude, gave her the space in which to think: of Samuel

telling her he loved someone else, and her decision to unmoor herself from Dorset; of her sister's death leaving her so alone in a
strange place. Honor at last began to cry, painful sobs reminiscent
of the heaves she had suffered on board the *Adventurer*.

The relief of her tears did not last, however. In between her muffled gasps, a sense came over her, just as it had on the road from
Hudson to Wellington, that she was not alone. Honor glanced behind her, but Belle was not in the doorway or the kitchen; indeed,
she could hear her voice back in the shop. And she could see no one
in any of the nearby yards. Then she heard behind her, in the lean-
to at the side of the house, the sound of a log falling from the
woodpile.

It could be a dog, she thought, wiping her eyes with her sleeve.
Or one of those animals we don't have, a possum or a porcupine or
a raccoon. But she knew they were unlikely to knock over a log.
And she knew, though she could not say how, that the presence she
felt now, and had felt on the road, was human.

Honor had never thought of herself as a brave person. Until
coming to America, her mettle had not really been tested. Now,
however, she resisted the urge to fetch Belle. Instead she put the
bonnet aside, rose from her chair, and crept down the back steps.
Hesitating would not help, she knew. She took a breath, held it, and
walked over to the lean-to to look in.

The light reached only a foot or two inside the woodshed; then
it was dim, leading to darkness. For a moment Honor could see
nothing as her eyes tried to adjust. Then she made out wood stacked
neat and high on the right; on the left there was a narrow gap between wood and wall, for access to the stack. In that gap stood a
black man. Honor sucked in a shocked breath on top of the one she
was holding, then let it out in a sudden exhalation. She stared at
him. He was of medium height and build, with fuzzy hair and wide

cheeks. He was barefoot, his clothes worn and dirty. That was all she could take in, or knew how to take in, for she was not familiar enough with Negro features to be able to gauge and compare and describe them. She did not know if he was frightened or angry or resigned. To her he simply looked black.

She did not know what to say, or if she should speak, so she did not, but stepped backward. Then she hurried to the porch, and began putting her sewing things back into her box. Piling the bonnets on top, she picked up everything and took it inside.

Belle did not seem surprised to see her. "Heat got to you?" she said as she adjusted a hat on a customer, sharpening the angle before sticking in a hat pin. Both women studied the effect in the mirror. "That's better, ain't it? Suits you."

"Dunno," the woman answered. "You've skimped on the violets."

"Think so? I can make you some more, now I got me an assistant. Penny a violet all right?" Belle winked at Honor. "You finished Miss Adams's bonnet? The green one. Yes? Good. You can work in the corner by the window—that's the best light." Before Honor could speak, Belle turned back to her customer to discuss violets.

She worked all afternoon on the bonnets, and gradually her hands stopped shaking. After a while she even wondered if she had imagined the man. Perhaps the heat and light and her own recent trauma had made her turn a dog or a raccoon into a man. She decided then to say nothing to Belle.

The shop had a steady stream of customers; all of them gazed on Honor as a curiosity worth commenting on, though they directed their questions to Belle rather than her. "What you got a Quaker in the window for, Belle?" they asked. "Where's she from? Where's she going? Why's she here?" Belle answered over and over again. By the end of the day every woman in Wellington must know that Honor was from England and on her way to Faithwell, but had stopped with Belle and was helping her out with sewing for a few days. She even made Honor into a feature of the shop. "She's got a fine hand—better than mine, even. You order a bonnet today and I'll get her to sew it for you. Last you a lifetime, her stitching's that strong, or till you're sick of it and want a new one. Then you'll regret buyin' one o' Honor Bright's bonnets—it just won't fall apart and give you the excuse for a new one."

Later, when the light was fading, Belle closed shop for the day and took Honor on a walk around Wellington. Little more than a cluster of shops and houses around a crossroads, its few streets were wide and laid out in a grid oriented north and south, east and west. Main Street had been widened so that there was a rectangular Public Square with a town hall, a church, a hotel and shops—one of them Belle's—arranged around it. Shops in the surrounding streets included several general stores, as well as a cobbler, a tailor, a blacksmith, a cabinet maker, a brickyard and a carriage maker. Most were two stories high and made of wood, with awnings and large windows displaying goods. A school had been built, and a train depot was almost finished for the railroad due to begin running to Wellington later in the summer. "This town's gonna explode when that train comes through," Belle declared. "Good for business. Good for hats."

As they strolled, Honor had the familiar uneasy feeling she had experienced when passing through American towns on her way to Ohio: that they had been built quickly, and could be destroyed just as quickly, by a fire or the extreme American weather she had heard about, hurricanes and tornadoes and blizzards. The storefronts might be relatively new but they had already been ravaged by sun and snow. The road was both dry and wet, dusty and muddy.

Wherever they went, the road and the planks laid above the mud were spattered with gobs of spit. Honor and Grace had been astonished when they reached New York at how often American men spat, walking around with a bulge of tobacco in their cheeks and letting fly both outside and in. Equally astonishing was that no one else seemed to notice or mind.

Belle nodded at everyone they passed, and stopped to speak a few words to some of the women. Most were wearing everyday bonnets, but a few wore hats that Honor recognized as Belle's, with their peculiar combinations of trimmings. Belle confirmed this. "Some of them make their own bonnets, but all the hats are mine. You'll see more of 'em Sundays, for church. They wouldn't dare wear a hat from one of them Oberlin milliners—they know I'd never do business with 'em afterward. Nothin' wrong with Oberlin, but you buy from your own, don't you?" Belle herself wore a straw hat with a wide orange ribbon around the brim, trimmed with flowers fashioned from pieces of straw.

On one corner of Public Square was the town hotel. For such a small town, it was surprisingly grand: a long, two-story building with a double balcony running all the way along its front on both floors, held up by several pairs of white columns. "Wadsworth Hotel," Belle remarked. "Only place in town to get a drink—not that you need to know that. You Quakers don't touch alcohol, do you?"

Honor shook her head.

"Well, I take my whiskey at home. And that's why." Belle nodded toward one end of the hotel, which faced the millinery shop across Public Square. Lounging on the porch out front were a cluster of men, bottles at their sides. Donovan was among them, his feet propped up on a table. On seeing Belle and Honor, he raised his bottle at them, then drank.

"Charming." Belle led her on. As they passed the last pair of columns, Honor noticed a poster tacked on one of them. It was not the

$150 REWARD in big letters that drew her in, but the silhouette of a man running with a sack over his shoulder. She stopped and studied it.

The description was remarkably specific. She pictured the man she had seen in the lean-to. Now that there were words for what he looked like, adjectives like *chunky* and *African* and *shrewd*, she could picture him, his calculating eyes taking her in, the strength in his shoulders—and his hair, bushy but parted on the side.

Donovan was watching her.

"Walk on," Belle hissed, taking her arm and marching her around the corner onto Mechanics Street.

When they were out of earshot, Honor said, "Did Donovan put up that poster?"

"Yes. He's a slave hunter. You worked that out, didn't you?"

Honor nodded, though she did not know there was a name for what he did.

"There's slave hunters all over Ohio, come up from Kentucky or Virginia to try and take back Negroes to their owners. See, we got lots of runaways through here on their way to Canada. In fact, a lot of traffic comes through Ohio, one way or another. Hell, you can stand at the crossroads here and watch it. East to west you got settlers moving for more land. South to north you got runaway slaves looking for freedom. Funny how nobody wants to go south or east. It's north and west that hold out some kind of promise."

"Why don't the Negroes remain in Ohio? I thought there was no slavery here."

"Some do stop in Ohio—you'll see free blacks in Oberlin—but freedom's guaranteed in Canada. Different country, different laws, so slave hunters got no power there.

"But Donovan's interested in you," Belle continued. "Funny, usually he's suspicious of Quakers. Likes to quote a politician who said Quakers won't defend the country when there's war, but are happy to interfere in people's business when there's peace. But it ain't good to get his attention: once you do it ain't easy to get rid of him. He'll bother you over in Faithwell too. He's a stubborn son of a bitch. I should know." At Honor's questioning look, Belle smiled. "He's my brother."

She chuckled at the change in Honor's face. "Two different fathers, so we don't look much alike. We grew up in Kentucky. But our mother was English—Lincolnshire."

A piece fitted into place. "Did she make the quilt on my bed?"

"Yep. Donovan's always tryin' to take it back from me. He's a mean son of a bitch. We gone in different directions, ain't we, even if we both come north. Now, we better get back." Belle stopped in front of Honor. "Look, honey, I know you seen things goin' on at my house, but it's best if you don't actually know anything. Then if Donovan asks, you don't have to lie. Quakers ain't supposed to lie, are they?"

Honor shook her head.

Belle took her arm and turned around to walk back toward the millinery shop. "Jesus H. Christ, I'm glad I'm not a Quaker. No whiskey, no color, no feathers, no lies. What is there left?"

"No swearing either," Honor added.

Belle burst out laughing.

Honor smiled. "We do call ourselves 'the peculiar people,' for we know we must seem so to others."

Belle was still chuckling, but stopped when they reached the hotel bar. Donovan was no longer there.

The next two days Honor sewed all day, first in the corner of the shop by the window during the morning, and on the back porch in the afternoon.

Belle had Honor work on bonnets again, finishing off some that customers were due to pick up that day. She edged one with lace, another with a double row of ruffles, then sewed clusters of cloth pansies to the inside rim of a stiff green bonnet and attached wide, pale green ribbons for tying under the chin. "Can you make more of them flowers if I give you the petals?" Belle asked when Honor had finished.

Honor nodded: though she had never made flowers, since Quak-

ers did not wear them, she knew they could not be harder than
some of the intricate patchwork she had sewn for quilts.

Belle handed her a box full of petals and leaves. "I already cut
out the petals after you went to bed last night. Just me and the
whiskey and the scissors. I like it that way." She showed Honor how
to construct the pansies, then violets, roses, clover and little clusters
of lace made to resemble baby's breath. Honor wished Grace were
there to see the things she was making: creations more and more
colorful and elaborate.

Belle's customers continued to comment on Honor's presence,
even those who had been to the shop the day before and already
discussed her. "Goodness, look at that Quaker girl's lap full of flowers!" they cried. "Isn't that the funniest thing! You'll turn her, Belle,
you will!"

Honor was only a short distraction, however, perhaps to be
mulled over later. For now, once they'd made their remarks, the
customers went on to the more important task of inspecting the latest goods and getting a bargain. Trying on the various hats and
bonnets displayed on stands, they questioned Belle's designs and
criticized the shape and trim in order to drive down the price. Belle
was equally determined to maintain her price, and a battle of words
followed.

Honor was unnerved by the haggling, with its underlying as-
sumption that the value of something could change depending on
how badly someone wanted to buy or sell it. The lack of a fixed price
made Belle's hats take on a temporary quality. Quakers never haggled, but set what they felt was a fair price for materials and labor.
Each product had what was thought of as its own intrinsic merit,
be it a carrot or a horseshoe or a quilt, and that did not change
simply because many people needed a horseshoe. Honor knew of
merchants in Bridport who haggled, but they didn't when she went

into their shops or to their market stalls. The haggling she'd witnessed was offhand, even embarrassed, as if the participants were
only doing it in jest, because it was expected of them. Here the
haggling seemed fiercer, as if both sides were adamant that they
were right and the other not simply wrong, but morally suspect.
Some of the women in Belle's shop became so indignant as they
argued with Belle that Honor wondered if they would ever return.

Belle, however, seemed entertained by the haggling, and unbothered when, more often than not, it reached a stalemate and the
hat remained unsold. "They'll be back," she said. "Where else can
they go? I'm the only hat maker in town."

Indeed, despite not managing to knock the price down, many
women placed orders. Belle rarely measured their heads—most she
knew already, and she could gauge a newcomer at a glance. "Twenty
inches, most of 'em," she told Honor. "German heads a little bigger,
but everybody else is pretty well the same, no matter how much or
how little they got up there."

Her choice of hat shapes and trim was often unusual, but most
customers accepted her judgment, saving their arguments for the
price rather than the style. From what Honor could see of the customers who came to pick up their hats, Belle usually *was* right,
often choosing colors and styles for them that were different from
what they normally wore. "Hats can go stale on you," she said to a
woman she had just convinced to buy a hat dyed green and trimmed
with straw folded and tucked to resemble heads of wheat. "You always want to surprise people with something new, so they see you
different. A woman who always wears a blue bonnet with lace trim
will start to look like that bonnet, even when she's not wearing it.
She needs some flowers near her eyes, or a red ribbon, or a brim that
sets off her face." She inspected Honor's plain cap so frankly that
Honor ducked her head.

"But *you* wear the same thing every day, Belle," the woman pointed out.

Belle patted her cap, which was almost as plain as Honor's, though with a limp frill around the edge and a cord at the back that when pulled made a little pleat in the fabric. "It don't do for me to wear anything fancy in the store," she said. "Don't want to compete with my customers—you're the ones got to look good. I wear my hats outside, for advertising."

Despite the haggling, the frivolous trimmings, the feeling at times that she was an entertainment for the hat wearers of Wellington, Honor liked working for Belle. Whatever she was making, she was at least kept busy, with no time to think about the traumas of the past, the uncertainty she was living in, or what lay ahead.

As she sat by the open window, Honor twice heard the thudding shoe of Donovan's horse and saw him ride past. One afternoon he stationed himself at the hotel bar across the square, leaning against the railing, his eyes on the millinery shop and, it seemed, on her. She shrank back in her seat, but could not avoid his gaze, and soon moved to the back porch, away from his scrutiny.

Belle had given Honor another pile of bonnets to work on, but before she began she sat for a few minutes, listening. There were no sounds from the woodshed, but Honor could feel that someone was there. Now that she knew who, and could even name and describe him, she felt a little less frightened. After all, it was he who would be frightened of her.

Belle had been so matter-of-fact about slaves before, but the idea was still new and shocking to Honor. Bridport Friends had discussed the shame of American slavery, but it had merely been indignant words; no one had ever seen a slave in person. Honor was astonished that one was now hiding fifteen feet from her.

She picked up a gray bonnet almost plain enough for a Quaker to wear. The lining was a pale primrose yellow, and she was to sew mustard-colored ribbons onto it, and add a yellow cord drawstring to the bavolet at the back of the neck where the cloth could be tightened and create a small ruff. Though at first Honor was doubtful of the color combination, by the time she'd finished it, she had to acknowledge that the yellow lifted the gray, yet was pale enough not to make the bonnet gaudy, though the ribbon color was more insistent than she would have chosen. Belle had unorthodox taste, but she knew how to use it to good effect.

During a lull in the shop, Belle brought out a tin mug of water. Leaning against the railing while Honor drank, she squinted into the yard. "There's a snake sunning itself on the lumber," she announced. "Copperhead. You got copperheads in England? No? Keep away from 'em—you don't want to get bit by one, it'll kill you, and it ain't a pretty death either." She disappeared inside, and came back out with a shotgun. Without warning, she aimed at the snake and fired. Honor started and squeezed her eyes shut, dropping the mug. When she dared to open them again, she saw the headless body of the snake lying in the grass, several feet from the planks. "There," Belle declared, satisfied. "Probably a nest, though. I'll get some boys in there to kill 'em all. Don't want snakes gettin' into the woodshed."

Honor thought about the man hiding there, almost three days now cramped in the heat and dark, and hearing the gunshot. She wondered how Belle came to be involved in hiding him. When her ears had stopped ringing, she said, "Thee mentioned that Kentucky is a slave state. Did thy family own slaves?" It was the most direct question she had dared to ask.

Belle regarded her with yellowed eyes, leaning against the porch railing and still holding the shotgun, her dress hanging off her. It occurred to Honor that the milliner must have an underlying illness to make her so thin and discolored. "Our family was too poor to own slaves. That's why Donovan does what he does. Poor white people hate Negroes more'n anyone."

"Why?"

"They think coloreds are takin' work they should have, and drivin' down the price of it. See, Negroes are valued a lot higher. Plantation owner'll pay a thousand dollars for a colored man, but a poor white man is worth nothin'."

"But thee does not hate them."

Belle gave her a small smile. "No, honey, I don't hate 'em."

The bell on the shop door rang, announcing a customer. Belle picked up her gun. "Donovan's gone, by the way. Saturday night he always drinks himself silly up at Wack's in Oberlin—that's one thing you can count on. Guess he's startin' early today. You can stop hiding from him back here if you want."

Dearest Biddy,

It grieves me to have to tell thee that God has taken Grace, six days ago, carried off by yellow fever. I will not go into details here—my parents can let thee read the letter I wrote them. How I wish thee were sitting here with me now, holding my hand and comforting me.

I think thee would be surprised to see where I am at this moment. I am sitting on the back porch of Belle Mills's Millinery shop in Wellington, Ohio. The porch faces west, and I am watching the sun going down over a patch of land, at the end of which glints the metal track of a railroad. When finished, it will run south to Columbus and north to Cleveland. The Wellington residents are very excited about it, as we would be if the railway in England were to extend to Bridport.

Belle is one of the many strangers who have taken pity on me and helped me along the way. Indeed, Belle more than most has been kind. Her shop is only seven miles from Adam Cox, yet when I arrived, she did not pack me off to Faithwell as soon as she could. She sensed without asking that I needed a pause to gather myself after Grace's death, and so has let me stay with her for a few days. In return I have been able to help with sewing, which has pleased me since it is a familiar activity, and I am able to feel useful rather than having to rely completely on others, or my purse, to look after me.

I am still stunned that Grace has been gone only a few days. Time and space have played funny tricks on me: the sea voyage seemed to go *on for years, though it was but a month, and I already feel far from Hudson, where Grace is buried, though I have only been in Wellington three days. For someone whose life was so ordered and without surprise, a great deal has happened to me in a short time. I suspect America will continue to surprise me.*

Already I am confused by its people, for they are so different from the English. Louder, for one thing, and they speak their minds in a way I am not accustomed to. Though they are familiar with Quakers, they think me odd. Customers in Belle's shop have been forthright in saying so, and in an overly familiar manner that jars. Thee knows I am quiet; being around Americans has made me even quieter.

Yet they have their secrets. For example, I am almost certain that, barely fifteen feet from where I write this letter, a runaway slave is hiding. I also begin to suspect he was hidden somewhere in the wagon that brought me to Wellington. But I do not dare to find out, for men are searching for the slave, and thee knows I cannot lie if asked. At home it was easy enough to be truthful and open. I rarely had to conceal anything from my family or thee. Only the business with Samuel was difficult in that way. Now, however, I have to keep my thoughts close. I do not ever want to lie outright, but it is more challenging to keep to that principle here.

I can at least be honest with thee, my dearest friend. I confess that I am nervous about Adam Cox's arrival tomorrow. He left for Ohio expecting only his future wife to join him, but now he has to contend with me without Grace. Of course I have known him and Matthew since the Coxes moved to Bridport, but they are older and not people I have been close to. Now they will be the only familiar faces amongst strangers.

Please say nothing of this to my parents, for I do not want them to worry about me. I do not think it is dishonest to withhold information about my feelings—they are not facts, and they are bound to change. Next time I write I hope to be able to report that I feel welcome in Faithwell and am content to live there. Until then, dear Biddy, keep me in thy thoughts and prayers.

Thy faithful friend,

Honor Bright

Silence

 HONOR WOKE EARLY on Sunday. Adam Cox would not come to pick her up until afternoon, after Meeting for Worship in Faithwell had finished, but anxiety made her lie awake in bed, listening to the dawn chorus of unfamiliar American birds, running her fingers over the outline of the Star of Bethlehem in the center of the quilt, and waiting for the changes to come.

Despite staying up much of the night with a bottle, Belle was also up early. As they ate breakfast—more eggs and ham, along with hominy grits, a white, thin sort of porridge Belle said she'd grown up with in Kentucky—Honor wondered if the milliner would go to church. But Belle made no move to leave; after clearing up the kitchen she sat out on the back porch reading the Cleveland *Plain Dealer* that a customer had left behind the day before. Honor hesitated, then got her Bible out of her trunk and went to join her.

The moment she sat down she knew the man was gone from the lean-to. There was a subtle shift in the atmosphere, and in Belle, who seemed more relaxed. She glanced over at the book in Honor's lap. "I don't go to church much myself," she remarked. "Me and the minister don't agree on most things. But I'll take you if you want. You got a choice of Congregationalist, Presbyterian or Methodist. I'd go for Congregationalist myself—better singers. I've heard 'em from outside."

"There is no need."

Belle rocked in her chair while Honor opened her Bible, trying to remember what she had last read, with her sister on her death-bed, a lifetime ago. She read a passage here and there, but could not concentrate on the words.

Belle was rocking faster. "Somethin' I want to know about Quakers," she announced, lowering the newspaper.

Honor looked up.

"You sit in silence, don't you? No hymns, no prayers, no preacher to make you think. Why's that?"

"We are listening."

"For what?"

"For God."

"Can't you hear God in a sermon or a hymn?"

Honor was reminded of standing outside St. Mary's Church in Bridport, just across the street from the Meeting House. The congregation had been singing, and she had been briefly envious of the sound.

"It is less distracting in the silence," she said. "Sustained silence allows one truly to listen to what is deep inside. We call it waiting in expectation."

"Don't you just think about what you're having for dinner, or what someone said about someone else? I'd think about the next hat I'm gonna make."

Honor smiled. "Sometimes I think about the quilt I am working on. It takes time to clear the mind of everyday thoughts. It helps to be with others also waiting, and to close one's eyes." She tried to think of words to explain what she felt at Meeting. "When the mind is clear, one turns inward and sinks into a deep stillness. There is peace there, and a strong sense of being held by what we call the Inner Spirit, or the Inner Light." She paused. "I have not yet felt that in America."

"You been to many Meetings in America?"

"Only one. Grace and I went to a Meeting in Philadelphia. It was—not the same as England."

"Ain't silence the same everywhere?"

"There are different kinds of silence. Some are deeper and more productive than others. In Philadelphia I was distracted and did not find the peace I was looking for that day."

"I thought Philadelphia Quakers are supposed to be the best there is. Top-quality Quakers."

"We do not think like that. But . . ." Honor hesitated. She did not like to be critical of Friends in front of non-Quakers. But she had started, so she must continue. "Arch Street is a big Meeting, for there are many Friends in Philadelphia, and when Grace and I entered the room, there were not many benches still free. We sat on one that was, and were asked to move, for they said it was the Negro pew."

"What's that?"

"For black Members."

Belle raised her eyebrows. "There's colored Quakers?"

"Yes. I had not known there were. None came that day to Meeting, and the bench remained empty, even though the other benches grew crowded and uncomfortable."

Belle said nothing, but waited.

"I was surprised that Friends would separate black Members in that way."

"So that's what kept you from God that day."

"Perhaps."

Belle grunted. "Honor Bright, you are one delicate flower. You think just 'cause Quakers say everyone is equal in God's eyes, that means they'll be equal in each other's?"

Honor bowed her head.

Belle shrugged and took up her newspaper again. "Anyway, I like me a good hymn. Give me that over silence any day." She began to hum, rocking in time to the simple, repetitive melody.

Later Belle had the neighbors' boys bring down Honor's trunk so that it was ready for Adam Cox's arrival. After dinner they sat together in the shop to wait for him. Though the other shops were also closed, people strolled up and down, looking in the windows.

"Thankee for your help," Belle said as they waited. "I'm caught up now. Won't be so busy again till September when they bring me their winter bonnets to be retrimmed."

"I am very grateful to thee for having me."

Belle waved her hand. "Honey, it's nothing. Funny, normally I don't take to company, but you're all right. You don't talk too much, for one thing. Are all Quakers as quiet as you?"

"My sister was not quiet." Honor gripped her hands so they would not tremble.

"Anyway," Belle said after a pause, "you can come here any time. Next visit I'll show you how to make hats. Now, I got somethin' for you." Belle went behind the counter and took down from a shelf the gray and yellow bonnet Honor had worked on the day before. "A new life needs a new bonnet. And this bonnet needs an adventure." When Honor did not take it, Belle pushed it into her hands. "It's the least I can do, as pay for all that work you did. And it'll suit you. Go on and try it."

Honor reluctantly took off her old bonnet. Though she liked the dove gray of the body of the bonnet, she didn't think the yellow rim would suit her. Yet when she looked in the mirror on the wall of the shop, she was startled to discover Belle was right. The yellow brim was like a soft halo that lit up her face.

"There you go," Belle remarked, satisfied. "You'll go to Faithwell lookin' smart, and maybe just a little more up-to-date. And here's a bit of the yellow left over—not enough for a lining so it's not much use to me. I know you quilters like your scraps."

Though she accepted that it was a silly thought, Honor wondered at first if Adam Cox was so cold with her because he didn't like the new bonnet.

When they heard a wagon approach from the north, Honor and Belle went out to the front of the shop to meet him, Honor's stomach twisting. Though she dreaded having to go through the details of Grace's death with him, to witness his grief and reignite her own, she was also looking forward to seeing a familiar face. When he drew up in front of the shop, slow and careful, she stepped forward eagerly, and was stopped short by his stiff gaze, as if he were far away and not engaged in what he was looking at. He could not seem to meet her eye. Nonetheless she said, "Adam, I am glad to see thee."

Adam Cox climbed down from the wagon. Honor had always been surprised that Grace chose to marry him. A tall man with the sloped shoulders of a shopkeeper, whiskers along his jaw, sober clothes and a broad-brimmed hat, he nodded at her as he approached the porch, but did not embrace her as a family member would. He looked uncomfortable, and it was confirmed to Honor even before he'd said a word that this would be a difficult reunion. There was no tie of blood or love to bind them, only circumstances and the memory of Grace. She felt tears welling, and struggled to keep them under control.

"I am glad to see thee too, Honor," Adam said. He did not sound glad.

"I thank thee for coming for me." Honor's voice emerged strangled.

Belle had been watching them, crossing her arms over her chest as she made up her mind about Adam Cox. But she was civil. "I'm real sorry about your intended's death, sir," she said. "God gives us a hard life, that's for sure. You look after Honor, now. She's had one hell of a time."

Adam stared at her.

"She's also got the finest sewing hand in town," Belle added. "I got a lot of work out of her. Well, now, Honor, I guess I won't see much of you—Faithwell's closer to Oberlin than to here, so you'll be goin' that way for your provisions. You watch out for them Oberlinites—they got opinions about everything and they'll be glad to tell you of 'em. You ever get tired of it over that way, come back—there's always work for you here. There, now, what's this?" For Honor was crying. Belle put her arms around her and gave her a hard, bony hug. For a thin woman she was very strong.

The road north from Wellington was wider and more established than the route Honor and Thomas had taken from Hudson. The trees had been cut further back so that the forest was less oppressive, and there were farms and fields of corn and oats along the way, as well as pastures where cows grazed. There was little traffic, though, it being Sunday.

Within a mile, Honor understood a little better Adam Cox's awkwardness: in terse words he told her that his brother Matthew had died three weeks before, of the consumption that brought Adam to Ohio to help with the business.

"I am so sorry," Honor said.

"It was expected. I did not want to burden Grace with the prognosis in my letters."

"How fares Matthew's widow?"

"Abigail is resigned to God's will. She is of strong character and will cope. But tell me of Grace."

Honor gave a brief account of her sister's illness and death. Then they lapsed into silence, and she could feel in its density the weight of unasked questions and unspoken comments. Chief among them, she was sure, was: "What is the sister to me now that the wife is gone?" Adam Cox was of course an honest and honorable man, and would accept responsibility for his would-be sister-in-law. But it was not easy for either.

Adam glanced over at Honor. "Is that bonnet new?"

Startled that he would show any interest in her wardrobe, Honor stuttered, "It—it was a gift, from Belle."

"I see. Thee did not make it."

"Is there something wrong with it?"

"Not—wrong. It is different from what thee normally wears—what a Friend would wear. But no, not wrong." It was strange to hear his Dorset accent so far from home. Adam cleared his throat. "Abigail—Matthew's widow—was not expecting thee. Indeed, I was not expecting thee either. We did not know thee was coming to Ohio until the milliner wrote the other day to say thee was with her."

"Thee did not get Grace's letter? She wrote the moment I decided to come. She sent it immediately—within a day." Honor kept adding information, as if by saying enough, the letter would appear.

"Honor, letters do not always arrive, or they arrive late—sometimes later than the person they announce. And by the time the letter arrives, the news is months old. Thee has written to thy parents about Grace, yes?"

"Of course."

"They will not know of her death for six weeks at the earliest. In the meantime thee will receive letters still asking after her. Thee must be prepared for that, upsetting as it is. The gap between letters can be disturbing. Things change before those affected are fully aware."

Honor was only half listening, for threaded through his words was the sound she had been expecting since leaving Wellington: the uneven hoofbeats of Donovan's horse approaching from behind.

He drew up alongside them, smelling of whiskey and stale smoke. "Honor Bright," he said, "you didn't think you could leave town without a good-bye, did you? That wouldn't be polite, after all. Wouldn't be friendly."

Adam Cox pulled on the reins to stop the wagon. "Hello, friend. Thee knows Honor?"

"This is Mr. Donovan, Adam," Honor broke in. "I met him on the road to Wellington." She did not add that he was Belle's brother: that would not help Adam's opinion of the milliner.

"I see. I thank thee for any kindness thee has showed Honor during this difficult time."

Donovan chuckled. "Oh, Honor's been quite the fixture in town, ain't you, darlin'?"

Adam frowned at the coarse familiarity. However, he knew no other way to be than honest. "I am taking her to live in Faithwell. If thee has finished, we will continue." He held up the reins expectantly.

"What, you gonna marry her now the sister's gone?"

Honor and Adam flinched and leaned away from each other. Honor felt physically ill.

"I have a responsibility to look after Honor," Adam said. "She is like a sister to me, and will live with my sister-in-law and me as family."

Donovan raised his eyebrows. "*Two* sisters-in-law and no wife? Sounds cozy for you."

"That's enough, Donovan." Honor's sharp tone was almost as surprising as her dropping of "Mr." Adam blinked.

"Ah, got your claws out! All right, all right, my apologies." Donovan half bowed from his saddle, then dismounted. "Now, I'll just have a look in your wagon. Down you get."

"What reason could thee have to search our things?" Adam demanded, the color rising in his face. "We have nothing to conceal."

"Adam, allow him," Honor whispered as she climbed down. "It is easier that way."

Adam remained on the seat. "No man has the right to search another's possessions without cause."

The violence when it came was so swift Honor caught her breath. One moment Adam was sitting hunched but defiant on the seat of the wagon; the next, he was lying in the dust of the road, crying out and holding his wrist while blood spurted from his nose. Honor ran and knelt by him, holding his head in her lap and mopping the blood with a handkerchief.

In the meantime, Donovan had opened her trunk once again, pawing through the contents and scattering them about on the wagon bed; he did not remark on the signature quilt. Then he lifted the seat they had been perched on and rummaged about. Satisfied at last, he jumped down and stood over them. "Where's the nigger, Honor? You know you can't lie to me, Quaker gal."

Honor looked up at him. "I do not know," she was able to say honestly.

Donovan held her gaze for a long moment. Though weary from his Saturday night carousing, his eyes were still lit with interest, and

Honor found them mesmerizing, for in the clear brown were little flecks of black like pieces of bark. He was still wearing her key under his shirt—she could see its outline.

"All right. Don't know why, but I believe you. Don't you ever lie to me, though. I'm gonna keep my eye on you. I'll be paying you a visit over in Faithwell soon." He swung up onto his bay horse. Turning its head back toward Wellington, he paused. "My sister's bonnet suits you, Honor Bright. Them colors are from a blanket we had when we was little." He clucked his tongue and the horse sprang away into a gallop.

Honor wished he would not tell her such things.

In the distance another wagon was coming. Honor helped Adam to his feet so that he would not be further shamed lying in the dirt in front of strangers. He clutched at his wrist.

"Break or sprain?" she asked.

"Sprain, I think, thanks be to God. It just needs binding." Adam shook his head at the mess of Honor's things in the wagon. "What did he think he would find? He knows we won't have any liquor or tobacco, and or indeed anything of value." He turned his bewildered eyes on Honor, who had retrieved his hat from the side of the road and was dusting it off.

She handed it to him. "He is looking for a runaway slave."

Adam stared at her until he had to move to make way for the approaching wagon. He said nothing until they were seated again, his wrist bound with one of Honor's neck cloths, and heading once more toward Faithwell. Then he cleared his throat. "It seems thee is quickly learning the ways of Americans." He did not sound pleased.

Faithwell, Ohio
6th Month 5th 1850

Dear Mother and Father,

It has been a very long journey from Bridport to Faithwell. The best part of my arrival was not lying down in a bed I knew I would not have to leave the next day, but seeing your letter awaiting me. Adam Cox told me it has been here two weeks: how can it have arrived so long before me when it had to make the same journey? I cried when I saw thy hand, Mother. Even though it was written just a week after I left, I relished every bit of news, because it made me feel I was still at home, taking part in all the daily events of the community. I had to remind myself by looking at the date of the letter that thy words and the things thee describes are two months old. Such a delay is so disorienting.

I am sorry to have to tell you that Matthew Cox has passed: the consumption he suffered from overtook him four weeks ago. This means the Faithwell household I have joined is now very different from what was anticipated. Instead of two married couples and me, there are just three of us, with tenuous ties to one another. It is awkward, though it is early days yet and I hope to feel more settled eventually, rather than a visitor, as I do now. Adam and Abigail, Matthew's widow, have been welcoming. But Grace's death has been a great shock to Adam, who of course had been looking forward to marrying and settling his wife into a new life in Ohio. My appearance was also a surprise, for the letter informing him that I had decided to accompany Grace to America never arrived.

I often find myself thinking of how Grace would have coped, how she would have smoothed the rough edges of the circumstances with her laughter and good humour. I try to emulate her, but it is not easy.

Adam's house in Faithwell—or Abigail's house, perhaps I should say, for she owned it with Matthew—is so different from what I am used to. I feel when I am in it as if the air around me has shifted and is not the same air I breathed and moved in back in England, but is some other substance. Can a building do such a thing? It is a new house, built about three years ago, of rough pine boards that smell of resin. The wood makes me think of a doll's house: it lacks the solidity of stone that made our own home on East Street feel so safe. The house creaks constantly, with the wood responding to the wind and the moisture in the air—it is very humid here, and they say it will get worse later in the summer. Apart from my bedroom it is spacious, for one thing America has is much land on which to build. There are two floors, and everyone knows when others go from one to the other, as the boards squeak so. The downstairs comprises a parlour, kitchen and what Americans call the sick room—a bedroom off the kitchen where whoever is ill at the time stays to be looked after. Apparently Americans get fever so often that they need such a room set aside for them—which is troubling, given what I have just witnessed with Grace.

There are three bedrooms upstairs: the largest, which Abigail would have shared with her husband, a medium-sized that Adam was expecting to share with Grace, and a tiny room that would have been for the baby if there were one. They have put me there, for now; the arrangement feels temporary, though what would be more permanent, I cannot say. Although there is room for little other than a bed, I do not mind. When I shut the door it is mine. The furnishings are adequate, though, as in many other American houses where I have stayed, they too have a temporary feel about them, as if they have been knocked together until there is time to build something more permanent. I always sit carefully in chairs, for fear they may break. The table legs often have splinters because they have not been properly sanded and finished. They are mostly made of maple or ash, which makes me miss the timelessness of our oak furniture.

The kitchen is not so different in principle from that on East Street:

*there is a hearth, a range, a long table and chairs, a sideboard for
crockery and pots, a larder—called a pantry here—for storage. Yet the
feeling is entirely different from the East Street kitchen. Partly it is that
Abigail is not so well organised as thee, Mother. She does not seem to
have "a place for everything, and everything in its place," as thee taught
me. She stacks wood haphazardly so that it does not dry out, leaves the
broom blocking the slops bucket rather than out of the way in the corner,
doesn't wipe up crumbs and so attracts mice, leaves dishes in a jumble
on the sideboard rather than neatly stacked. Then too, the range and
fireplace take wood instead of coal, so the kitchen smells of wood smoke
rather than the deeper earthiness of burning coal. We don't have to clean
up coal dust, but the wood ash can be just as trying, especially when
Abigail is clumsy.*

*It is unfortunate that Abigail and I did not get off to a good start.
The first meal she served on my arrival was a steak pie: the meat was
tough and the pastry hard. I said nothing, of course, and chewed away
at it as best I could, but Abigail was embarrassed—and was made more
so by giving me sour milk the next morning. I am hoping to be helpful
to her, using gentle persuasion over time.*

*I have ventured out into town a little—though 'town' is perhaps an
ambitious word for a row of buildings along a rutted track. Bridport
must be a hundred times its size. There is a general store—what we
would call a chandler—a smithy, the Meeting House, and ten houses,
with farms in the surrounding fields. The community comprises some
fifteen families, most of whom moved from North Carolina to get away
from the slavery that is engrained in society there. I have not yet been to
Meeting here, but the people I have met are friendly, though absorbed
in their own concerns, as many Americans I have met seem to be. They
do not practise the art of conversation in quite the way the English do,
but are straightforward to the point of bluntness. Perhaps this will
change when I have got to know the community better.*

Beyond us the road extends into forest, except where farms have been hacked out of the trees. I had no idea before coming to America just how hard it is to create farmland out of woods. There are stumps everywhere. England is very ordered, with the feeling that God has put trees in their place, and meadows in theirs, and that the fields have always been there rather than needing to be created. I look at the woods here from the window of my little room and it feels as if they are creeping towards the town, and axes will only temporarily keep them back. You know I have always loved trees, but here they are so overwhelmingly abundant that they feel threatening rather than welcoming.

The general store is sparsely stocked with everyday items. For everything that the general store doesn't carry, we must go to Oberlin, three miles away. It is much larger, with a population of two thousand as well as a collegiate institute full of students. I have not yet visited, though Adam's shop is there and he goes most days. Eventually if Faithwell grows large enough he would like to move the shop and sell primarily to Friends, but that may take some time. He has said I can help at the shop when they are busy. I shall be glad to be useful.

Daily life here feels more precarious than it did at home. What Bridport did not have Dorchester or Weymouth was sure to. In the American towns I have visited on my way here, and especially now in Faithwell, I sense that we must be self-sufficient, that we cannot rely on others because they are not always there to be depended upon. Most here grow their own vegetables, as we did, but there is no one selling lettuces should one's own be eaten by rabbits, as Abigail's were—here one simply goes without. Many keep their own cow as well. Abigail and Adam do not have a cow, though they do keep chickens; we buy milk and cheese from one of the outlying farms.

I have painted only a very brief portrait of Faithwell. I do not yet have a place here, but with God's help and the support of Friends, I *hope to find one. Please be reassured that I am safely arrived, and am well looked after. I have a bed and enough to eat and kind people about me. God is still with me. For these things I am grateful and have no reason to complain. Yet I think of you all often. Though it is too warm to use it now, I have laid the signature quilt across the end of my bed, and at the beginning and end of the day I touch the signatures of all who are dear to me.*

Your loving daughter,

Honor Bright

Appliqué

SHE COULD NOT stay. Honor knew this within half an hour of arriving at Adam and Abigail's in Faithwell. It was not the messy kitchen, where dishes left over from dinner were still piled in the sink, or the mud that had not been swept from the hallway, or the inedible supper, or the smokiness from a stove that did not draw well. It was not the mouse droppings she spied in the pantry, or the tatters of cobwebs fluttering in corners, or the tiny room Adam showed her that held no more than a bed, so that her trunk had to sit in the hallway. None of these things would have put her off.

She could not stay because Abigail clearly did not want her there. A tall woman with a wide forehead and dark, staring eyes, she had broad shoulders and thick ankles and wrists. On meeting Honor she hugged her, but there was no warmth in the contact. Defensive after the unpalatable meal she served, she rattled off a list of excuses as she showed Honor around the house. "Watch thee doesn't trip on that rug—it needs tacking down, doesn't it, Adam?" "This lamp does not usually smoke—I was in such a fluster about thy coming so unexpectedly that I didn't have time to trim it properly." "I would have swept, but knew thee and thy trunk would bring in dust I would have to sweep away again." Abigail had a way of making the faults of the household seem the result of everyone but herself. Honor began to feel guilty for being there at all.

As a child she had been taught that everyone has a measure of the Light in them, and though the amount can vary, all must try to live up to their measure. It seemed to her now that Abigail's measure was small, and she was not living up to it. Of course she had recently nursed and then lost a husband, and so could be forgiven for being somber. But Honor suspected her unfriendliness was part of her nature.

Adam Cox did not try to defend Honor or make her feel welcome, but sank further into himself, sober and quiet—stunned by the double loss of his brother and his fiancée, Honor suspected. Though their courtship had been conducted almost entirely through letters, he must have looked forward to the arrival of a lively, beautiful wife. Now he was stuck with the quiet sister and a difficult sister-in-law.

He only became animated as they were sitting on the front porch after supper and Abigail brought up Honor's decision to come to Ohio. "Adam told me about Grace's family," she said, rocking vigorously in her chair, her hands idle, for it was too dark to sew. "He said thee was to be married. Why is thee here instead?"

Adam sat up, as if he had been waiting for Abigail to bring up the difficult topic. "Yes, Honor, what happened with Samuel? I thought thee had an understanding with him."

Honor winced, though she knew eventually this question would have to be answered. She tried to do so in as few words as possible. "He met someone else."

Adam frowned. "Who?"

"A—a woman from Exeter."

"But I am from there and know most of the Friends there. Who is it?"

Honor swallowed to ease the tightness in her throat. "She is not a Friend."

"What, he married out of the faith?" Abigail practically shouted.

"Yes."

"I assume Bridport Meeting disowned him?" Adam asked.

"Yes. He has gone to live in Exeter, and joined the Church of England." That was what was hardest: Honor could almost manage the thought of Samuel no longer loving her, but for him willingly to leave the faith that was the very foundation of her life was a blow she did not think she could recover from. That, and the embarrassment in Samuel's parents' eyes whenever she ran into them, and the pity in everyone else's, had made her say yes to Grace's suggestion to emigrate.

Thinking of this, she found she was gripping her hands in her lap. She took a deep breath and tried to relax her fingers, but her knuckles were still white from being forced to think of Samuel.

Abigail shook her head. "That's just terrible." She sounded almost gleeful, but then frowned, perhaps recalling it was those circumstances that brought her this unwelcome guest. Something hard and cruel in her sidelong glance gave Honor the guilty feeling that, once again, she was at fault.

Though it was warm, that night she huddled under the signature quilt in the tiny bedroom, seeking solace.

Later Honor admitted to herself that she had not hidden her dismay at her new home well, and Abigail might easily have taken offense. The ramshackle, frontier nature of the house extended to Faithwell itself. When Adam brought her from Wellington, she'd thought the scattering of houses had been just the announcement of a larger settlement nearby. The next morning she discovered otherwise when she and Abigail went for a walk. Though it was raining and the road in front of the house had turned to mud, Abigail insisted on going out. It was as if she dreaded being alone with Honor—Adam had left early for the Oberlin shop. When Honor suggested they might wait until the rain let up, Abigail frowned and continued putting on her bonnet. "I hear it rains all the time in England," she countered, tying the ribbon tight under her chin. "Thee should be used to it. Thee won't wear that gray and yellow bonnet, will thee? It's fancy for Faithwell."

Honor had already decided to store Belle's bonnet; she wondered if she would ever find a place to wear it. Grace would have managed to wear it here, she thought.

She followed Abigail along the track, picking through the mud to planks that had been laid alongside for this purpose, though the mud covered them as well. They passed a few houses, similar in construction to Adam and Abigail's, but no one else was out. The general store was also empty apart from the owner. He greeted her kindly enough, with the sort of open, honest face she was familiar with among Friends back home. The shop itself was small and basic, the space given over primarily to barrels of flour, cane sugar, cornmeal and molasses. There were also a few shelves carrying a jumble of bits and pieces such as candles and bootlaces, a tablet of writing paper, a dishcloth, a hand broom—as if a peddler had come along and convinced the shopkeeper he needed one of each in case someone asked for it someday.

Honor maintained a strained smile as she looked around, trying to mask what she was thinking: that these barrels and shelves represented the limitations of her new life. A metal pail, a packet of needles, a jar of vinegar: these lone items, sad on their shelves, were all there was to Faithwell. There was no additional room full of tempting sweets or beautiful cloth, no corner to turn with another row of shops on a mud-free street, no duck-egg-blue floorboards. Adam's letters to Grace had not been lies, exactly, but he had made the town out to be thriving. "It is small but growing," he had written. "I am certain it will flourish." Perhaps Honor should have paid more attention to Adam's use of the future tense.

Back at the house she tried to help Abigail: she washed dishes and scrubbed pots, shook out the oval rag rugs scattered throughout the house, brought in wood for the range and hauled out ash from the stove to dump in the privy—"Outhouse," she murmured. With every task she asked for instructions so that she would not offend Abigail with different ways of doing things that might imply her hostess was in the wrong. Abigail was the sort of woman who thought that way.

She made her big mistake while sweeping the kitchen and pantry. "Does thee have a cat?" she asked as the mouse droppings accumulated in the pile of sweepings, thinking this gentle suggestion might solve the mouse problem.

Abigail dropped the knife she was using to peel potatoes. "No! They make me sneeze." She disappeared into the pantry and came back with a jar of red powder, which she tapped into bellows and began blowing into the corners, her movements jerky and accompanied by sighs. Honor tried not to stare, but curiosity overtook her, and she picked up the jar. "What is this?"

"Red pepper. Gets rid of vermin. Doesn't thee use it in England?"

"No. We had a cat." Honor did not add that their cat, a tortoiseshell called Lizzy, was a good mouser. She used to sit next to Honor while she sewed and purr. The thought of her old cat made her eyes sting, and she turned back to her sweeping so that Abigail would not see her tears.

In the evening when Adam returned, Honor heard Abigail whispering to him out on the porch. She did not try to listen; from the tone she knew what Abigail was saying: she could not stay. But where could she go?

The next afternoon, when Abigail decided they had done enough housework for the day, she settled into the rocker on the front porch with a quilt she was working on and a bowl of new cherries from a tree behind the house. Honor had picked them so the blue jays wouldn't eat them all. Fetching her sewing box, she joined Abigail. She had not worked on a quilt since being on board the *Adventurer*— her journey since then had been too disjointed, and her sewing time at Belle's was spent on bonnets.

Though she'd thrown into the ocean all of the hexagons her mother had cut out for her, Honor still had some bits of cloth from home, a few shapes she had already pieced, and fabric tacked around templates, ready to be sewn together. Most women who made quilts had half-started projects waiting for the right moment to be taken up again. Honor looked through the rosettes and stars she had already made, wondering what she should do with them. The shapes and colors—brown and green rosettes made from Grace's and Honor's old dresses, the beginning of a Bethlehem Star in different shades of yellow—reminded her of Dorset, and seemed foreign in the bright American sunlight. She did not think she could make something from them that would complement Ohio life. However, she was not ready to sit with pen and paper and work on a new design: it was too soon, and she needed a clear head, and inspiration.

Honor glanced at Abigail's quilt; if she were with her mother, or Grace, or her friend Biddy, she could offer to help if she did not want to work on her own project. However, she did not dare ask

Abigail, who would doubtless take the offer the wrong way. Besides, Abigail's quilt was in a style Honor could not imagine making: a floral appliqué of red flowers and green leaves spilling out of a red urn, sewn onto a white background. Honor had always preferred patchwork to appliqué, feeling that to sew pieces of fabric on top of large squares of material was somehow cheating, a shortcut compared to the harder task of piecing together hundreds of bits of fabric, the colors blended so that the whole was graduated and unified and made a pleasing pattern. Though some quilters despaired of the rigid geometry and the accuracy required for making patchwork, to Honor it was a happy challenge. Since coming to America she had seen these appliquéd quilts—usually red and white, sometimes with green as well—everywhere, in inns and guest houses, hanging on lines and over porch railings for airing. They were bright, cheerful, unsophisticated. Some of the quilting patterns were beautifully executed, of feathers or vines or grapes, sometimes padded so that the pattern stood out. But the overall look was not to her taste.

The block-piecing style of other American quilts was a little more appealing. Such a quilt consisted of a dozen or more blocks made up of squares and triangles set out in patterns with names like Bear's Paw, Monkey Wrench, Flying Geese, or Shoo Fly. More challenging than the appliquéd quilts, they were still too simple for Honor. She preferred her templates.

However, she must work on something—piece more shapes she might use later, when her head was clear and she had longer stretches of time. Honor began threading needles. She had poked five threaded needles into her pin cushion when she felt Abigail's eyes on her.

"What is thee doing?" Abigail demanded. "Why so many needles?"

"I get them ready so I do not have to stop each time I run out of thread," Honor answered. Belle Mills had not been surprised by her needle threading, but Belle was a seamstress.

"Now isn't that efficient," Abigail said in a tone that suggested efficiency was not something to be aspired to.

Honor pinned together two green and brown hexagons already tacked to templates, and began a quick overhand stitch in white thread, her preferred color for sewing, whatever the color of the cloth. She paused at the end of the row to fit in another hexagon, run the thread under the cloth, and begin sewing, two sides now.

Abigail was staring again. "How does thee sew so fast?"

"I keep my thread short." Honor had noticed that when Abigail threaded her needle she cut off thread as long as her arm.

Abigail picked up one of the rosettes Honor had already made. "Look at those stitches," she declared, pulling at the seams. "They're so even. I haven't seen stitches that fine since I was a girl in Pennsylvania. One of our neighbors had a hand this good." She crinkled its petals. "Is that paper in there?"

"Yes. Thee has not made patchwork using paper templates?"

"No."

"In England we sew cloth around paper shapes to keep them accurate, otherwise they won't fit when we sew them together to make the quilt. See?" Honor handed Abigail some paper hexagons.

"But then the comfort will crackle!"

"We take them out once we have sewn them all together." Honor loved removing the paper templates from a finished piece, a design that had been stiff and formally held in place by paper growing soft and comfortable.

Abigail was peering at the paper templates. "Ten pound flour," she read. "One cake rennet. I did not want . . . away from Dorch . . . will soon return . . ."

Honor froze. Even as Abigail read out the scraps of words, she knew it was in Samuel's hand—a brief note telling her he was visiting relatives in Exeter and would be back in a week. The letter had seemed unimportant at the time, enough that Honor sacrificed it for use as templates. Now it carried more meaning, Exeter being where Samuel had met the woman he married.

Honor held out her sewing box so that Abigail could put the templates back. Abigail took her time, though, continuing to inspect the words on the scraps of paper while Honor waited. At last she dropped them in. "I prefer appliqué," she said, smoothing out her square of red and green and white. "It makes a simple, pretty comfort." Honor could see that her stitches were ragged, and of different lengths. It was no surprise that her sewing was so uneven, for to make even stitches the seamstress herself had to be steady. Abigail tended to hunch over her patchwork, her fingers and thread a snarl, and sew a few stitches before abandoning it to look down the road toward the houses near the general store, or to get up for a drink of water. Honor knew such restless sorts, even among Quakers, for she had taught several to sew in Bridport. She attributed her own fine sewing to the prolonged periods of silence at Meeting; these had made her thoughts level and her hand steady, which was reflected in her even stitching. But it seemed that silence did not have that effect on everyone's sewing.

Honor did not try to teach Abigail, to adjust the way she held her needle or advise her to sit up straight and to use a thimble so she wouldn't prick her fingers and get blood on the white cloth, or show her how to do a double back stitch instead of making a knot in the thread. It was enough to be able to sit with her and work side by side in a familiar rhythm Honor had known her whole life.

"Wait till the others see thy stitching," Abigail remarked. "They'll be asking thee to quilt for them at the next frolic."

———

Slowly Honor began to meet other Faithwell residents. Passersby came up to be introduced when they were sitting on the front porch. Abigail took her to the farm west of town that sold milk and cheese, and she met the farmers as well as a few other customers. On the Fifth Day it was raining so hard Abigail declared she would not attend Meeting in such weather. So it was not until the First Day Meeting that Honor met the whole community.

Faithwell Meeting House consisted of a bright, square room with bare whitewashed walls and windows on all sides. It was about the size of Bridport's, but for half the number of Members, so it did not have the crowded feel Honor knew from home. Benches on four sides faced inward, one of them reserved for Elders—the senior Members whom the community looked to for guidance. An unlit stove sat in the center, its pipe zigzagging up to a hole in the roof.

Honor had been looking forward to Meeting, for she had not attended one since Philadelphia and craved the sense of peace it normally brought. It always took some time for a Meeting to grow still and quiet, like a room where dust has been stirred up and must settle. People shifted in their seats to find comfortable positions, rustled and coughed, their physical restlessness reflecting their minds, still active with daily concerns. One by one, though, they set aside thoughts about business, or crops, or meals, or grievances, to focus on the Inner Light they knew to be the manifestation of God within. Though a Meeting started out quiet, the quality of the silence gradually changed so that there came a moment when the air itself seemed to gather and thicken. Though there was no outer sign of it, it became clear that collectively the Meeting was beginning to concentrate on something much deeper and more powerful. It was then that Honor sank down inside herself. When she found the place she sought, she could remain there for a long time, and see it too in the open faces of surrounding Friends.

Occasionally Friends felt moved to speak and give testimony, as if God were using them as a medium. They spoke thoughtfully, sometimes quoting passages from the Bible. Though anyone could speak if they wished to, Elders spoke more often than others. Honor had never spoken: the feeling she reached at Meeting was not something she could describe in words. Trying to would ruin it.

Yet, though Faithwell Meeting was similar in form to English Meetings, Honor found as she sat, still and silent, that she could not drain her mind. The space was different, the light and the air and the smell, and the many new faces. Then, too, there were the crickets and grasshoppers, and something Abigail called katydids, all noisier and more persistent than any insects Honor had heard in England. Their buzzing and droning and whining produced a wall of sound difficult to ignore.

All of these things were distractions. But Honor had been to unfamiliar Meetings before, in Exeter and Dorchester and Bristol, and she had managed to experience the same silence as at Bridport. At Faithwell, however, she was conscious of being in a place she would be expected to consider home, and because of that, she could not relax and let her mind go. When the silence began to deepen, Honor could not connect to that communal gathering and follow the others. Instead she found herself thinking about Grace's last, terrible days; about Abigail, beside her, and Adam, across from them on the men's bench, and the strained atmosphere in the house, and the looks that passed between them which she tried to ignore; of the black man hiding in Belle's woodpile; of Belle's jaundiced skin and surprising hats; of Donovan, pawing through her trunk and looking at her with light in his eyes. A few days after her arrival, he had ridden through Faithwell while she and Abigail were hanging out laundry, and had slowed and lifted his hat. Abigail had been horrified.

Honor was not a fidgeter like Abigail, who crossed and recrossed her ankles, blew her nose, wiped sweat from her neck. Honor had always sat very still at Meeting—indeed, could sit for two hours without changing position. But it was possible to sense that someone was not part of the silence, even when they did not move. Perhaps Abigail was disturbed by Honor's lack of concentration. She shut her eyes and tried again. When that did not work, she opened her eyes and looked for an inspiring face. There was one at every Meeting: someone—often a woman—with a face so attentive and anticipative that they provided silent leadership, even among a group who functioned by consensus. It was almost painful to watch them, for it seemed a violation of their private communion with God. Yet they were a good reminder of the open approach a Friend should take at Meeting.

At Faithwell, Honor found the face on the Elders' bench perpendicular to where she sat. She was an older woman, with white hair under her cap and bright eyes focused on a distant point outside the room, indeed probably somewhere in her mind's eye. Her arched eyebrows gave her an open, surprised expression, and the natural line of her mouth fell into a half-smile accentuated by round cheeks. Honor kept glancing at her, and had to force herself to look down so that the glance would not become a stare. Though immensely compelling, the woman's face was not necessarily friendly. She was someone you admired and respected rather than loved. She did not enable Honor to concentrate as she had hoped, however.

At length a man stood up to quote from the Scriptures. That at least gave Honor something to think about, even if she could not find a way to her own communion with God.

After Meeting she was introduced to many people, but found it hard to remember a long list of unremarkable names: Carpenter, Wilson, Perkins, Taylor, Mason. Only a few stood out: Goodbody, Greengrass, Haymaker. The last she recognized as the dairy farmers they bought milk from; it was Judith Haymaker with the compelling face on the Elders' bench. Now that Meeting was over her expression was less intense, but she still had widely arched eyebrows over a pale, blue-eyed gaze that Honor found hard to meet for more than a second or two. Her daughter Dorcas was with her; a similar age to Honor, she smiled obediently when introduced but seemed indifferent to this potential new friend. Indeed, though the Faithwell community was polite enough, they did not ask Honor any questions. It was not that she wanted them to—she was not eager to repeat the story of Grace's death—but her new neighbors seemed solely interested in their own affairs.

Judith Haymaker nodded at a young man standing among the others. "My son, Jack." As if hearing his name from afar, he looked over, his eyes snagging on Honor's as none of the other men's had. His messy brown hair was lightened by blond strands like stalks of hay, and his half-smiling mouth was like his mother's, but warmer.

Oh, she thought, and looked away, catching Dorcas Haymaker's pale blue eyes as she did. Dorcas did not have the perpetual smile of the rest of her family, but a forceful nose like a carrot and a frown that reminded Honor of Abigail. She looked down at the ground. Were all American women so difficult to talk to?

No. She said a little prayer of thanks for Belle Mills.

Dearest Biddy,

I write this letter from the front porch of Adam and Abigail's house
in Faithwell. One of the benefits of American houses is that most have
porches where one can sit and catch what little breeze there is and yet be
sheltered from the sun. It is hot here, as hot as Dorset ever was, and I
have been told that next month will be worse. It is not just the heat
that enervates, but the inescapable humidity that makes one feel
enveloped in a cloud of steam. My dress is damp, my hair frizzed, and
sometimes I can barely take in a breath. In such heat it is difficult to
summon the energy for work. If only thee were here beside me, to talk
and laugh and sew. Then the strangeness of this place would be more
bearable—as it would have been if Grace were here. Had she lived, she
would have made our lives into the adventure the ship that brought us
to America promised. Without her it is more like a trial I am being put
through. I wish I could tell thee that I am settling happily into my new
life in Ohio. I know that is what thee wishes for me, and I for myself.
But I confess, Biddy, if it were not for the impossible journey to reach
Bridport, I would immediately buy my place east on a stage from
Cleveland. There is little to keep me here.

I do not mean to sound ungrateful. Adam Cox has been welcoming,
if rather silent about how I will fit into the household without Grace as
the natural reason for my presence. Perhaps he does not know himself
what to think. Abigail will think for him, I suspect.

I must try to be fair. Abigail too has welcomed me, in her way.
When I first arrived she threw her arms around me, as American
women like to do; I had to remain very still and not flinch. Then she
cried and said how sorry she was about Grace and how she hoped we
would be like sisters. Since then, though, she has not been very

sisterly. Indeed, at times I have caught her studying me in a way that is not friendly, though she tries to cover it with questions about how I am, or offers of cups of tea, or a loud cough at nothing. Underlying all that she says and does is the iron rod of an inflexible spirit. Whatever her plans were for Grace's arrival, they have been put into disarray now that I have come instead. Abigail does not like her plans to be altered.

Of course it cannot be easy to have an unexpected stranger arrive to live in one's house, especially when that house is as chaotic as hers. She does not seem to have an order to her work; I have not yet discerned which day is wash day, for example, or on which day she bakes. Most noticeable is that the kitchen is not the comfortable centre of the house. Always when I worked with Mother in the East Street kitchen there was a sense of clarity, of light and warmth and happy industry. I could not be miserable in such a kitchen, even when there were things to be unhappy about. By contrast, Abigail's kitchen is dark and muddled and temporary. It is hard to feel settled in a place that itself is so unsettled. I would like to scrub every inch of it, air it, and make a place for everything so that I may put it in its place. I have tactfully tried to put things in order without offending Abigail, but with little success. Though she said nothing about my scrubbing and sweeping, when I rearranged the crockery on the sideboard, the next morning I found the bowls and plates back in their random stacks. She does her work with such clattering and rattling and slamming that I grow weary just hearing her.

Perhaps thee will best understand what Abigail is like if I tell thee that when she quilts she prefers to stitch in the ditch, hiding her poor stitches in the seams between the blocks. I do not think thee or I has resorted to such a technique since we were girls!

But I am being unkind. Abigail too has had her own unhappiness. She lost her husband to consumption after a long struggle, and she and

Matthew were married for three years before he died, yet had no children. That must be a sorrow, though of course we have not spoken of it.

Perhaps it is simply me. I have been unsettled since leaving home— and before then, in honesty, for Samuel's change of heart shook loose my solid life. So I am seeing my surroundings in that light. We are an odd trio, Abigail, Adam and I, for it is only indirect bonds of duty that hold us together. That is truly what makes the house feel temporary— my position in it is so precarious. After twenty years of living in the secure arms of family, it is a strange and terrifying feeling to be so adrift.

Faithwell itself is a tiny, rough sort of place. I know Adam did not deliberately lie in his letters describing it, but when he called it a 'town' he was clearly exaggerating. They boast that this part of Ohio is cleared and populated, much more so than ten years ago, but to me it feels like a frontier, with a few houses scratched out of the wilderness. Thee would be amazed at what is called the 'general store' here—a shop with mostly bare shelves and little to choose from, set on a track that a coach could never manage. Even wagons frequently get stuck in the mud, or the ride is so jolting one would rather walk.

The Meeting House is pleasant at least, and the Friends kind. I do not know why, but I have not been able to settle at Meeting yet; this is a great disappointment, as I normally take much comfort from the collective silence, and it would do me good now truly to wait in expectation with others. I need to be patient, I know, and a way will open once again.

I have not yet got to know the other families, nor discerned who might become a friend. The women in general here are straightforward, in conversation, in dress, even in the way they walk, which is flatfooted and rather graceless. Thee would smile. At least thee may be content that there is no rival here who would ever take thy place as my dearest friend.

I must stop criticising my new country. I will leave thee with something to smile at: in Ohio they like to call quilts 'comforts'!

Thy faithful friend,

Honor Bright

Dandelions

TWO WEEKS AFTER her arrival, Adam Cox asked Honor to help him at his Oberlin store on a Sixth Day, as Abigail, who usually helped him when needed, was unwell. Sixth Days were busy ones in towns, with the stores in Oberlin remaining open late for farmers coming in from the fields. Honor was pleased with the prospect of going to a larger town, for she was finding the isolation of Faithwell trying. She was also glad to have time away from Abigail, who had become increasingly hostile.

Adam normally rode his horse to the store, or walked if he had the time. For Honor, however, he borrowed a buggy. Just as they drove past the general store, Judith Haymaker came out carrying a sack of flour. Honor hoped her eyesight was not keen enough to spot the gray and yellow bonnet she was wearing. She had not touched Belle Mills's gift since arriving in Faithwell, but thought that it might be appropriate while working in Adam's store—smarter than her everyday bonnet but not ostentatious. Of course it should not matter what she wore, as long as it was clean and modest. She should not care. But Honor did care about that inner rim of pale yellow, its reflection lifting her face from the gray of the rest of the bonnet, just as she cared about the inch of white cloth edging the necklines of her dresses. Such details made her feel clearer and more defined. She suspected, though, that Judith Haymaker would not approve. Adam himself had raised his eyebrows when Honor came down wearing the bonnet, but said nothing.

Now he nodded at his neighbor, and Judith Haymaker nodded back, otherwise standing motionless to watch them pass.

East of Faithwell the trees closed in, and Honor swallowed several times to force down a rising panic. She wondered if she would ever grow used to the monotonous Ohio woods. It made her miss the ocean—not traveling on it, but the shoreline, with its definitive break from the land and its open, promising horizon.

Once they had turned onto the road north to Oberlin, however, she could relax a little, for it was clearer, running past farms and fields of corn, and the pressure of the woods receded. There was enough sunlight along the road that wildflowers could grow, chicory and Queen Anne's lace and black-eyed Susans. There was also more traffic: other buggies and wagons and horses heading their way, or passing them in the opposite direction toward Wellington.

"Why do all the roads run north and south or east and west?" Honor asked. She had been puzzling over this regularity since first riding with Thomas from Hudson to Wellington. In England roads followed the contours of the landscape, which did not conform to rigid compass directions.

Adam chuckled. "Because they can. This part of Ohio is very flat, so there is nothing the roads need go around to avoid. Except for one dogleg by the Black River a few miles south of here, this road runs dead straight between Oberlin and Wellington for nine miles. The towns are more or less evenly spaced too, every five miles or so in either direction, like a net."

"Except Faithwell."

"No, we stand apart," Adam agreed.

"Why did they place the towns so evenly?"

"Perhaps the surveyors of this territory were trying to bring order to a land they felt they had no control over." Adam paused. "It is very different from Dorset." It was the first time she had heard him compare Ohio to home since coming to live with him.

Adam drove Honor around Oberlin before stopping at the shop. It was a pretty town, more substantial than Faithwell and twice the size of Wellington. The buildings looked sturdier and more permanent, with a few even built of brick. In the center of town, four streets formed the sides of a square, which had been created by felling all the trees. Half the square had college buildings on it; the rest was a park planted in diagonal lines with new oaks and elms. Honor was glad to see trees that were familiar and ordered, so different from the thick, indistinguishable woods surrounding Faithwell.

Two of the streets making up the square were taken up by other college buildings. Honor sat in the buggy and watched the young people hurrying back and forth, so busy and earnest. Some were women, and some were black. "Are they all students?"

Adam nodded. "Oberlin was founded on principles of equality similar to Friends. Indeed, it began as a religious community, with strict rules of conduct. No alcohol is sold in town, or tobacco."

"No spitting, then."

"Yes, no spitting." Adam chuckled. "It is surprising, isn't it? Funny, though, one gets used to it. I don't notice the spitting now when I go to Cleveland."

Oberlin's shops were for the most part on Main Street, and the variety after Faithwell dazzled Honor, with several groceries, two butchers, a cobbler, a barber, a dentist, a milliner, two bookstores and even a daguerreotype artist. The roads were better than the one running through Faithwell—wider and less rutted, though still prone to thick mud when it rained. Planks had been laid in front of the shops for pedestrians.

Cox's Dry Goods on Main Street was modest compared to the shop Adam's brothers had run in Bridport, where there had been bolts of cloth stacked in open cupboards from floor to ceiling and a ladder on runners they slid along to climb for out-of-reach material. Here the floor space was bigger but there was less stock, laid out on tables in the center of the room. Adam's brother had not managed to make the shop into a thriving business before he fell ill. In the year since, Adam had built it up only slowly. It was perhaps the very principled nature of the town that drew Quakers like Matthew and Adam to run a shop there, but those principles were also the cause of the limits to its success. Apart from restrictions on diet and behavior, original Oberlin settlers were discouraged from wearing clothes made from expensive fabrics. Although the town population was now diluted by newer, less principled settlers, there were still few buyers for the more profitable soft velvets and bright satins the Cox family had sold to non-Quakers in Bridport. In fact, there was little Adam sold that Honor could not have worn herself. Full of gingham and chintz—which American customers called calico—and only a little damask or dimity for curtains, the shop's brightest fabrics were the bundles of offcuts Adam kept in stock for quilters. There were no restrictions on what an Oberlinite or a Quaker could use in making her quilts, even if the bright reds and greens of Ohio quilts might never be seen in her dresses.

Adam kept Honor at his side for the first hour to teach her how to measure cloth against the marks made on the edge of the table, make a small cut and rip the fabric along the weave, and wrap it in brown paper and string. She had bought cloth often enough to be familiar with the procedure, which did not differ between Oberlin and Bridport. At least some things were the same in the two countries. Once Adam was confident that Honor knew what to do, he left her to deal with customers alone while he handled money and oversaw a boy he'd hired to sharpen scissors and needles brought in by customers, a recent initiative he hoped would help the shop's prospects.

Honor was glad to have contact with new people. While living in a community of Friends was familiar, after just a few weeks in Faithwell, among the same people day after day, she was finding its limitations trying, and craved variety. At home she had been more used to the mingling of Quakers and non-Quakers, and with the coming and going of ships there was always something different to see, and strange faces to ponder. In Adam's store she studied people's clothes and listened to their talk about politics or the weather or crops, or what foolish Oberlin students had been up to. She watched boys run by with hoops, and smiled at a girl dragging a carved toy dog on a string. She held a baby while a customer spread out a bolt of cloth, and helped an elderly woman around the corner to the buggy waiting for her on College Street. All of these interactions made her feel vital rather than the unwanted extra she was at Abigail's.

Among the steady stream of customers, several black women came in to buy cloth or needles or pins, or to have their scissors sharpened. Honor tried not to stare, but she could not help it, as they were like exotic birds blown off course to land among sparrows. They all looked the same to her, with brown skin like polished oak, high cheekbones, wide noses and dark, serious eyes. They conducted themselves similarly too. After glancing at her, they went over to Adam, waiting for him if he was helping someone else, then asking him for material, or giving him the scissors or needles for the boy to sharpen. It was as if they had established that Adam was safe, and so they did not have to approach her. Clear about what they wanted, they chose quickly, paid and left, saying little to Adam and nothing to Honor. They certainly would not have asked her to hold their babies for them.

When there was a lull in the shop, Honor went out for a brief walk to escape the heat inside, and discovered a few doors down a confectioner's where a crowd of black women were gathered, chatting and laughing in groups. The man behind the counter, selling peppermints and shaved ice, was also black and clearly in charge. Honor had not expected Negroes to own their own businesses. Donovan had been right: Oberlin was radical.

As a Quaker, Honor had been used to the feeling of being set apart, and she was an outsider in almost every place in America. She knew the black women must feel more comfortable with one another, just as she did with other Quakers. However open-minded, people tended to gravitate to those like themselves. And Negroes had reason to be wary of whites, where one family could produce two people as different as Donovan and Belle Mills. But as she watched the women so clearly at ease, where they hadn't been in Cox's Dry Goods, she felt a pang. I am excluded even from the excluded, she thought.

Late in the day, as she was folding cloth, Honor heard a throat cleared beside her. "Excuse me, miss. How much is that a yard?"

A black woman stood next to her, intent on the fabric in Honor's hands: a cream cotton dotted with tiny rust-colored diamonds. She was as small as Honor, and older, her cheeks smooth and shiny and crisscrossed with lines, like the palms of hands. She wore spectacles and a straw hat trimmed with dandelions limp from the heat.

Honor glanced toward Adam: he had disappeared into the back

room. "I will look for thee," she said, pleased to have been asked. Each bolt was wound around a flat piece of wood; on one end Adam had written the price. Honor searched for that now, pulling back the layers of cloth. "Fifty cents a yard," she announced.

The woman grimaced. "I can manage that, just about." She pulled out a lace collar yellow with age but beautifully made, and laid it on top of the cloth, smoothing it with long fingers tipped with pale oval nails. "This go with it?" She said this more as a statement than a question, and Honor did not know if she should answer. The collar went well enough with the material, but something finer like silk would have been preferable. She did not think she should suggest this, though, as silk cost much more.

"Is it for thee?" she asked.

The woman shook her head. "Daughter's wedding dress. She need somethin' she can wear after, for everyday or for church."

She is like any woman, Honor thought, concerned that her daughter should look her best and yet have a practical dress. "Then it is a good choice," she said. "How many yards would thee like?"

"Six—no, five, please. She's a little thing."

Her hands shaking, Honor measured and cut the cloth with more care than she had for any other customer that day. As she wrapped the cloth and tied twine around the paper, she thought, This is the first time I have helped a black person.

She felt eyes on her and glanced up. The woman was studying the yellow rim of Honor's bonnet. "Where you get that bonnet? Not from Oberlin, did you?"

"No. Belle Mills's Millinery in Wellington." Several other women had already asked about the bonnet and had been disappointed that they would have to go all the way to Wellington for one.

Recognition sparked in the woman's eyes; she gazed at Honor, a steady look unhampered by her glasses. She might have been about to say something when Adam appeared from the back room. "Hello, Mrs. Reed. Has Honor been able to help with everything thee needs?"

Mrs. Reed's eyes disappeared behind a flash of spectacles as she turned to Adam. "Yep, she did. Where Abigail at?"

"I'm afraid she was unwell this morning."

"Was she, now." Mrs. Reed pressed her lips together and handed Adam the money for the fabric. She made it seem as if she had much to say but was holding it back behind her clamped mouth, only letting some of her thoughts seep out from her eyes. She picked up her package from the table. "Thankee. Good day." She turned and departed without looking back.

Honor refolded the cloth and put it away, deflated. Clearly their encounter had meant much less to Mrs. Reed than it had to her.

Faithwell, Ohio
7th Month 5th 1850

My dear parents,

I was overjoyed to receive your letter this morning—the first I have had since the letter that awaited my arrival in Faithwell. As I read it I could hear your familiar voices, and imagine exactly how Mother sat at the desk in the corner to write it, looking out of the window now and then while considering what news to tell me.

My pleasure was only tempered by the pain of reading your address to Grace as well. Even as I write this, you, indeed the whole community, still do not know of her death, and it is an odd feeling, that news of such importance suffers a delay of almost two months. By the time you receive this letter, other things may have happened that you will not know of. Similarly, the news I have had from your letter may already have been overtaken by other events. I can only hope and pray that our lives will not be so full of drama as to outdate our letters before they reach their destination.

Since last writing, I have been slowly getting to know the other residents of Faithwell, and to help Abigail more effectively than I did at first. I am no longer trying to reorganise the house, for when I do make a suggestion she takes it as a criticism against her. Of course I don't mean it in that way—I am only trying to help her establish a household that runs smoothly. But she is very sensitive. Adam has refused to become involved other than to ask me to respect Abigail's right as mistress of the house to organise it as she prefers. And so I have had to step back.

However, in one way I have managed to make real improvements. Abigail does not like to work in the kitchen garden—it is unbearably hot, with the sun shining more than in England and the air so thick and still. One might think that since she is a native to American

summers she would be more tolerant of the heat than I. But she becomes
very red in the face and complains so bitterly that I pity her. Then there
is the constant struggle against animals and insects, which she finds
trying. When I offered to do the work myself, Abigail looked grateful for
the first time since my arrival. That in itself is worth the heat.

In the garden we are growing many of the vegetables one would find
in thy garden, Mother: potatoes, beans, carrots, lettuces, tomatoes. But
they are different from what I am used to, even when the varieties are
meant to be the same. The potatoes are larger, with more eyes. The
carrots are thinner and more tapered—though as tasty. The beans have
a smoother skin, and the lettuce leaves grow much faster.

Much of the garden is given over to corn. Where at home it is only
grown to feed livestock, here corn seems to be the primary staple, even
more than wheat or oats. It grows everywhere, and though it is still too
young to eat fresh, I am assured it is tender and sweet. I have, however,
eaten much that is made with cornmeal. Too much, I sometimes think.
Abigail insists on doing the cooking, though she will allow me to wash and
chop and scrub for her. Everything seems to be corn-based, from the mush
favoured for breakfast to the bread that accompanies dinner to the batter
for the occasional fried fish to the cakes we have with coffee. Of course I do
not complain; I am grateful for any food served. It is just that the
underlying sweet vegetable flavour begins to make everything taste
similar.

I have much to do in the garden. Abigail and Adam started it off
well enough, but in the summer heat it needs constant watering. The
weeds seem to grow faster and more luxuriant than the crops. Then
there are the deer and rabbits, the birds, the slugs and snails and locusts
and other insects I am unfamiliar with. The rabbits are particularly
clever at digging under fencing—I am sure American rabbits are more
intelligent than English ones—to the point where I am almost tempted
to sleep out in the vegetable patch to scare them away. Now that Abigail

has handed over the responsibility for the garden to me, she has become very critical of my methods, without making useful suggestions herself. It can be rather trying. Luckily the corn does not need too much attention. I am glad, for whenever I go down the rows of it I always scare out a few snakes. I have never seen so many snakes; I have had to stifle a few screams. Most of them are harmless, though there are enough that are poisonous to keep me wary.

They say here that the corn should be 'knee-high by the Fourth of July'. Ours is much higher than my knee, and I thought it must be doing exceptionally well, until I was told that it meant one's knee when mounted on a horse. There are so many words and phrases that I don't understand, sometimes I wonder if American English isn't a language as foreign as French.

Yesterday was the Fourth of July. One subject Americans feel strongly about is their independence from Britain. They are very proud of having become a separate country. I did not know what to expect, though I had heard there would be celebrations in many places. However, neither Faithwell nor Oberlin celebrated, for it would be supporting the Declaration of Independence, a document that I have learned does not include Negroes as equal citizens. Instead some of the Faithwell Friends went along to the college park in Oberlin to listen to anti-slavery speeches, bringing with us a picnic deemed necessary rather than celebratory. In general northern Ohioans oppose slavery, and Oberlin has a reputation for being the most vehemently anti-slavery of all the towns in the area.

For once it was not too hot, with a breeze that kept us comfortable. The spread of food was enormous, all laid out on trestle tables. Americans take their picnics very seriously. Where at home we would carry modest provisions, here it is considered important to display and eat as much as possible. I did not think that Faithwell Friends would find a way to show off—indeed, in terms of dress and deportment they are as modest as any Bridport Friend. But they laid out more food than ever we could eat, with much care taken over the baked goods. This seemed to be the case with Oberlinites as well, as I noted when Abigail and I strolled about the square. I have never seen so many pies.

I was interested to witness a small group of Negroes also picnicking. While my passage in America to Ohio took me only through states where slavery is not permitted, I did come across a few Negroes, usually working on the docks or the stagecoaches, or in the kitchens and stables of inns. I never saw any at their leisure. Here I studied them—out of the corner of my eye, for I did not wish to stare—and found they are not so different from everyone else. Their picnic was certainly as abundant, though it may have differed in content: many Ohio Negroes are originally from the South, where I have heard the cooking described as more vigorous. The Negro women dressed with more frills than a Quaker would, though the cloth was not so fine. The men wore dark suits and straw hats. Their children were boisterous, and played with balls and pinwheels and kites, as did the white children in the square— though they did not play together.

The speeches were long, and I confess I did not understand much of what they said. It was not just the American accents, which are varying and at times baffling. It seems that even those opposed to slavery disagree about how it should be ended, with some advocating immediate emancipation, while others argue that such a drastic action would ruin the economy, and that freedom needs to be handed out incrementally. They talked too of Congress—the American equivalent of our Parliament, I think—debating a bill about fugitive slaves, and the men who spoke grew very heated, at times their words descending into personal insults towards politicians I had not heard of. However, their speeches gave me much to think about.

Then the blacksmith from Faithwell recited a poem in a deep simple voice that was welcomed by the crowd. I asked afterwards and

*discovered it was a poem by Whittier: 'Stanzas for the Times'. I have
written down some of the lines I want to remember:*

> *. . . guided by our country's laws,*
> *For truth, and right, and suffering man,*
> *Be ours to strive in Freedom's cause,*
> *As Christians may,—as freemen* can!

*When it grew dark the students of the college hung paper lanterns in
the trees, and fiddlers played songs I was not familiar with. It was very
beautiful, and I felt at ease for perhaps the first time since leaving
England.*

*Only one thing marred the day. I was at the picnic table, looking for
food with no corn in it, when I overheard Judith Haymaker, a
dairywoman who sells us milk and cheese and is one of the Elders of
Faithwell Meeting, say to Adam, 'A man living with two young
women who are neither sister nor wife nor daughter is an arrangement
that cannot continue.' I did not hear Adam's response, but he looked
very grave.*

*I would like to report that I was astonished by her words, but I was
not. She has voiced the thought that has nagged at me ever since I
arrived in Faithwell. Neither Adam nor Abigail has spoken of it, but
there is a tension at times that I know stems from our unusual
household. However, please do not be troubled on my account. You may
take comfort in the knowledge that by the time you read this letter, we
will have found a suitable arrangement to satisfy everyone.*

Your loving daughter,

Honor Bright

Woods

THE FIRST DAY after the Fourth of July, Honor had a visitor. She was sitting on the porch with Abigail and Adam, sleepy and a little queasy from the Sunday dinner they had just finished, in which fatty, oversalted ham played a large part. Honor had never eaten so much pork. She longed for lamb, and fish—delicate tastes simply served.

"I got a bone to pick with you, Honor Bright!"

Honor started and opened her eyes. A light buggy had pulled up in front of the house, with Belle Mills holding the reins. She threw them over the white picket fence in front of the house and hopped down. "You been sending me too many Oberlin ladies sayin' 'I want that gray and yaller bonnet the Quaker girl's wearing.' How am I gonna keep up with orders without you helping me?" Belle nodded at Adam and Abigail. "You must be Abigail. I already met Adam. I'm Belle Mills, the milliner over in Wellington. Don't know what Honor told you about me—probably nothin'. She don't talk much, do she? Now, you gonna invite me out of the sun? It's mighty hot."

Honor stood and waited for Abigail to ask Belle, deferring to her as the mistress of the house. But Abigail was staring at Belle's hat:

straw with a wide brim trimmed with a band of white lace over red ribbon, a clump of silk cherries pinned to the side.

Honor gave up on Abigail and greeted Belle herself. "I am very glad to see thee. Please join us."

Belle stepped onto the porch and sank into the rocker Adam offered. "Oh, that's good—no more jolting along that track," she said, pulling off lace gloves. Honor had not seen her wear gloves in Wellington, not even when they went for walks. These dainty ones looked odd on her, especially when they were taken off to reveal Belle's big hands and squared fingers. The gloves and her hat jarred with her lean frame and wide shoulders, so different from the plump curves and rounded shoulders that were the fashion. If women were meant to look like doves these days, Belle resembled a buzzard.

"Abigail, perhaps our guest would like something to drink," Adam suggested.

"Oh!" Abigail hurried inside, embarrassed at having to be reminded.

"Well, ain't this something," Belle remarked, looking around. "I never been out this way. That the rest of Faithwell?" She nodded toward the general store.

"There are a few outlying farms, but yes," Adam replied. "It is growing, however. New families are moving here all the time."

"Sure they are. All of 'em Quakers, right? I can't imagine anyone else willing to go down that track. What's it like in the rain? Mud's bad enough on the road between Wellington and Oberlin."

When Abigail reappeared with four glasses, a bottle of dark liquid and a pitcher of water, Belle nodded. "Blackberry cordial, is it? I'm impressed you managed to save some from last summer. I would've drunk it all by October."

Abigail paused in the act of pouring, as if she couldn't do so and think at the same time.

"Don't worry, honey, that's a compliment," Belle added. "It takes a good housekeeper to hold back the best stuff so she's got something to give guests." She turned to Honor. "I was wonderin' if we would see you in Wellington for the Fourth of July, but I expect it was too far for you, wasn't it?"

"We do not celebrate the Fourth," Adam replied.

"Really? What, Quakers don't like to have fun?"

"We do not wish to celebrate a document that does not include all men as citizens of America."

"We went to Oberlin to listen to speeches opposing slavery," Honor added.

"Of course you did. I should've guessed Quakers would be more entertained listening to abolitionists than shootin' guns in the air. Me, I like the guns. How's business up in Oberlin?"

"Fair," Adam said. "I would like to see it a little busier."

"Bet you don't sell much satin or velvet, do you?"

"Not much, no."

Belle chuckled. "Them Oberlinites don't go in for anything fancy, do they? I wouldn't be a milliner there—I'd never get to make anything fancier than Honor's bonnet." Belle glanced at Abigail's and Honor's plain dresses, at Adam's collarless shirt and braces. "Which fabric supplier do you use in Cleveland?"

While Abigail finished pouring cordial and Honor passed it around, Belle discussed business with Adam with an ease Honor envied. But then, much of her job involved talking to people. Belle more than many managed to combine sincere interest with casual humor and offhandedness.

"You got a similar accent to Honor," she remarked. "You two from the same place in England?"

Adam concurred, and Belle asked him and Honor question after question about Bridport. As they discussed their home town, Abigail began to rock faster and faster until she suddenly stopped. "Would thee like more cordial?" she interrupted, jumping up.

"Sure would, thankee." Belle held out her glass, winking at Honor as Abigail filled it. "Where you from originally, Abigail?"

"Pennsylvania."

"Well, there you go. We're all from somewhere else. That's how Ohio is."

"Where was thy home?" Adam asked.

"Kentucky—can't you tell from my accent? I came up here 'cause my husband went to Cleveland to speculate on steamboats on Lake Erie. I thought Cleveland would be more interesting than a Kentucky hollow. Well, it was, sort of."

"Thee was married?" Honor exclaimed.

"Still am. Rascal ran off—encouraged by my brother, I'm sorry to say. Them two never saw eye to eye. No idea where he is now. Oh, he was no good, and I was a fool, but I would've liked to do the chasin' off rather than leave it to Donovan. Bastard." Belle paused. "Sorry for cursing. Anyway, just as well he left—railroads set to take over steamboats soon enough. In Cleveland I learned how to make hats—it's one of the only businesses a woman can run on her own. Then I came out to Wellington to set up shop. Thought about Oberlin, but they don't like feathers, or color, and I do. Now, Honor," she continued, draining her glass, "you gonna show me the rest of Faithwell? I'm ready to stretch my legs. And wear that gray bonnet—I want to see it in action."

Still reeling from the thought of Belle Mills being married, Honor ran to get her bonnet. It was not what she would have worn for a walk in Faithwell, but she could not say no to its maker.

Belle pulled Honor's arm through her own as they walked west along the rutted track, nodding at the families gathered on their own porches in neighboring houses. All stared at Belle and her hat, and Honor and her bonnet. Belle seemed not to notice. "Donovan bothered you any since you been here?" she asked.

"He has ridden by a few times, but not stopped." Honor did not mention that his grin and wave each time brought grimaces from Abigail and Adam.

"Good. Don't expect that to last, though. He never can resist payin' people attention when they don't want it."

They passed the smithy, then the general store. Belle peered in the windows, though it was closed. "Not much to choose from, is there?" she remarked. "How many families live here?"

"Fifteen, including the outlying farms."

"Lord, that's the size of the speck I came from in Kentucky. I know what it's like. How we gonna get you out of that house?"

"What does thee mean?"

Belle paused and shook Honor's elbow. "Oh, come on, now, you ain't gonna stay there with those two, are you? Not with Abigail giving you those looks. Did you see how rattled she got when you and Adam were talkin' about England? Thought she would rock the runners off that chair. Any time she felt left out she had to interrupt."

"But—" Honor stopped.

Belle's hazel eyes were laughing. "She's jealous of you. Surely you can see that? Or maybe you're too nice to. No, she wants Adam to herself, and she don't like another woman—a nicer woman, and better looking, certainly better at sewing, and probably a better housekeeper—in her way. Hell, I think she was jealous of *me*, till I mentioned the husband."

As they began walking again, Honor repeated to Belle what Judith Haymaker had said to Adam about their irregular household.

Belle snorted. "I ain't surprised. You'd get comments about your setup in Wellington too, and we ain't so strict as Quakers."

"This is her farm where we come for milk," Honor said in a low voice. "That is Judith Haymaker."

The older woman was sitting with her two children on the porch of a large white house with green shutters. It was set far enough back from the road that Honor and Belle could simply wave without being obliged to walk up and say hello. Jack Haymaker nodded; Dorcas stared; Judith rocked. Honor could feel three pairs of eyes on her bonnet as they continued along the track, the Haymakers' orchard to their right. The cherries were finished, the plums and peaches not quite ripe.

That is the second time Judith Haymaker has seen this bonnet, Honor thought. And we have to walk past them on the way back.

"Farm looks well run," Belle remarked. "Good herd too." She nodded toward the brown cows in the pasture behind the barn. Honor had not even noticed them.

They reached the end of the orchard, where the trees began again and the road became little more than a path crisscrossed with roots, winding through a thick wood Honor had not dared to enter. To her this was the West, wild and unknown and unwelcoming. Even Belle, who did not seem frightened of anything, stood at its edge without suggesting they go on. The trees were mainly maples and beech, with a sprinkling of ash, elm and oak—their leaves long and smooth rather than with the curled edges Honor was used to. Even a tree as solid and steady as an oak was transformed in America into something alien. As she peered into the dim woods, a raccoon scurried away, its humped back swaying back and forth. Only when it had climbed high into a maple did it feel secure enough to turn its masked face toward the women. Grace would have loved to see a raccoon, Honor thought.

"Belle, I do not know what to do," she said.

Belle was rearranging the cherries on her hat. "About what?"

"Living here the way I am, in that house."

"All right, let me ask you something: Do you want to marry Adam Cox?"

"No!"

"Then you're gonna have to look around. Any other men in Faithwell take your fancy?"

The press of Jack Haymaker's eyes flashed through her mind—and then Donovan, grinning at her, the ribbon that held her key around his neck dark with sweat.

"It's simple, Honor Bright, you got a choice to make," Belle declared. "Go back home to England, or stay here. If you stay, you got to find a man to marry. What's it to be?"

Honor shuddered, making Belle laugh. "It ain't easy, findin' a man you can stand. C'mon, honey." She took Honor's arm. "Let's parade past them Haymakers again and show off our headwear. You get nervous, just have yourself a look at the marigolds in the front yard. Planted in *rows*!"

Faithwell, Ohio
7th Month 11th 1850

Dearest Biddy,

It made me very happy to receive thy letter yesterday with all the news from home, even if it is now six weeks old. Reading it, I almost felt I was with thee, walking along the familiar streets and stopping in on various friends. I was especially keen to read about thy visit to Sherborne and the new people thee met there. I wish I had been able to go too.

I am sitting out on the porch now in the cool evening—my favourite place to sew and write. Adam and Abigail have remained inside, saying the mosquitoes will come out with the damp. I do not mind the bites, if it gives me a few moments alone. Earlier there was a thunderstorm—they occur almost every afternoon during the summer. The storms are much more violent and frightening than the few we witnessed in Bridport, which managed only a bolt or two of lightning, usually remaining over the sea and not threatening us. Here they come on suddenly, with the sky turning from blue to black in just a few minutes. The rain falls in torrents, sometimes accompanied by hail that damages crops if it lasts long. The roads turn to mud in an instant. One afternoon last week the sky turned green, which Abigail said indicated a tornado was close. We had to crouch under the table, though I am not sure it would have given us much protection if the tornado had passed through. I have heard they can toss a house up in the air and completely destroy it.

Once the storm is past, though, the air is clear and fresh, and blessedly cooler. I had heard of Ohio heat, but not believed it could be so extreme. Sometimes I can barely move, it is so thick and relentless, even at night. So I welcomed today's thunderstorm.

I have surprising news: Adam and Abigail's banns were read out at Fifth Day Meeting today. They are to be married in ten days. I had *thought banns were to be read out over a three-week period to give the community time to consider the match, but apparently they are willing to do things faster here.*

Adam and Abigail did not tell me of their intentions before Meeting, so I was as surprised as the rest of the community when the announcement was made. Afterwards they were congratulated by other Members, though I felt the words were rather perfunctory. There was not the joyous feeling in the air one normally senses when a marriage is announced. Adam and Abigail were both subdued and even a little embarrassed. I expect they felt this was a practical solution to the awkward arrangement of our household.

Grace died only six weeks ago. I would like to have reminded Adam of that. He has not been able to look me in the eye all day. Indeed, he and Abigail have avoided me—and I them, if I am honest. Though it was very hot and close, I spent much of the afternoon after Meeting out in the garden, weeding. Only the thunderstorm drove me inside.

Some of the women have quickly organised what they call a quilting "frolic" for tomorrow, to help Abigail with quilts for her marriage. Where at home Grace and Mother and I would have quilted a coverlet over several days, here they sometimes quilt it all in one day, with many hands helping. I had been looking forward to attending one, but I wish this frolic were not to do with Abigail's marriage: it takes some of the pleasure out of the day.

I know thee will want to hear about it, so I shall delay sending this letter in order to report back.

Later

The frolic took place at the Haymaker farm where we get our milk. I do like their name, though the mother is full of steel and the daughter resembles Abigail a little in mood. We arrived with a side of ham and a cherry pie, only to discover there were four other cherry pies and two sides of ham. The 'comfort' we were to work on had been stretched over a square frame. I had expected we would make a whole-cloth bridal quilt, but instead it was an appliqué pattern of flowers in vases and fruit in bowls, the predominant colours red and green on a white background—a look common throughout Ohio. Abigail has worked hard these last few weeks to finish sewing the cover. She does not sew much, so perhaps I should have guessed the reason for all of this activity. Appliqué is very popular here. To my eye it has a facile look about it, as if the maker has not thought hard but simply cut out whatever shape has taken her fancy and sewn it onto a bit of cloth. Piecing together patchwork, on the other hand, requires more consideration and more accuracy; that is why I like it, though some say it is too cold and geometrical.

Judith Haymaker had marked out with chalk and a taut string simple double parallel lines for us to quilt in a diamond pattern, with stitching in the flowers and leaves as well, copying their shapes. For backing Abigail had used the familiar blue cloth thee will know from Friends' quilts in England; some customs have successfully crossed the ocean. However, the batting was cotton rather than the wool thee and I would have used. There was some discussion about the origins of the cotton, whether it had been grown and picked by slaves. Judith Haymaker assured us that Adam Cox had bought it for her from a merchant in Cleveland who had dealings with plantations in the South that do not use slaves. I have heard of a store in Cincinnati, run by a Friend, where all of the goods are guaranteed to be of slave-free provenance. But I did not know of such a store in Cleveland. I was glad, however, that Faithwell Friends are concerned about such things.

Eight of us sewed for several hours and, as has happened before, even in England, much was made of the speed and evenness of my stitches, and of my doublehanded sewing as I quilt. Most of the women controlled

*their needle with one hand, and were astonished at how quickly I was
able to sew in and out of the layers using both hands. Indeed, I was so
much quicker that I had to change places with the slower quilters. Some
also crawled under the frame to look at my underside stitches. Thee
knows I have always managed to quilt evenly on both sides. I do not
write this to boast, but rather to point out how displaced I often feel here,
even when performing the most familiar of tasks. Instead of
complimenting my quilting, the others stared as if I were some sort of
strange fruit being sold at a market. Compliments in America can take
an almost aggressive form, as if the speaker needs to defend her own
shortcomings rather than simply to rejoice in another's ability. However,
Judith Haymaker did ask me to quilt the appliquéd fruit and flowers, as
they will be noticed more; that was a compliment of sorts.*

*There was much talk as we quilted, though I was quiet unless asked
a direct question, which was not often. The other women were pleasant,
though I confess that, apart from the discussion on the origin of the
cotton, I found their conversation dull. I do not want thee to think I
have become judgemental. Perhaps if one of them were sitting with us
in Bridport, they too would find our conversation tedious as we discuss
people they don't know and places they haven't visited. In time I expect
I will get to know those people and places, and conversations will hold
more interest. In general, though, I have found that American women
seem to be interested in little other than themselves. Perhaps the struggle
to live here is enough of a challenge that they prefer not to think much
beyond their immediate circumstances.*

*No one spoke of Abigail's marriage, though I sense there is relief that
our unusual household will be made more regular now. No one asked
me what I am to do. I am wondering that myself. I do not wish to
continue to live with them, but there are few alternatives within such a
small community.*

At the end of the day when the quilt was done, the men came in from their work and we all ate. As well as ham, there was roast beef, mashed potatoes, baked sweet potatoes—which have orange flesh and taste more like squash than potato—green beans (which they call 'string' beans), fresh corn as well as corn bread, a wide variety of preserves, and many pies, mostly cherry, as they were recently in season. I was most pleased by a bowl of gooseberries, which I had not thought were grown in America. Their simple, fragrant taste reminded me of our garden at home in the summer sun.

I was glad to be at the frolic, for quilting is always a pleasure to me, whatever the conversation. The even repetitiveness of the work soothes me. I only wish there had been another sitting around the quilt who might become a friend. There were two others close to my age—Dorcas Haymaker, the daughter of the house, and another named Caroline, but they were more suspicious than friendly, and I believe both felt threatened by my sewing. It made me miss thee all the more.

I am sorry, Biddy. In each letter I feel compelled to apologise for my judgements and complaints. I am surprised myself at how hard I have found it to adjust to this new life. I had thought that I would take to it easily. But then, I had never been far from home and so had no true idea of what lay ahead, and how challenging it would be to my very spirit. And of course I thought I would have Grace here to support and encourage me.

I promise thee that in my next letter I shall not complain, but show thee how I can truly embrace life in America.

Thy faithful friend,

Honor Bright

Corn

JACK HAYMAKER WAS like a pulled muscle that Honor sensed every time she moved. She found she was looking out for him on the days when she went to the Haymaker farm to buy milk. Usually he was out of sight, and his absence was both a disappointment and an anticipation of his eventual appearance. Occasionally, though, she caught a glimpse of him coming out of the barn, or walking behind the cows in the pasture, or hitching the horses to a wagon full of surplus milk. When she did see him, it was like looking at the sun—she could not do so directly, but only glance, and hide her reaction. And whenever she did look, Jack was already smiling, even when not looking back at her. He always seemed to know that he had her attention.

At Meeting, when he sat across the room from her in the men's section, his presence was so disruptive Honor began to think she would never be able to concentrate on the still small voice inside herself while he was in the same room. Afterward, when everyone stood chatting outside the Meeting House, she hoped he would not approach her and Abigail and Adam. In such a small community, every gesture was noted. He must have understood this, for he remained talking with the other young men, laughing and scuffling in the dried mud on the road so that his white shirt grew dusty. But though his eyes were not directly on her, Honor could feel him there, and wondered that no one else seemed to notice the connection.

He was not an especially handsome man: his features were flat and his eyes small and close set—though he was clean shaven, which Honor preferred to the beard that lined the jaws of most Quaker men. What made him most attractive was that he was attracted to her. Another's interest can be a powerful stimulant. She could feel his eyes on her as an almost physical pressure.

At the Haymakers' frolic, Honor was glad she had the familiar, steadying task of quilting to keep her occupied. Yet even as she worked, she knew Jack Haymaker would arrive at the day's end to join the women for supper. While she was skilled enough to keep the mounting tension from affecting her stitches, after a few hours her wrists and lower back ached and her shoulders were tight. Coupled with the heavy heat she had not yet grown used to, she felt a headache creeping up. By the time Jack appeared with the other men she could barely see him for the pulsating lights before her eyes and the pain at her temples.

As the porch and parlor began to fill with people, Honor slipped through the kitchen and out of the back door, where she stumbled to a well in the center of the yard. After drawing up the bucket, she leaned against the curved stone wall and drank from a tin mug left out for the purpose. Then she took a deep breath and gazed up at the darkening sky, dotted with a few stars. It was still and hot, and fireflies blinked in the farmyard. Honor watched them flickering and marveled that insects could light up from within.

"Is thee all right, Honor?"

Of course he had followed her out, though she had not meant him to. "I was a little hot."

"'Tis a hot night, even outside. I wonder at everyone willingly crammed into the parlor." Jack Haymaker spoke with a faint drawl.

A firefly landed on Honor's sleeve and began walking up her shoulder, its tail still blinking. As she craned her neck to look down at it, Jack chuckled. "Don't be scared. It's just a lightning bug." He placed his finger in its path. Honor tried not to think about the pressure of his touch. When the firefly crawled onto his finger, he lifted it up and let it fly off, signaling its escape route with sparks of light.

"We do not have fireflies in England," she said.

"Really? Why not?"

"Many things are different there."

"Like what?"

Honor looked around. "The land is more—ordered. Fields there are divided by hedgerows and are greener. It is not so hot there, and there are not so many trees."

Jack folded his arms. "Sounds like thee prefers England."

"I—" Words had tripped her. It would have been better to say nothing. "That is not what I meant."

"What did thee mean?"

Thinking back over what she had said, Honor understood she had made the mistake of presenting England in a better light. She would have to praise Ohio somehow. Americans liked that. "I do like the firefl—the lightning bugs," she said. "They are cheerful and welcoming."

"More so than the people?"

Honor sighed. Again he was taking her few words and twisting them. It exhausted her. This was why she so often kept quiet.

"It cannot be easy, living with Abigail and Adam," he continued.

Honor frowned. Though she welcomed sympathy from the right person, she did not know Jack well enough to accept it from him. As much as his physical presence drew her in, she wanted to back away from his words.

"I'd best go in," she said.

"I will come with thee."

They went back through the kitchen and into the crowded parlor, where Dorcas Haymaker and her friend Caroline turned their faces toward them like two silver plates catching the light. Caroline's cheeks were red—rubbed with mullein, Honor suspected, a trick Grace had used to brighten her cheeks when she thought she was looking too pale. Quaker rouge, she'd heard outsiders call the plant.

Jack did not seem to notice his sister's friend. "Will thee eat?" he said. "Quilting all afternoon must give thee an appetite."

Honor could not tell whether he was teasing her or not. It was hard to know with Americans: they laughed at things she did not find funny, and were silent when she wanted to smile. She said nothing, but stepped up to the tables heavy with food, hoping he would not follow, and that the buzzing in her head would subside. She did not know why he had such a physical effect on her. His easy manner unnerved her, much the way America itself did. Honor was accustomed to an efficient, organized life, and hers had been anything but that since leaving Dorset. Jack Haymaker was part of the American chaos that pulled at her, making her want to step back.

She surveyed the field of food laid out before her. It was already predictable: the shoulder of ham, the roast beef, the mounds of mashed potatoes, the string beans, the johnnycakes, the army of pies. She swallowed a surge of nausea. What she longed for was a buttered crumpet, smoked mackerel pâté, a lamb cutlet, strawberries and cream—food prepared simply and easily digested, not served in a heap. Then she spied a bowl of gooseberries, pushed to the back of the table, and reached for it.

At that moment there was a stirring in the crowd around the food, and it parted to reveal Judith Haymaker, carrying a large platter piled with ears of steaming corn, stripped of their husks and tassels. "Corn's ready!" she cried, her face bright with heat and anticipation. For once she was smiling fully. There was a scramble as women moved dishes so that she could set the plate down in the middle of the table.

"First corn of the season," Jack explained as people surged forward to pick out ears. "The ears are smaller than they will be next month, but they're tenderer too. Where is thy plate? They will go fast." He reached over and picked up an ear between thumb and finger. "Quick, it's hot!"

Honor had no choice but to take a plate, and Jack deposited two ears of corn upon it. "I—" she began to protest, but Jack talked over her.

"Thee can have it with butter, if thee likes. See the plate there with the slab of butter? That's for rolling corn in. But I think the first corn is better plain. It's so sweet, it doesn't need butter's help. Come." He led her to a bench pushed up against the wall and waited for her to sit so that he could hand her the plate and join her. Honor could feel more eyes on them besides Dorcas and Caroline—Adam and Abigail, Judith Haymaker, Caleb Wilson the blacksmith. Caroline had glittering eyes and a hard stare.

Honor ducked her head and studied her ear of corn, each kernel like a translucent tooth. Jack was already gnawing at his, turning it around and around as his teeth cut away the kernels with a chomping sound like a horse, or a deer crashing through undergrowth. Honor could not bear to look. Her brothers, Samuel, even Adam

Cox would never make such a noise when they ate. Jack Haymaker ate joyously, brutally.

Dropping his spent corncob onto the plate they shared, he stood to go for more and noticed hers, untouched. "Does thee not like corn?"

Honor hesitated. "I have never eaten it on the cob."

"Ah." Jack smiled. "Then thee has a treat in store. This I must see." To her embarrassment he remained in front of her, looking down, with his broad grin and his hair messy and a kernel of corn sticking to his chin. If they hadn't been watching Honor and Jack before, everyone was now. She flushed a deep, hot red but knew she had no choice. To hesitate longer would draw even more attention. Picking up the ear, she turned it as if trying to find the best place to begin biting.

"Go on, Honor," Jack said. "Jump in."

Honor closed her eyes and bit down, slicing the kernels with her teeth. She opened her eyes. Never had she tasted anything so fresh and sweet. This was corn in its purest form, a mouthful of life. Turning the cob, she bit again and again, to savor the taste, so different from the other corn dishes she'd eaten over the past weeks. Then she couldn't stop, and bit all the way up and down the cob until it was bare.

Jack laughed. "That did thee good. Welcome to Ohio, Honor. Shall I fetch thee another?"

Jack Haymaker came into Cox's Dry Goods the day after the frolic, toward the end of the afternoon when the final rush was over and Honor was folding material while Adam Cox recorded the day's takings. Though she tried not to show it, she started when Jack entered, and her chest grew tight. She greeted him, then concentrated on the fabric she was wrapping around the bolt—the same cream with rust diamonds that Mrs. Reed had bought for her daughter the month before. Earlier she had asked Adam's permission to cut a small piece of it to add to the scraps she'd saved from Grace's brown dress and Belle's yellow silk.

Jack turned to Adam, who had paused in his writing, his pen steady over his accounts book. "I have finished delivering a batch of cheese to the college," he announced, "and thought I'd offer Honor a lift back, if thee is done with her. She must be tired after a long day here."

Adam glanced between Jack and Honor, the relief that crossed his face telling her more than any words could: Jack was courting her, with Adam's tacit blessing. Her life, which had been so uncertain these last few months, now had a needle hovering over it, ready to tack it into place. She did not feel secured, though, but rather as she had when she stepped off the *Adventurer* in New York, the land pitching and heaving under her feet.

"Of course," Adam replied. "I can finish up here." He began to write again. As Honor reached for her shawl—redundant in the heat, but a woman always carried one—hanging on a peg on the wall behind him, she glanced down at his ledger. *11 needles sharpened @ 1 cent/needle: 11 cents. 5 pairs scissors sharpened @ 5 cents/pair: 25 cents. 3 yards coarse calico*, he was writing. From this angle she could see the bald spot on top of his head.

It had not rained that afternoon to break the heat. Driving south down Main Street in the Haymakers' wagon, they could hear thunder rumbling in the distance, and the sky west of them was dark. Jack glanced sideways at her. "Don't worry, it is still a ways off. I will get thee home before the storm."

"I am not frightened," Honor said—though she was, a little. American thunderstorms were much more dramatic than any she had witnessed in England. The air would thicken over the course of a day until the tension was almost unbearable, the far-off thunder and lightning promising release. Then the rain would burst out from the massed black clouds, the lightning that had been held back suddenly overhead and simultaneous with the crashing thunder. It was loud, ruthless, violent. Honor had never been caught outside in an Ohio thunderstorm, and did not want to be now. Adam's borrowed buggy would have been quicker than the Haymaker wagon, or she could have waited out the storm in the safety of the shop. But she could not ask Jack to turn back.

As they passed Mill Street, Honor caught sight of Mrs. Reed turning down it. The black woman looked over and noted Honor and Jack together, then nodded, but did not smile. Her straw hat was trimmed this time with clusters of tiny white flowers that Honor had seen along roadsides.

"Thee knows her?" Jack did not sound pleased.

"She is a customer. What are the flowers on her hat?"

"Boneset. Used to treat fever. Don't they have it in England?"

"Perhaps. Flowers look different here, even when they have the same name."

Jack grunted. In the distance, thunder rumbled again, louder now.

Sitting next to Jack in the wagon felt nothing like sitting next to Adam, or Old Thomas from Wellington; nor was it like what she had felt when walking with Samuel back home. It was not just that he smelled of fresh hay even when covered with the mud and sweat of a day's work. It was the raw, wordless connection, the buzz of electric tension in the air around them and the space between them that surprised her. She was painfully aware of him. Every breath he took, every toss of his head or roll of his shoulder or flick of his wrist as he guided the horses registered deep within her. She let her eyes rest on his forearm, exposed by his rolled sleeves so that she could see each blond hair pointing in the same direction, like wheat in the wind.

This is what lust is, she thought, her cheeks burning with shame. She had not felt such a thing with Samuel: she had known him since they were children, and he was more like a brother. Perhaps what he felt for the Exeter woman was like this with Jack, she thought. For the first time, she allowed herself to consider with a steady mind how Samuel had felt and why he had done what he did.

"Corn's growing," Jack commented as they passed cornfields cut out of the woods between Oberlin and Faithwell. He said little else on the half-hour drive other than to reassure Honor that the lightning hadn't come any closer. Otherwise he hummed a tune under his breath that she did not recognize.

At Abigail's house—Abigail on the porch, gaping—Honor thanked Jack for the lift as he helped her down, his hand lingering on her elbow. He nodded. "We beat that storm, eh?"

By the day's end at Adam's store she had been hungry and exhausted. But that night Honor ate nothing and slept little. The storm never came, and the next morning it was as hot and still and close as before.

"Corn's almost tall enough," Jack said the following Saturday as he again gave her a lift back from Oberlin. "Not quite ready, though."

The third time she rode with him, he pulled the wagon off the road by a cornfield. They sat looking over the corn, now higher than a man, the ears swollen, the tassels long and silky, the stalks rustling.

"Honor, this corn is ready. Does thee agree?"

Honor swallowed. Was this how American courtship proceeded? One conversation at a frolic, three rides in a wagon, and a coupling in a field? Then the banns would be read and they would marry: first greeting to marriage bed in less than two months. In America time seemed to be buckling: stretching and contracting before her, the steady rhythm Honor had been accustomed to disrupted. Either it was slowed down—on board the *Adventurer*, while waiting for letters to and from her family, during hot afternoons with Abigail on the porch; or it speeded up—Grace's death, Abigail and Adam's marriage, Jack's expectations. It made her breathless and unable to think.

"Honor?"

Did she have a choice? She could say no, and Jack would gee up the horse and they would continue along the road to Faithwell, where he would drop her off and never give her a lift again, and never smile at her except in a neighborly way. She would be stranded at Adam and Abigail's house. They had married the week before, yet she felt just as awkward living with them.

Honor had always assumed she would have a deep familiarity and connection with her husband, born of a shared history and community. But then, that did not guarantee success either; Samuel's abandonment had been as sudden as Jack's courting of her was now. And the deep familiarity she had relied on turned out to be hollow when not accompanied by physical attraction. At least she felt lust for Jack. That was something.

"Yes," she answered at last. "The corn is ready."

Jack jumped down and held out his hand. As he led her into the corn, shaking and rattling the stalks above their heads, the long fibrous leaves pressed in, snagging Honor's sleeves and gently and insistently scratching at her cheeks. Though they were walking in a straight line along a row, she became disoriented, with the rustling green all around and the hot dark sky buzzing, and swallows flying fast above them, looking for their roost for the night.

Jack laid her down on the sandy dirt between two rows of corn. He looked at her for a moment with a small smile, as if searching for the certainty in her face before he continued. He did not kiss her immediately, but pulled the white scarf from her neck and ran his mouth along her collarbone, gently biting the ridge. Honor sucked in a gasp. No man had ever touched her there—or anywhere, really. Her stalled courtship with Samuel had involved hand-holding and brief kisses, and occasionally she had leaned against his arm when they sat side by side. The touch of Jack's mouth stirred a part of her she had not known was waiting to be moved.

All around them crickets were blaring their endless song. Honor's breath quickened when he loosened her dress from her shoulders, pushing it down so that the white arrow of her neckline crumpled like a ribbon at her waist. As he followed down with his lips, Honor closed her eyes and allowed herself to enjoy the pressure of his mouth on her breasts. When he pulled up her skirt and stroked her inner thighs, though, she realized she was picturing Donovan, his speckled brown eyes pulling at hers, his tan hands assured on her white skin. She opened her eyes, but it was too late to stop what they had begun. Jack touched her between her legs, opened her and pushed himself inside. Shocking, and painful, and animal, yet she responded almost unconsciously to the rhythm he set, which she somehow recognized though she had never experienced it before. Faster and faster, stroke after stroke, Honor could not hold on to what she felt, the pain and excitement mixed up so that she lost track of herself in the pounding rhythm. Then Jack thrust and held himself rigid with a gasp. When he collapsed over her, Honor wrapped her arms tight around him, her nose buried in his neck while their breathing slowed together. Turning her face to one side to gulp air, she heard the crickets again, and felt the hard ground against her back. A rock bit into her waist. She gazed, unfocused, at the dark rows of corn, wondering if there were snakes nearby; nothing was moving but it was only a matter of time before one appeared, pulling its weight through the stalks, its gold and brown pattern flashing.

The next day the banns were read. Before they left for Meeting, Honor came upon Abigail vomiting in the backyard. When she straightened, she had the same sweaty upper lip and look of elated nausea that Honor had seen in other women, and she knew at once that Abigail was carrying a child—she who had just married. Honor said nothing when Abigail announced she was going back to bed. Everything is happening so fast, she thought. Too fast.

As they walked toward the Meeting House, she told Adam of her decision to marry Jack Haymaker. Adam simply nodded, without offering reassuring words or expressing pleasure.

Jack would have told his mother before Meeting as well, for as an Elder, Judith Haymaker would have to know of the banns. Honor was relieved not to have been with Jack to witness her first reaction. She was a sober, principled woman, from the brief exposure Honor had had of her at the frolic, at Meeting, and when she bought milk and cheese at the farm. Judith would have had a clear idea about the course her son's life should take, and it was unlikely that her vision had included a rope merchant's daughter untutored in dairy farming, small and quiet, and homesick.

Haymaker mother and daughter were already seated: Dorcas in the women's section; Judith on the Elders' bench. As Honor sat down, Judith Haymaker was gazing at the whitewashed wall opposite, her arched eyebrows giving her face its usual bright, hard openness. Dorcas was frowning. At least Jack smiled at her from the men's section. For once Honor missed having Abigail at her side—she felt exposed to the community and would have liked more solidarity than Adam could provide from across the room.

She lowered her eyes and sat absolutely still, as if by not moving she could absent herself from the room. She could not concentrate, however. When Meeting settled into a deeper searching, Honor could not follow the silence down and still her troubled thoughts. Instead she felt her back aching, her nose itching, the heat of the day sending sweat trickling down between her breasts. By the time Meeting ended two hours later, she was more agitated than she had been when she sat down.

The reading of the banns was met by surprised murmurs. Honor turned red, and flinched when she heard a stifled sob from Caroline, Dorcas's friend who had stared at her at the frolic. Honor knew little of her except that she was a farmer's daughter. In such a small place as Faithwell, an eligible man like Jack Haymaker was likely to have had a potential wife already earmarked, by the community as well as his family. Now Caroline would either hastily marry another—likely a man from a nearby Quaker community such as Greenwich, twenty miles away—or she would go west with cousins, to Iowa or Wisconsin or Missouri. Honor closed her eyes, unable to bear seeing the defeated face. I am sorry, she thought, hoping that somehow this message would cross the room and settle like a balm on Caroline. I am sorry, but marriage is the only way I can make a place for myself here. Otherwise I am afloat, with no idea how to find land again.

As they rose from their benches, Caroline hurried from the room. Dorcas started after her, but stopped when Judith Haymaker placed a hand on her arm. Honor felt all eyes in the room on her and her future mother-in-law as Judith stepped over to join her, Dorcas trailing behind. Her hands folded so that she would not wring them, Honor faced her future family, as she knew she must—she could not live with her eyes permanently fixed to the ground.

Judith wore a dark gray dress and a flat white bonnet firmly tied with white ribbon. Despite the heat, she did not sweat. Like Dorcas, her shoulders were not sloped as was the fashion of the day, but were almost as square as a man's, her arms bulging with muscles developed from a lifetime of milking cows. Her mouth was in its perpetual half-smile that Honor now understood held little warmth. "Thee and Adam must come over after dinner," she said. "We have much to discuss."

Honor nodded, noting that Judith had avoided inviting them for a meal. It was just as well, for she did not think she could swallow in the older woman's presence.

It seemed what Judith Haymaker most wanted to discuss was quilts.

Honor had been to the Haymaker farm several times with Abigail to buy milk, and to the frolic a couple of weeks before. But she had not inspected it then with an eye to living there. As she and Adam walked along the track from Faithwell west toward the farm, each step took her farther from the cleared village and closer to wilderness. As they approached the farm, she looked at it anew. It was very different from Dorset farms, which, being older, had sunk into their natural surroundings, while Ohio farms had been boldly hacked out and stood perched on the surface of the landscape. The buildings were laid out carefully rather than higgledy-piggledy, and made of wood rather than stone, the boundaries lined with rail fences rather than stone walls, the whole of it surrounded by thick woods rather than manageable green meadows and hills and small clumps of trees. The two-story clapboard house was set back from the road, and the front yard had some lawn—an unusual feature here, as it required clearing every stump, diligent watering and a dog good at keeping away the rabbits and deer. They had one: Digger, a clever English shepherd who ran at them now, snarling and barking as he had never done when Honor came for milk. He seemed to sense that this visit had a different, more ambivalent purpose. Behind the house were various outbuildings, dominated by an enormous barn, much bigger than the house, painted red but now faded, and with a steeply sloping roof and a bank of earth built up to its entrance. The doors were open, and Honor could see hay in bales piled almost to the rafters.

The Haymakers waited for them on the front porch. Judith Haymaker held a Bible in her lap, Dorcas a shirt she was mending, and Jack sat with his eyes closed—though he jumped up to call off the dog. While Dorcas went inside, Judith ushered them to straight-back chairs before reseating herself in a rocking chair Honor suspected no one was to use but her—the first of many Haymaker rules she was going to have to learn. Digger sat near her, just out of reach of the chair's runners. He was clearly Judith's dog; Honor knew he would never come and lie at her feet. Perhaps she would have more luck with the calico cat slinking across the lawn and disappearing into the flower beds laid out on either side of the porch steps. It looked much wilder than her English cat.

Adam and Jack talked briefly about the oats and when the crop would be harvested, about business at Adam's store, about a new slave law Congress was debating that Caleb Wilson the blacksmith had spoken of at Meeting. Honor wanted to listen but she was too nervous to pay much attention. She had brought with her some patchwork, and got out the brown and green hexagons she had already been working on. As she began to whipstitch them together into a rosette, the familiar gesture calmed her. Wherever she was, however foreign and awkward the place and the people, sewing at least felt familiar.

Judith glanced at Honor's quick, even work. "Such intricate patchwork will take some time," she remarked. "Does thee never do appliqué? It goes much faster. Even pieced blocks in patterns like Shoo Fly or Flying Geese or Ohio Star would be quicker than what thee is making."

"In England we have always made patchwork like this."

"Thee is not in England any longer."

Honor bowed her head.

When Dorcas brought out a pitcher of water and glasses, Judith stopped rocking and the men broke off their conversation. "I would like to know what Honor brings to this marriage," she announced as her daughter began to pour out the water.

There was a silence apart from Dorcas clinking the pitcher against a glass.

"She brings very little, Judith," Adam replied. "Thee knows her circumstances. Honor has never presented herself to be more than she is."

"I know that. But does she bring anything at all? Quilts, for example." Judith turned to Honor. "How many comforts does thee have ready?"

"One."

"One?" Judith was aghast. "I had been led to believe thee is an expert quilter. I saw thy stitching at the frolic. Look how fast thee works now." She leaned across and took up Honor's hexagons. "Thee has the best hand in Faithwell. What has thee been doing back in England?" Behind that question Honor could hear other unvoiced ones: How did a rope merchant's daughter spend her time? Was she lazy? How would she be useful to the Haymakers?

"I did have more quilts," Honor explained, "but I gave them

away, as they would be too unwieldy for the journey. Grace and I only brought two with us, and Grace's marriage quilt had to be burned, as there was worry it could be infected with yellow fever." She looked down, ashamed that she had no quilts to be married with. Marriage had not been her expectation, at least not so soon, and she was unprepared. She should count herself lucky that Jack wanted her anyway.

"Did thy sister not bring more quilts with her for her marriage to Adam?"

"She was not concerned about the quilts, and thought she could make them once she got here."

Judith grunted and handed back her patchwork. "Thee must ask for thy quilts back from England. Write and explain the circumstances, ask that the comforts be sent. It will take several months, but at least thee will have them. How many can thee get back?"

Honor hesitated—it seemed rude to ask for quilts she had willingly given away. She tried to think of who would be least offended. "Three, perhaps."

"I do not know what the traditions are in England," Judith said, "but here young women should have a dozen quilts ready for marriage, and a thirteenth made, a whole-cloth one in white. Perhaps Abigail and Adam did not tell thee, as theirs is a second marriage, where the tradition is different. Now, if thee can provide the white material," she directed at Adam, "we will hold a frolic later this week to quilt it. We are busy now with crops, but we will simply have to make the time. And we will give thee three of Dorcas's comforts—with the quilts sent from England that will make eight."

Dorcas clattered the pitcher onto the table with a stifled cry, red dots coloring her cheeks.

"Of course I will provide the material," Adam agreed. "I thank thee for accepting Honor into thy family. If the quilts are a problem, perhaps there is no need to rush into the marriage. Honor can remain with us while she makes the quilts she needs." He did not sound confident in this suggestion, however.

"That would take far too long, if the quality is to be good," Judith Haymaker replied. "To make five good quilts—"

"Eight!" Dorcas interrupted. "Three to replace mine."

"Eight quilts, she would need two years, with us helping."

Adam looked startled, clearly unaware of the work involved in quilting. Though he dealt in cloth, he had not grown up around sisters making quilts.

"Though if she would make appliqué rather than patchwork, it would go faster." Judith gestured at Honor's diamonds. "It is time to put those away and take up Ohio patterns."

Honor stopped sewing and laid her hands in her lap. It was not a great hardship to set aside the hexagons, and she could make appliqué quilts if needed. But she had always assumed that when the time came to make her marriage quilt, she would have plenty of time to design it and oversee the quilting, even if as the bride she was not meant to work on it herself. She would have chosen one or two hands to do it, and had them quilt carefully. At the frolic Judith would organize, however, many hands would quilt it, with varying degrees of skill. At least a patchwork design hid bad stitching; on a whole-cloth quilt of one color the stitching was everything, and the unevenness of the different hands helping would show. She and Jack would begin their married life under a quilt of dubious quality. It was not an auspicious start.

I must not cry, she thought. I will not cry. To keep the tears from spilling over, she gazed out into the front yard for distraction. Then she noticed a tiny form hovering around the morning glory that twined up the porch columns. Honor blinked. It was a minute bird, almost a bee but with a needle beak, moving its wings so fast she couldn't see them. As she watched, it inserted its beak to draw out the flower's nectar.

Jack followed her gaze. "That is a hummingbird," he said. "Has thee ever seen one, or is it another thing England does not have, like lightning bugs?"

Honor shook her head, the movement sending the bird away, though it soon returned. "I have never seen one."

"We have brought in two crops of hay," Judith continued, frowning at the interruption, "and we will get in one more this summer. The oats are ready, and then the corn, and there is all the kitchen garden to put up. We are not expecting Honor to work in the fields, but she can cook and look after the garden and milk the cows and sell cheese. It is always a difficult time of year, with just three of us. With four we can manage more easily. If Honor is to be of any help to us, she and Jack must marry as soon as possible." She shook her head. "But eight quilts for a wedding. I've never heard the likes."

Honor noted that Jack said nothing about the quilts, but allowed his mother to negotiate; perhaps he felt he had already played his part in the cornfield. However, when his mother had finished, he took them around the farm, eager to show off what the Haymakers had built up. It was then that Honor truly began to understand how much her life was about to change. At Abigail and Adam's at least there were other houses within sight, and the general store—basic as it was—was nearby. The Haymakers' was only a quarter-mile beyond Faithwell, but the road had turned into a rutted track by then and the farm felt remote. And though it had been cleared so that there were front and back yards, a kitchen garden, an orchard and a pasture for the cows, there was still a sense that the wilderness was close at hand, pushing in on the farm from all sides, particularly the woods to the west where she and Belle had stopped before. Honor had always thought she loved trees, but now the beech woods her brothers had climbed in, the apple orchard behind their house, the horse chestnuts they collected conkers from each autumn, all seemed tame next to the bur oaks and black ash and beeches and maples that made up the woods by the farm. "Wieland Woods," Jack called it. "Named for my father." When Honor looked questioningly at him, he added, "He died in North Carolina. Fire."

She did not ask for details: Jack's face had shut down.

Almost as worrying as the press of the trees were the animals. The Brights had kept eight chickens for eggs, and bought every-thing else they needed from the town butcher and dairy. The Hay-makers had eighty chickens: twenty layers and sixty pullets for eating. There were two horses, two oxen they shared with another farm, eight cows ("We are adding a cow a year," Jack explained proudly), and four pigs, huge and so smelly her stomach turned. Indeed, the whole farm smelled of raw animal; she could not imag-ine living with such a pervasive odor. But Jack had Honor and Adam inspect every animal. As they went around, Adam was polite and seemed genuinely interested, while Honor felt only a growing dread. She could never be proud of a cow. In Bridport she had lived far from barns, and close to the shops that did the selling. Here she would be at the heart of the making. It was a very different life, full of alien smells and sounds and textures and spaces. Seeing Jack in his home made him more of a stranger; she would have to grow used to him too.

The only place on the farm where she felt any ease was in the haymow. There the hay's sweet, dry, dusty scent masked the stench of piss and manure, and it was quiet, with the animals in the stalls below and the people going about their work. Here she could imag-ine coming to escape the rest of the farm for a few minutes. New bales from the recent harvest were stacked high. Only the straw in

one corner was low. "When we are harvesting the oats, we will replenish the straw," Jack reassured Honor and Adam. Honor picked
up a strand—dull and dead compared to the hay, its life cut off
when the seeds were threshed from it.

The house was a little more familiar, since Honor had now been
in enough American houses to expect square rooms with large windows, plain furniture made of ash and pine and elm, and oval rag
rugs laid on the floor. Judith led them through each room, including the pantry and the cooler cheese-making room off the kitchen.
Honor was surprised when she then led them upstairs and showed
them each bedroom, plainly furnished but for the red and green and
white quilts on each bed. Honor was not expecting to see bedrooms—
at home she would never have showed strangers the bedrooms,
which she considered private. She glanced at Adam, but he did not
raise his eyebrows. In Pennsylvania the families she stayed with had
also showed her each room, as if to give her a clear idea of how they
lived and what they possessed. In England it would be considered
showing off, but here such things were natural and important. Besides, the bedrooms were no longer private to her, she reminded
herself, for she was joining the family. Somehow she would have to
think of this house as home.

Faithwell, Ohio
8th Month 4th 1850

My dear family,

I am writing to tell you that I am to be married this morning, to Jack Haymaker. We will live with his mother and sister on their dairy farm just outside of Faithwell.

This is very sudden, I know, but I hope you will give us your blessing and think fondly of us.

Please if thee could, Mother, ask for the Star of Bethlehem quilt back from Biddy and send it, along with those I gave to William and Aunt Rachel. I need them here. I am sorry to have to ask, but it is required of me by my husband's family to have in possession a sufficient number of quilts when married. I hope thee and the others will understand.

Your loving daughter,

Honor Bright

Fever

 HONOR DID NOT spend her first married night in Jack Haymaker's bed. Their bed, as she would have to learn to think of it. After the marriage Meeting and a community feast hosted by the Haymakers, when the last neighbors had left and the sky was finally turning to ink, Jack led her upstairs and down the hall to their bedroom. "This will be more comfortable than the cornfield," he said, smiling as he brought her to the bed. It was spread with the whole-cloth white quilt made at the frolic earlier that week—quickly and unevenly quilted by whoever could be spared. Honor held on to the iron bedstead to keep from swaying.

Jack removed his braces—"suspenders," she must call them— and his shirt before noticing that she had not moved. "Will thee get undressed? Here, I'll help thee." Reaching over to unfasten the buttons that ran down her back, he let his hand rest on her neck for a moment, then frowned. "But thee is hot!" Jack turned her around and took in her flushed face, then made her sit while he felt her cheeks and forehead. "When did thee begin to feel like this?"

"I—'tis a hot night." And it was—so stifling and still that Honor's hot brow had seemed to her simply an extension of the weather.

Jack called for his mother and sister, and Honor, having held herself together all afternoon, let herself slump on the bed.

Judith and Dorcas led her back downstairs and settled her in the sick room off the kitchen, a small, square room containing a single bed, a wooden chair, and a basin and pitcher set into a cabinet with a chamber pot inside. Above the cabinet a medicine closet hung on the wall, filled with strips of linen and bottles of camphor, mustard and other medicines unfamiliar to Honor. The bed was made up with old linen sheets and a gray wool blanket that she found unbearably scratchy. A window faced onto the backyard. The women left it open and the door to the kitchen ajar so that some air could circulate, though little did and it was very close.

For the first few days of her fever Honor swung between hot and cold, delirium and lucidity, a desire to have the Haymakers with her and a longing for them to leave her alone. Sometimes she pretended to be asleep when Dorcas looked in on her or Jack sat by her bed. Conversation—either speaking or listening—was too draining, particularly when she barely knew them. She had not yet built up the hours of talk about the weather, the cows, the chores, how well she had slept, the neighbors' comings and goings, the milk souring in the heat, wonder over letters from relatives and friends. When Jack sat with her or Judith Haymaker spooned broth into her mouth or Dorcas hung in the doorway, they too seemed at a loss as to what to say, and often resorted to talking to each other, or rinsing the chamber pot when it didn't need it, smoothing the sheets, opening or shutting the window, sweeping the clean floorboards.

Alone Honor lay and watched the light change on the walls, too weak and dazed to sit up and read or sew. At times the room was so hot she felt she and the air had lost any boundary between them and become one. Even in her delirium she knew this was nonsense, and then she welcomed the intrusion of a Haymaker or, once or twice, Adam, to remind her of who and where she was.

Apart from her seasickness on the *Adventurer*, she had never been so severely ill for so long. She was in bed a week before she could sit up, and another week before she could get out of bed even briefly.

Though the Haymakers were attentive in looking after her, they did not seem alarmed by the length or severity of her illness. "It's ague," Judith Haymaker replied when Honor wondered why she was not yet better. "It likes to settle in for a long visit. Everyone gets it."

Her illness overlapped with the harvesting of the oats, though she was well enough by then that all the Haymakers could leave her to go to the fields, as every hand was needed. Honor regretted not taking part, as she had hoped it would help her to feel more a part of the farming community. She said as much to Jack when he came to see her briefly after the first day of the harvest. "There will be other years," he said, and then fell asleep in the chair.

The window of the sick room looked out over the yard between the barn, the wagon shed and the henhouse, and Honor watched it for hours. Often it seemed nothing changed, but after a while she noticed small movements, of yellow and black butterflies hovering, of a breeze blowing leaves about, of the slowly shifting shadows across the dusty ground.

One day while the Haymakers were in the fields, Honor lay and watched two chipmunks chase each other around the well in the middle of the yard while the calico cat crept toward them, her belly low to the ground. She was not fast enough, however, and the chipmunks ran off. Later the cat recrossed the yard, three half-grown kittens following and then stopping to fight, the mother watching with indifference. The well cast no shadow now, for it was noon. A tin mug sat on its curved edge. Honor blinked, and then knew she must have slept, for there was a shadow to one side of the well. She blinked again. The mug was gone.

A pullet had managed to escape from the henhouse and pecked at the ground, unprotected from foxes, for Digger had gone to the fields as well. Honor wondered what she would do if a fox stalked the chicken, though she suspected it was unlikely to in daylight. She could now walk across the sick room, but she doubted she could get out into the yard and save the chicken without fainting.

Studying the shadow by the well, Honor thought she must be delirious again, for the darkness there was not a reflection of the shape of the well, but more like a sack of potatoes. As she watched, an arm extended from the dark shape and set the mug back on the well. If she hadn't been looking, Honor would not have heard the metallic tap as mug met stone.

She sat up carefully so that she would not rustle the sheets. The idea of being alone on this farm, surrounded by woods, with someone crouching by the well, made her stomach twist with fear; she wished she could close her eyes and open them to find the man gone. Taking a deep breath, she sought inside herself to find steadiness. Everyone has a piece of God in them, she reminded herself, even a man hiding in the yard. But she was shaking as she slid out of bed to kneel at the window.

Honor had hoped the sun's glare would blind the man so that he could not see her, but as she peered at the dark form she sensed a gaze back. He remained very still, so still that the pullet pecked close by. Honor did not move either. Beneath her nightgown she could feel sweat trickle down her back. As she watched, the darkness unfolded itself, stood and took the shape of a young black woman, barefoot, in a yellow dress. Around her hair she wore a strip of cloth torn from the hem of the dress. The chicken ran off, but she did not try to run as well. Instead she held out a hand toward Honor. A small, ambiguous gesture, it still had the power to untwist Honor's stomach, for it said: I am running away. Help me. She and the woman were now linked by that gesture. She had grown up with the understanding that slavery was wrong and must be opposed, but that had been all thoughts and words. Now she must actually *do* something, though she did not yet know what.

The black woman lowered her hand then and stood by the well. All the movement in the yard seemed to have stopped. The chicken remained out of sight. There was no breeze. Even the crickets and grasshoppers were not chirping and ticking. It was as quiet as Honor imagined Ohio could ever get.

She stood, slowly so that she did not grow dizzy. Then she made her way to the kitchen, touching the doorway and walls to steady herself, and picking up the heel of a loaf of bread as she passed the sideboard. Out on the back porch she hesitated, then stepped down into the yard. There the hot bright sun stopped her. Honor held her hand up to shade her eyes, and squinted, but was still so blinded that her eyes streamed. It had been over two weeks since she was last in the sun.

The woman did not come to her, but remained by the well, her hand resting on its edge. She reminded Honor of a sheep who had to be approached carefully so that she would not bolt; even then, you knew it was almost impossible to get close enough to touch her. Once when she was younger, Honor after much patience had managed to place her hand on the neck of a lamb. It did not spring away as she'd expected, but seemed to submit to the attention. This woman did not look ready to submit; every part of her was poised to run.

Honor tried to think of something to say, but knew that gestures were more effective. Stepping closer, she held out the bread. The woman reached over, took the crust and nodded, but did not eat it, instead tucking it into the pocket of her dress. She was tall, much taller than Honor, with long thin legs and arms like fence posts. The dress had been made for someone shorter, as it only reached her calves, and her bony wrists poked well beyond the cuffs. It was filthy, rumpled and torn, as if she had lived in it day and night for weeks. Her face was shiny with sweat, and on her wide flat nose was a sprinkling of pimples. The whites of her eyes were yellowed, and the corners crusted. Honor wondered if she would agree to come inside for a wash, but doubted it. She needed quick, practical help, not a bath.

Before Honor could open her mouth to speak, the woman jerked her head, as if connected by a string to a sound far away. Honor listened, and heard what she had not for some weeks: the irregular hoofbeats of a horse with a thick shoe.

The woman's eyes flashed, and Honor read in them the despair of having come so far only to be caught so close to her goal. She took a breath and tried to think, though the sun was confusing her and stars were swimming in her eyes. She could feel herself swaying. Just as her knees buckled she said, "Go inside to the cool room."

When Donovan rode into the yard, Honor was lying in the dust. Dismounting, he ran to her, knelt and pulled her into his lap. "Honor, what's happened? Did someone—" Donovan looked around at the empty yard, then peered at her pinched face. "You got the summer fever. What are you doing out here, you silly woman?"

The smell of his sweat was awful and intoxicating. Honor did not try to struggle out of his arms, as she did not want to offend him. "I—the chickens are loose. I must catch them." This at least was true. As if it had heard her, a chicken appeared now near the barn, jerking its brown head and clucking in indignation at Donovan's presence.

"I'll round 'em up. Let me get you inside first. Don't fight me." Donovan scooped her up like a sack of flour and carried her inside. "Where is everyone?" he asked as he looked around the empty kitchen.

"Harvesting oats." Honor indicated the sick room. "In there, please."

He laid her down gently for such a rough man. "Honor Bright, what in hell's name are you doin' here?" he demanded, sinking into the chair next to the bed. "I ain't seen you in weeks. Thought you was hidin' from me at that other Quaker house, but turns out you're here!" Donovan looked put out, as if she had been a poor friend not to tell him.

Honor took a deep breath. "Please could thee fetch my—my husband. Jack Haymaker. In the field south of here, a little west along the road. Please."

A look crossed Donovan's face before he covered it with a smirk. "Husband. Huh. Somebody got in there already, did they?"

Honor just looked at him. She should be frightened that they were alone. But she was not. She should despise him for what he did for a living. But she did not. There is a measure of the Light in him, she thought, if only I can find it.

"You want anything?" Donovan glanced in the white pitcher on her bedside table, a lace doily draped over it to keep out flies. "You want some cold water? I can get you some from the well, or the cool room if they got one."

"No." Honor tried not to snap.

"It ain't no trouble." For once Donovan was being solicitous when she didn't want him to be.

"There is something I would like," she began, to distract him from searching for the cool room, where he would find the woman among the shelves of cheese. "Does thee remember the signature quilt that was in my trunk the first time we met?"

"Yep."

"Could thee get it? It is upstairs in my trunk. This blanket is so scratchy."

"Sure." Donovan bounded out, clearly pleased to have something concrete to do. She heard his footsteps on the stairs and then over-head, shaking the hallway and bedroom. Honor prayed the woman in the cool room would keep still and not panic.

Donovan returned with the quilt in his arms. Spreading it over her, he paused, then crouched and smoothed it so that his hand ran slowly down the outline of her body. His eyes glowed bright in his tanned face. Honor thought of how she had lain in the corn with Jack and imagined Donovan, and blood rushed to her face. It must be the fever confusing me, she thought—though she knew it was not.

Donovan watched her deepening red and responded with a flush of his own up his neck and cheeks. "Dammit, Honor. You didn't give no one else a chance, did you?"

Honor swallowed. She had never imagined she would have such a conversation with him. "Friends marry Friends," she said, "else we must leave the community. Besides, I could never—associate with a slave hunter."

"But you're *associatin'* with me now."

She shivered, and gazed at him, helpless. "Please get Jack," she whispered.

The reminder of her husband seemed to rouse him. "I'll just get the chickens 'fore the foxes do."

"Don't worry about the chickens. Jack will see to them."

"No, I'll do it. I want to have a little look around while I'm at it.

That's what I come here for, anyway—I'm lookin' for somethin'. Didn't know I'd find you." Donovan paused. "How'd those chickens get out, d'you think?"

Honor shook her head.

Donovan looked at her. "All right then, Honor Bright. I'll be seein' you."

He went back outside. Honor watched him walk through the yard, past the well with its mug gleaming on the wall like a beacon. Now that he had mentioned water, she was desperately thirsty. She closed her eyes. She could hear him whistling; then he pulled the barn door open and the whistling faded. It reappeared a few minutes later, and the chickens began to squawk as Donovan rounded them up.

Soon she heard his horse cantering toward the oats field. She must have slept for a few moments. Then she jerked awake, sure of a presence nearby. The room was empty, but a mug of water sat within reach on the table next to her bed. It was cool as if freshly drawn from the well, and tasted better than any water she had ever drunk.

Honor had not expected Donovan to accompany Jack back, but her husband must have been worried enough to accept a ride from the slave catcher. She heard the horse return, then Jack rushed into the sick room, knelt and felt her forehead. Donovan hung in the doorway, his hat in his hands. His eyes moved immediately to the mug of water, the only thing in the room that had changed in the last half-hour. Honor stared at him. Instead of the anger she expected, however, a slow smile spread across his face, along with an admiring expression, as if she had played a particularly skillful hand of cards. He wagged his finger at her. "Haymaker, you better tell your wife about the Fugitive Slave Law. I hear the president's gonna approve it soon enough. Once it comes in, I won't be so easy on her—or you. Maybe I'll get you to help me catch a nigger."

Jack stared up at him. Honor could not bear the tension of having them both in the same room. "Please go now, Donovan."

Donovan grinned. "You got a feisty little wife there, Haymaker. Better keep your eye on her. I know I will." He winked at Honor, then replaced his hat and backed from the room.

Honor closed her eyes and prayed that the woman had had enough time to find a better hiding place.

Jack began to question Honor even as Donovan's horse could still be heard clattering through the yard. "He—that man, Donovan—he said he knew thee. Where did thee meet him?" Jack was trying to keep his face neutral, but it only exaggerated his suspicion.

"Wellington." Honor reached for the mug by her bed.

Jack stared at it. "He brought thee water?"

Honor did not answer, so that she would not have to lie, but allowed Jack to think what he wanted. She sipped the water, then set the mug back on the table.

"But how—how would thee meet a man like him?" Jack continued. "A slave hunter."

Honor closed her eyes to avoid his intent gaze. I have nothing to hide, she reminded herself. "He is the brother of the Wellington milliner."

"What was he doing here? Had he come to visit thee?"

"No."

"Did he speak to thee about a runaway? Did—" Jack stopped and his eyes narrowed. "Did a colored man come here and ask thee for help? And did thee help him?"

"No," Honor was able to say. "No man was here apart from Donovan. Why would a runaway come here?"

"There are many runaways in Ohio, and established routes, with safe houses and helpers along the way. I believe they change often, to confound the slave catchers. They call it the Underground Railroad."

Honor had not heard the phrase before.

"Most runaways pass through Oberlin," Jack continued, "but now and then one strays this way. That must be what happened to bring Donovan here. If ever a runaway comes to the farm, thee must not keep them here, but indicate the way to Oberlin."

"What if they are hungry—or thirsty?" Honor did not dare look at the mug.

Jack shrugged. "Of course give them water if they need it. But do not get involved. It could get thee—all of us—into trouble."

She slept then. Later that evening when he came back from the fields, Jack sat next to her. "Donovan caught a colored woman in Wieland Woods," he said. "He rode past here with her, but thee was probably asleep."

He was watching her carefully, and Honor was equally careful not to react.

"I am glad he caught her," Jack added.

Honor stiffened. "Why?"

Jack shifted on the edge of the bed. "It is better not to have people like Donovan chasing others across the countryside, disrupting honest people and scaring women."

"Does thee think slaves should not try to escape?"

"Honor, thee knows we do not support slavery. It goes against our beliefs in the equality of all in God's eyes. But—" Jack stopped.

"But what?"

He sighed. "It is difficult to explain to someone like thee, who comes from a country that has not had slavery woven into the very fabric of its foundation. It is easy to condemn slavery outright, without considering the consequences."

"What consequences?"

"Economic consequences. If slavery were abolished tomorrow, America would fall apart."

"How?"

"One of this country's main products is cotton and the textiles made from it. The southern states grow it using slaves. The free northern states make the cotton into cloth. Each relies on the other. Without slaves to harvest the quantity of cotton needed at the right price, the northern factories would shut down."

Honor considered this, wishing her head weren't so fuzzy so that she could supply a coherent response.

"I know English Friends have strong principles about slavery, Honor," Jack continued, "as do Americans. But we are perhaps a little more practical. Putting beliefs into practice is harder than preaching them. Think of all the cotton thee has used for thy quilts. Much of it, even what thee bought in England, is made using slave labor. We try when we can to buy cloth with no associations to slavery, but that is difficult, for there is little of it." He fingered a rectangle of green chintz that made up part of a block on Honor's signature quilt. "This bit of fabric was probably made in Massachusetts with cotton from a southern plantation. Will thee now throw away the quilt because of it?"

Honor found herself curling her fingers around an edge of the quilt, holding on to it as if she expected Jack to try and yank it away. "Does thee think that we should not help slaves who run away?"

"They are breaking the law, which I do not condone. I would not stop them, but I would not help them. There are fines, and imprisonment—and worse." As he spoke Jack's jaw tightened.

There is something he is not telling me, she thought. Shouldn't a wife know everything about her husband? "Jack—"

"I must help with the milking." Jack bolted from the room before Honor could say more.

Later, alone in the sick room, she wept for the black woman who had brought her water and was now in Donovan's hands.

The next afternoon she woke to find Belle Mills sitting beside her. Honor blinked to make sure she wasn't dreaming. But no: she could never have dreamed up Belle's bonnet, with the widest oval brim she'd ever seen, lace ringlets cascading down on each side and tied with a bright orange ribbon. It accentuated the yellow tone of her skin, though, and while the bonnet was very feminine, it had the effect of making Belle's face, with its strong jaw and staring eyes, more masculine.

"Honor Bright, you went and got married and didn't even tell me! I had to find out from my brother, and I hate getting news from him. I'd a mind not to even come out here, 'cept he told me you were sick and I had to see for myself that your new family's lookin' after you. Don't look like they're doin' much. Ain't even here."

"Harvesting oats," Honor murmured. "They have to get it in before the storms that are expected tomorrow."

Belle chuckled. "Honey, listen to you, talkin' 'bout the harvest. Next you'll be tellin' me how many jars of peaches you put up." She laid a cool hand on Honor's brow—Honor wondered how she managed to remain so in such heat. The gesture reminded her of her mother, and she closed her eyes for a moment to relish the kindness.

"Well, you still got a fever," Belle announced, "but it ain't too bad. You'll live. Now then, I'm glad to hear you took my advice about marryin'. And it's no surprise you chose Jack Haymaker, with a farm like this. Course you got the mother-in-law to go with it. I remember her stare. Oh, honey, what is it? There you go again." For Honor was crying, tears rolling in hot rivers down the sides of her face to pool in her ears. Seeing Belle Mills was like discovering a sweet plum in a bowl of unripe fruit.

"There, now." Belle slid her arm around Honor's shoulders and held her tight until she had stopped. She did not ask what the tears were for.

"Guess what's come to Wellington," she said when Honor was quiet. "The train! Had her maiden run from Cleveland a couple weeks ago. Whole town was out to see it come in, and of course most of the ladies had to have new hats. Told you the train would bring business."

"I would like to see it."

"It's like the biggest blackest snorting horse you ever saw. Did you know it goes fifteen miles an hour? Fifteen! Only two and a half hours to Cleveland. I'm gonna ride on it soon. You should come with me."

Honor smiled.

"Oh, I brung your wedding present," Belle said. "You didn't think I'd come empty-handed, did you?"

"We—thee didn't have to—I thank thee—Jack and I thank thee." Honor went through a series of corrections to find the right words. In general, Quakers did not give gifts, as material possessions should not be given heightened status. But she did not want to criticize Belle's generous gesture. And so she took the flat, paper-wrapped parcel tied with a blue ribbon.

"Go on, open it. You don't have to wait for your husband. I didn't come all this way not to see if you like 'em."

Honor pulled off the ribbon and unwrapped the paper to find two linen pillowcases edged in fine lace. She was not meant to care, but she loved them.

"Here's what I think," Belle said. "Whatever's happened to you during the day, as long as you got a nice pillowcase for your head at night, you'll be all right. You got yourself a place to lay your head, Honor Haymaker. Things are lookin' up."

Faithwell, Ohio
8th Month 27th 1850

Dear Belle,

 I am writing to thank thee for visiting me when I was ill. I am feeling better now, though still weak.

 I thank thee too for the beautiful pillowcases thee has given Jack and me. No one has ever given me such a gift. I will treasure them, as I treasure the hand of friendship thee extends.

     Thy faithful friend,

     Honor Haymaker

Blackberries

A FEW DAYS later, when her head was clearer and she had regained her strength enough to be up and about, Honor found a response to Jack's argument about slavery and cotton. It came so plainly to her mind that she wanted to pass it on before it lost its shine. And so at supper, to the astonishment of all three Haymakers, Honor spoke out without having been asked a question first. She was so eager to say what she was thinking, and so unused to leading a conversation, that she did not preface her words with any explanation. Into the silence—the Haymakers did not talk much when they ate—she stated, "Perhaps we should all pay a bit more for our cloth, so that cotton growers may use that extra money to pay the slaves, making them workers rather than slaves."

The Haymakers stared at her. "I would pay a penny more a yard if I knew it was paying to dismantle slavery," she added.

"I did not know thee had the pennies to be generous with," Dorcas remarked.

Judith Haymaker passed her son a platter of ham. "Adam Cox would have to shut down his business if he raised the prices on the cloth he sold," she said. "There are few pennies to spare these days.

Besides, southerners would rather stop farming than pay their slaves a wage. It is not in their nature to make such a change."

"'The stranger that dwelleth with you shall be unto you as one born among you, and thou shalt love him as thyself.'" Though she had heard the words many times, Honor spoke them without as much force as she would have liked.

Judith frowned. "Thee does not need to quote Leviticus at me, Honor. I know my Bible."

Honor dropped her gaze, ashamed of her attempt to engage in a true discussion of the issue.

"We come from a slave state," Judith continued. "We moved to Ohio from North Carolina ten years ago, as many Friends did at the time, for we could no longer live in the midst of slavery. So we understand the cast of the southern mind."

"I am sorry. I did not mean to judge."

"There are a few farmers in the South who have given their slaves freedom, or allowed them to buy it," Jack conceded, "but they are rare. And it is difficult for free Negroes to find a living. Many come north, leaving families behind, to settle in places like Oberlin, which is more tolerant than most. But even in Oberlin they are a separate community, and those who have run away are not entirely safe. That is why we support colonization. It seems a better option."

"What is colonization?"

"Negroes come originally from Africa, and they would be happier living back there, in a new country of their own."

Honor was silent, thinking about this. She wondered how Jack knew what would make Negroes happy. Had he asked them?

She had an opportunity to do so herself the following week. Jack was driving the wagon to Oberlin to have a corn husker repaired, and Honor accompanied him. Ten days before she could not imagine having the strength to cross a room, much less go to town, but when the fever abated, her recovery was quick, as others told her it would be, and she was eager to go to Oberlin again. Adam had promised that once the harvest season was over, he would ask Jack if she might occasionally help him at the store on Sixth Days. She did not know what her husband would say: probably that she should learn about cows instead of fabric. Judith had said she would soon have her milking, which Honor dreaded, for the cows seemed big and alien. Because of her illness, so far she had remained in the house and garden, and managed to avoid the animals, with their insistent hunger and muck. She could not escape the smell, however.

Each time Honor's life changed, she found she missed what she'd had before: first Bridport, then Belle Mills's Millinery, now Cox's Dry Goods. But there was no use in dwelling on what her life might have been: such thinking did not help. She had noticed that Americans did not speculate about past or alternative lives. They were used to moving and change: most had emigrated from England or Ireland or Germany. Ohioans had moved from the south or from New England or Pennsylvania; many would go farther west. Already since she had arrived in Faithwell three months before, two families had decided that after the harvest they would go west. Others would come from the east or south to take their place. Houses did not remain empty for long. Ohio was a restless state, full of movement north and west. Faithwell and Oberlin too had that restless feel. Honor had not noticed it when she first arrived, but now she was discovering that all was in flux, and it seemed to disturb only her.

In the center of town she and Jack parted, he to the blacksmith, Honor to Cox's Dry Goods to say hello and search for fabric for a

new quilt she was making for Dorcas. The boy was sitting out front,
sharpening a pair of scissors; he barely looked up as she stepped
inside. The shop had just one customer: Adam Cox was helping
Mrs. Reed. Today she was wearing black-eyed Susans on her hat.
Honor nodded to them both, and out of habit went over to one of
the tables to fold and restack bolts of cloth. Gazing across the sea
of colors, she was reminded of the discussion at supper several days
earlier. She had always loved fabric, admiring the weaves and patterns and textures, imagining what she could make. A length of
new cloth always held possibilities. Now, though, she understood
that much of it was not innocent, unsullied material, but the result
of a compromised world. To find fabric without the taint of slavery
in it was difficult, as Jack had said; yet if she refused all cotton, she
would have to wear only wool in the intense Ohio heat, or go na-
ked.

"I will just step next door to get change," Adam was saying to
Mrs. Reed. "Honor, will thee look after the shop for a moment?"

"Of course."

As they waited for Adam to return, Honor continued to fold,
while Mrs. Reed walked around the tables, patting the odd bolt,
letting her hand linger on the material.

"May I ask thee a question?" Honor ventured.

Mrs. Reed frowned. "What . . . ma'am?" Honor did not wear a
wedding band, as Friends did not need such a reminder of their
commitment; yet somehow Mrs. Reed knew she was married.

"Please call me Honor. We do not use 'ma'am'—or 'miss.'"

"All right. Honor. What you want to know?"

"What does thee think of colonization?"

Mrs. Reed let her mouth hang open for a moment. "What does
I think of colonization?" she repeated.

Honor said nothing. Already she regretted asking the question.

Mrs. Reed snorted. "You an abolitionist? Lots of Quakers is." She glanced around the empty shop, and seemed to reach a decision. "Abolitionists got lots o' theories, but I'm livin' with realities. Why would I want to go to Africa? I was born in Virginia. So was my parents and my grandparents and their parents. I'm American. I don't hold with sending us all off to a place most of us never seen. If white folks jes' want to get rid of us, pack us off on ships so they don't have to deal with us, well, I'm *here*. This is my home, and I ain't goin' nowhere."

Suddenly Adam was at Honor's side. "Is there a problem, Mrs. Reed?"

"No, sir, no problem." Mrs. Reed held out her hand to take the change, then nodded at him. "Good day to you." She left without looking at Honor.

"Honor, thee must never discuss politics with customers," Adam said in a low voice. "They will bring them up—Americans often do—but thee must remain neutral."

Honor nodded, holding back tears. She felt as if she had been slapped twice.

A few days later Honor and Dorcas went to pick the last of the season's blackberries at the brambles on the edge of Wieland Woods. Though it was still hot when the sun was overhead, the heat had had its back broken, and evenings were becoming cooler.

Honor's sister-in-law was almost as tricky to get along with as Abigail had been. She mimicked Honor's accent, took offense at offers of help, and did not attempt to include Honor in conversation. Honor tried to feel sorry for her. It must be hard to have a stranger in her home who brought disruption and difference, particularly since she had been expecting her own friend to take that place. As Honor expected, Caroline had recently announced she was going west. And a week before, Honor had moved from the sick room back to the bedroom she shared with Jack. It was next to Dorcas's room, and she must be aware of what went on there. Although they were quiet, the rhythmic movements of their coupling shook the bed and wall, and Jack sometimes groaned softly. Honor was getting over the shock of the demands made on her body, and beginning to enjoy what they did together.

On her own, however, without anyone else to make a point to or her mother to perform for, Dorcas was friendlier. As they bent over the brambles, she chattered on about picking enough blackberries to make pies for an upcoming frolic, the last they would have before the push to harvest the corn and put up produce from the kitchen garden and the orchard. Blackberry-picking for a frolic was a frivolity they would soon have no time for.

Ohio blackberries were subtly different from what Honor knew: larger than English berries, and sweeter, but not as tasty, the sweetness masking their unique fruitiness. Honor was hoping to surprise the Haymakers with blackberry junket, a sieving of the berries to turn them into a thick paste that concentrated the nutty flavor. She began to suspect, however, that these berries would be better for jelly or cordial.

As she worked, Honor had been only half listening to Dorcas, but a pause made her look up. Her sister-in-law was standing motionless, arms held out stiff from her sides, her fingers splayed. A swarm of yellow jackets hovered around her. As Honor watched, frozen, the wasps seemed to reach a collective decision, and swooped. "Ow!" Dorcas yelped, then began to scream, her face swelling. "Get them off me! Honor, help!" she cried, swatting at her skirt.

In Dorset, tamed by centuries of settlement, the worst that had happened to Honor when she went for a walk was a nettle sting. The American landscape was much wilder, with more dangers and sudden crises. People responded to them methodically, digging storm cellars for tornadoes, shooting bears, lighting fires to smoke out caterpillars. Belle had shot the copperhead in her yard as if it were an everyday event, like swatting a fly or chasing rabbits from a vegetable patch. Honor knew she should do something equally competent. But, while she had been stung once or twice as a child, she had never had to cope with so many wasps, and had no idea what to do. When there was a pause in the yellow jackets' attack, she had the presence of mind to take Dorcas's arm and lead her away from the nest she had stepped on. A few of the yellow jackets briefly followed, one of them stinging Honor's arm.

As she hesitated, a low voice spoke behind her. "Take her to the crick, strip her an' roll her in the water. Then put mud on them stings."

Honor turned around. A young black man was crouching by the brambles, his eyes flicking between Honor and Dorcas, whose face was now so swollen she could not see. He was sweating with nerves as much as heat, it seemed, and looked poised to run.

"Crick?" Honor whispered.

"The crick, yonder." The man waved a hand deeper into Wieland Woods. "Cold water and mud'll bring them stings down." His eyes held Honor's for a moment, his look bright and serious and fearful all in one. "Can you tell me which way to go? I get lost during the day without the northern star to follow."

Honor hesitated, thinking of what Jack counseled her to do, and then pointed. "Oberlin, three miles that way. Ask any Negro for Mrs. Reed. She will help thee." She was making this up, but she had to assume that Mrs. Reed would not turn the young man away.

He nodded. Then he smiled, a sudden flash of teeth that made their being out in the woods seem as if it were a game of Hide and Seek. It surprised Honor so much that she smiled back. She watched the man run off through the trees north toward Oberlin and freedom, and wished she had been able to give him some food for his journey.

She took a deep breath, then plunged into the forest, pulling Dorcas along in the direction the man had indicated. She had not gone into any woods since the trip between Hudson and Wellington with Thomas. She strode through the undergrowth, stepping on soft wet ground, nettles and brambles scratching at her. The woods turned out to be less frightening—and less thick—once you were in them, and had a destination.

They passed through a clump of beeches, with their smooth bark and the clear forest floor beneath them, and reached a stream. "Thee must take thy clothes off. Here, I will help thee." Honor began unbuttoning Dorcas's dress, and helped her out of her petticoat, yellow jackets falling out from the layers of clothes, some crushed, others attacking again as Honor swatted them away. Without her clothes Dorcas looked skinny and vulnerable, her hip bones knobby, her shoulder blades like chicken wings, her head incongruously large. She reminded Honor of a cow standing in a field, bereft of its herd and scrawny after a winter in a barn without fresh grass. Over her arms and legs and torso red welts from the stings were scattered.

"Come, thee must get in the water," Honor instructed.

"It's cold!" Dorcas shrieked as she rolled in the shallow pool. Honor knelt, scooped up some mud and plastered it on Dorcas's back and arms. Dorcas began to cry again, this time from shame rather than pain. "I want to go home," she moaned.

"Soon. Hold still." Honor smeared mud on Dorcas's face, and had to hide a smile. She resembled etchings Honor had seen of native tribesmen in Australia.

The water and mud helped to bring down the swelling, as the man had said. After a few minutes Dorcas climbed out of the water, and Honor helped her to dress, though they both hesitated about putting clothes on over mud. It couldn't be helped, though—Dorcas could not walk back with flesh bared.

They did not speak as they trudged through the woods. Honor collected the pails of blackberries they had abandoned on the edge of the trees, yellow jackets still circling above. There was no sign of the man. Dorcas had said nothing about him, and Honor hoped she had been too distraught to notice him.

Upon reaching the farm, Dorcas began to cry again as her mother caught sight of them and hurried over. Judith had her daughter sit in a cold bath, then applied a paste of baking soda and water to the stings—nineteen of them, Dorcas announced to Jack when he returned that evening, and to anyone who came for milk over the next few days. Forgotten were the tears and pain and embarrassment as she recounted her battle with the yellow jackets. Honor too was cut from the story, and Dorcas seemed to have retreated from her friendliness. Honor did not mind, as long as Dorcas did not mention the black man.

When Honor next met Mrs. Reed, it seemed the older woman had been waiting for her. Honor had come to town with the Haymakers, who were buying more jars for putting up the last vegetables from their kitchen garden. Honor went first to visit Cox's Dry Goods, then for a walk through the college square before rejoining her in-laws. Under the shade of the elms planted in the park, their leaves now edged with yellow, she heard a low voice beside her. "That was just foolishness, sending him to me like that. And usin' my name! You one foolish child. I see I got my work cut out for me."

Honor turned. The first thing she noticed was bright yellow buttons and fern-like leaves wrapped around the brim of a straw hat. She recognized the flowers: tansy, which her mother used to gather for a tea to brew when any of them had a sore throat. The distinctive spicy odor surrounded her; Mrs. Reed must have picked them just a few minutes before.

She was pursing her wrinkled mouth. "Keep walkin'," she commanded. "Don't want no one to wonder why you actin' like a dumb mule. Come on." Mrs. Reed stepped rapidly along the wooden walkway, nodding to black passersby and the odd white one. Honor followed, holding up her skirt so that it would not get snagged on the loose nails. She hoped the Haymakers were still busy with their jars, for she was not sure what they would think if they saw her with Mrs. Reed.

"He could of asked the wrong person about me, then what kind o' trouble I would of been in," Mrs. Reed continued. "Course they's mostly sympathizers here, but not so many as you might think, and you can't always tell 'em apart. Best to be cautious. Next time, tell 'em to look for a candle in the rear window of the red house on Mill Street. Then they'll know it's safe to come. If that signal change I'll let you know." Mrs. Reed increased her stride, and Honor hurried to keep up.

"Usually springtime's when you get the most runaways—winter too cold, summer they busy in the fields and their masters lookin' after 'em. But they's gonna be a flood of passengers this fall now it look like the Fugitive Slave Law comin' in. People who thought they was safe up here now thinkin' twice and headin' for Canada. Even coloreds in Oberlin lookin' over they shoulder. Not me, though. I'm stayin' put. My running days behind me."

Donovan had mentioned the Fugitive Slave Law to Jack, but at the time Honor had been too feverish to ask what he meant. She wanted to ask Mrs. Reed now, and why there would be more runaways, and who else was helping. But Mrs. Reed was not someone of whom you asked too many questions. "What more can I do?" she said instead.

Mrs. Reed gave Honor a sideways look and rolled her tongue over her teeth. "Get you a crate and put it upside down behind your henhouse. Put a rock on it to weight it down so animals can't get at it. Put you some victuals there—anything you got. Bread's best, and dried meat. Apples when they come in. Y'all make peach leather?"

Honor nodded, remembering the hot peach pulp that scalded her arms as she stirred it, drying into tough strips that softened in her mouth into tangy sweetness.

"That kind o' thing. Food that'll travel. Even dried corn better than nothin'. I'll get word to the people sending runaways your way so they know what to look for. Don't ever talk to me about it, though."

They were getting curious looks—not hostile, as Honor suspected would be the case in other towns, but nonetheless an acknowledgment of the rarity of a white woman and a black woman talking together in public. By now they had reached the First Church, a large brick building on the northeast corner of the square. Mrs. Reed shook her head as if to say, "I'm done with you," and hurried up the steps. Honor dropped back, for Quakers did not go inside what they called steeple houses. Mrs. Reed probably knew that.

"Was thy daughter pleased with her wedding dress?" she called as the black woman was about to disappear inside.

A wide smile cracked open Mrs. Reed's sober face. "She looked good, oh yes she did. That was a success."

———

The next time a runaway came to the farm, Honor was more prepared. One evening when she and the Haymakers were sitting on
the front porch to catch the last of the daylight, Donovan rode by.
Jack lowered the newspaper he had been reading, Dorcas stopped
sewing a tear in her skirt, and Honor paused, her needle half in and
half out of the red appliqué she was working on for the new quilt.
Only Judith Haymaker continued to rock back and forth in her
chair as if there had been no interruption. Donovan raised his hat
and grinned at Honor but did not stop, disappearing down the
track into Wieland Woods.

"Must be a runaway somewhere nearby," Jack said. "There is no
reason for him to be over this way otherwise." He glanced at Honor
as if to reassure himself.

"They were saying at the store that a Greenwich family who had
been helping runaways has stopped because of the Fugitive Slave
Law," Dorcas remarked. "Now that part of the Railroad is disrupted, some of them are ending up over this way rather than going
through Norwalk."

"That Greenwich family has sense," Judith Haymaker declared,
"though doubtless another will take their place."

"What—what is the law?" Honor asked.

"It means a man like that"—Judith jerked her head at Donovan's
back—"can demand we help him capture a runaway or be fined a
thousand dollars and imprisoned. We would lose the farm."

"Congress is on the verge of passing it," Jack added. "Caleb Wilson led a discussion of the law at a Meeting for Business during thy
illness, Honor, so thee did not hear. It was decided that each individual must follow his own conscience when it comes to helping
fugitives or obeying the law."

Honor looped the thread through itself, pulled tight, and bit off
the end.

———

The next morning when she went to collect eggs, there were two fewer than usual, and the chickens—normally laying like clockwork—seemed upset. Honor told her mother-in-law she had stepped on the eggs and broken them, though she hated lying, and suspected Judith did not believe her anyway.

Later, though, she took some leftover corn bread, smeared it with butter, folded it in a handkerchief and hid it beneath a crate she had taken from the wagon shed where Jack kept farm tools, a rock on top to weigh it down and signal that something was concealed there. It was a risk—any of the Haymakers might find it, or Donovan if he came snooping. The next morning when Honor went to collect eggs, the corn bread was gone, the handkerchief neatly folded. She left a few pieces of bacon that evening, but in the morning they were still there, crawling with ants. Runaways must not linger, she reasoned, or people would notice.

She began to keep a closer eye out for signs of runaways: rustling in the woods; Digger's barking in the night; the shifting of the cows in the barn. More than these clues, though, Honor began to be able to sense when a presence hovered on the outskirts of the farm. It was as if she carried an inner barometer that measured the change in the surrounding area, as one senses the air swelling before a thunderstorm. The shift was so clear that she marveled none of the others seemed to notice. To her, people's beings gave off a kind of cold heat. Perhaps that was what Friends meant by an Inner Light.

Often she did not see the runaways, and could only be sure they were out there when the food she hid disappeared. Each time she waited for one of the Haymakers to find the crate and accuse her. But no one went behind the henhouse unless a chicken got out or Jack took the hoe to the snakes that lived in holes there and stole eggs. He normally announced he was doing this, and Honor hid the crate until he was done. To her surprise, and sometimes shame, she was growing used to stealing, and to hiding what she was doing. It was not like her, and it went against Quaker principles of honesty and openness. But since she had come to America, Honor was finding it harder and harder not to lie and conceal. At home her life had been simple and open, where even the heartbreak of losing Samuel was conducted in front of family and community. Among the Haymakers, Honor felt she was constantly working to keep from speaking out, and maintaining a blank expression so that her thoughts and behavior did not clash openly with her new family.

Yet while she said nothing and accepted that it was for her to adjust to the Haymakers, she could not agree with their stance on slavery and fugitives. And so she kept watch, and noted when she became aware of a presence, and looked for ways to help that would not bring attention to what she was doing. She must not seem to be disobeying her husband's family. Underneath it all, though, she was.

It was not easy to hide her activities. A farm is run communally, with all taking part and working together. Honor was rarely alone. If she was working in the garden—as she often did, for it felt more familiar to her than the rest of the farm—Judith or Dorcas was at the kitchen window, or shaking rugs outside, or making butter on the back porch, or pegging out laundry in the yard. Once the cows were milked, Jack led them out to pasture for the day, and then mended fences, or chopped firewood, or delivered cheese to neighboring towns, or mucked out the pigs, or groomed the horses, or worked in the fields. He was constantly busy with different tasks, and his movements were unpredictable.

Slowly Honor found gaps where she could be alone. Though she was not keen to help with the cows, she willingly took over the chickens, for it was harder to make mistakes with them. Every morning she fed them and collected their eggs; once a week she cleaned out the henhouse. Jack and Dorcas were busy milking then, while Judith was at the stove making breakfast, and Honor was free to check the food crate. When she went to the outhouse to use it or empty chamber pots, she could fill an old mug with water and leave it under the crate or at the edge of the woods. She did these things, always expecting that eventually she would be found out, and not knowing what she would do then.

While the weather was mild, passing fugitives remained in Wieland Woods, only venturing out to look for food under the crate. Honor never saw them, or heard of them, unless they were caught by Donovan or another slave hunter. Donovan in particular liked to advertise his victories to Honor, making sure to ride by the Haymakers' farm, even when it was out of his way. Often he had the runaway shackled and bound and forced to ride behind him, struggling not to be bounced off the horse's back.

One evening when the Haymakers were sitting on the porch, Donovan rode up, raised his hat, then nudged the man he had caught off his horse. Honor leaped up, but Jack grabbed her and held her back. "Do not get involved, Honor. He wants thee to."

"But a man needs help. He may be hurt." The runaway was lying facedown in the dust, kicking his legs to try to roll onto his side.

"It is a victory to a man like Donovan if thee goes to him."

Honor frowned.

"Do what thy husband tells thee," Judith Haymaker said. "And do not look at me like that."

Honor winced at her sharp tone, and looked to Jack to soften his mother's command. He did not: he was watching Donovan, arms folded across his chest.

"Haymaker, help me out here," Donovan called. "I got a live one tryin' to escape." When Jack did not immediately move, Donovan grinned. "You want me to quote the law? I'm happy to oblige you: 'All good citizens are hereby commanded to aid and assist in the prompt and efficient execution of this law wherever their services may be required.' See, I learned to read just to be able to quote words like that. Now, you gonna be prompt and efficient or you want me to bring you in for breakin' the law? Or maybe you'd like a little stay in jail, away from your pretty wife."

Jack's jaw flexed. He is caught, Honor thought, just as I am caught. Is it worse to have no principles, or principles you cannot then uphold?

She stood on the porch and watched while her husband helped Donovan pick up the black man and heave him back into the saddle. The man's face was bruised, his clothes torn, but as Donovan rode away the slave's eyes met Honor's for a moment. Donovan did not see the exchange, but Jack did. He glanced at his wife, and she dropped her gaze. Even looking was becoming dangerous.

Dearest Biddy,

I have been meaning to write to thee these last several weeks, but each time I pick up my pen I fall asleep over my words. We have been so busy bringing in the crops that I am too tired to do anything other than eat and wash before falling into bed. Then I am up at dawn for the milking. Yes, I now know how to milk a cow! Judith has insisted on it, and I do understand that if I am truly to be a Haymaker I must take part in the milking.

I confess at first I was terrified of the cows. They are so big and solid and bony, and would do what they like rather than what I wish them to, shifting and stamping and pushing at me. I was frightened that they would step on my foot and break it, and was always jumping out of the way. Even when Judith gave me the more placid cows, I found it hard to master the technique. My hands are small and my arms are not strong. (Judith and Dorcas's forearms are as thick as fence posts!) For a time it took me twice as long to milk a cow as the others. I think they despaired of me, especially as I wasted so much milk from the cows kicking over my pail.

It is an odd thing to touch a cow's udders. At first it did not feel right, and I thought it would upset them. But Dorcas taught me to spit on my hands so that I would not chafe them, and the cows seem not to mind. Little by little I have become more confident, and in the past week I have not had one pail spilled. Perhaps my arms are stronger, for now I can milk a cow in fifteen minutes. That is still slower than the others, who take only ten minutes. But I am persevering. I have even begun to enjoy the milking: there is something calming about leaning against a cow's flank and coaxing milk from her. Sometimes I even have that sinking-down feeling that I get at Meeting.

I am glad to be able to help. Indeed, I must help, if the farm is to grow. Each year the Haymakers try to add a cow to the herd, if they have brought in enough extra hay to support one. Jack is very pleased that we managed three good crops of hay this summer, which means that we can afford to keep the calf born last month.

I can picture thee now, smiling at my talk of cows and hay and crops. I too never thought I would live such a life. If thee could see the pantry here, thee would be amazed at the rows and rows of jars filled with all the food from the garden: beans and peas and cucumbers and tomatoes and squash. The cellar is full of potatoes and turnips and carrots and beets, and apples and pears. The cherries and plums are in syrup or dried. We are now making apple sauce, apple butter, and drying apple rings as well.

Of course back home we put up our garden too, but not as extensively as here. We must have five times the produce that Mother put up. It was a great deal of work, and I stank of brine and vinegar, and have burns on my hands and arms from hot syrup or the wax we used to seal the jars. At times I thought of the ease of going to the shops in Bridport and simply buying what we needed. But here we haven't the money. Moreover, the Haymakers—indeed, everyone— take great pride in being self-sufficient. It is satisfying to look in the pantry and see it brimming. And the hay is topping the haymow; the corn crib is full of dried corn. The pigs are fattening fast and will be slaughtered in a month or two, the chickens will be bottled (yes, they put them in jars!), and Jack is going hunting for deer. In short, the farm is ready for the winter, which they say is long and very cold. I do not think I will mind it—I prefer snow to the suffocating heat. Actually I am enjoying the autumn here—fall, they call it, for the falling leaves. It has been quite mild, though the nights are sharp, and there was a frost two weeks ago. The leaves are glorious colours, far more vivid than any I have seen in England: bright red and orange maples, so plentiful here, gold birches, purple oaks. The sight makes my heart glad.

I am getting on a little better with Judith and Dorcas, now that they see I can be useful. I have learned to defer to Judith and let her tell me what to do, for if I go my own way I always err, in her eyes. It is wearying at times, but easier than trying to justify my methods. And, by submitting to her, it gives me more freedom, as she does not scrutinise me quite so much. Also it lessens the strain I feel at times with Jack, that he is being pulled between us. It is not easy, joining another family.

I am afraid that I have failed in my cooking. They do not like it; they say it is too delicate. Indeed, the ingredients here do not respond as I would like them to. When I try to make a posset, the milk burns rather than curdles. The flour is so coarse that my pastry falls apart. The beef is tough and I don't know how to make it as tender and tasty as English lamb. There is no lamb—cows fare better here than sheep. The ham and bacon are so salty I can barely eat them. The Dutch oven is too hot and burns everything. And whatever I cook tastes of corn, whether I am using it or not. Now I simply do what Judith asks of me— chopping, scrubbing, sweeping.

The one thing I am truly valued for here is my sewing and quilting. Judith has handed over all of the sewing, and I have happily taken it. At several of the frolics I have been asked to quilt the central panel, as that is the one most noticed on a bed.

I am now working on a quilt for Dorcas to replace one of those she gave me for my marriage—the first of three I owe her. I am making good progress on it. Dorcas has settled on an appliqué pattern they call a President's Wreath, made of circles of red flowers and green leaves on white fabric arranged in repeated blocks. They are bordered first in solid red, then with an outer border of a trailing green vine, with more red flowers all around. The colours, being complementary as well as

standing out against the white, are very bold. The effect is striking but
much less subtle than what thee and I are accustomed to. I drew it out
for her, with her changing her mind several times about the details—
vines in green or red, the size of the wreaths, daisies alternating with
tulips or not. Then she changed her mind again after I had already cut
out the pieces! I thought I would have to throw away a great deal of
cloth, and be considered wasteful, but for once Judith came to my rescue
and told Dorcas to let me decide what is best. In that one area, then, I
am my own mistress.

I did manage to convince Dorcas to let me use printed material
rather than plain, so the red has tiny blue dots, the green tiny yellow.
That way the appliqué will look less flat. It was one small victory, and
makes me more willing to work on the quilt. Then, too, appliqué does go
much quicker than patchwork, so at least I will not be working on this
one for too long. By the time I make the next, perhaps I will have
persuaded her to allow me to make her an English patchwork quilt,
even if it takes much longer.

I wonder sometimes why I don't make quilts for myself and simply
give back hers when they are done. We have not used them yet
anyway—at the moment Jack and I are sleeping under my signature
quilt and the whole-cloth white quilt made for us the week before our
wedding. I have not suggested this idea to Judith, however, for I sense
that she and Dorcas would not like the suggestion. Mine will be the
better made, and Dorcas would prefer that, as long as she gets the
pattern she wants. I look forward to the quilting, as she has fewer
opinions about that element of the work, and I can quilt the patterns I
prefer. I think I will quilt a running feather border, though it is more
difficult than other patterns. Then when one looks past the red and
green wreaths and flowers, one may see that bit of sewing which is
truly me.

I expect by now Mother will have asked thee for the Star of

Bethlehem quilt I gave thee before leaving for America. I was ashamed to have to ask for it back, but I know my dearest friend will understand. Circumstances have led me to marry much sooner than expected, and I was not ready, in terms of quilts—and other ways too. I hope one day to make another quilt and send it on its long journey to reach thee.

Thy faithful friend,

Honor Haymaker

Pole Star

AS IT GREW colder, Honor began to worry about the runaways sleeping outside. Those she had glimpsed had few clothes with them, and nothing warm. Most fugitives passed through during the night, simply taking the food Honor left out. Occasionally, though, one got stranded there at daylight, and hid in Wieland Woods. As the frosts came, and then dustings of snow, she looked for a warmer place to hide them during the day, in case any needed hiding. The haymow was the most obvious place, where there was also straw for bedding. But since it was obvious, slave hunters were more likely to search it. Moreover, she and Judith and Dorcas milked the cows in the barn twice a day, and Jack was in and out, mucking out dirty straw and replacing it with fresh, and feeding the animals with hay from the loft. It was a busy place to hide someone in. However, she could not think of a better spot: the chickens would make too much noise with someone in the henhouse, and the cows and pigs and horses would be stirred by a presence in their stalls beneath the haymow. The wagon shed was less used but more exposed, and cold and uncomfortable. The woodshed was too close to the house. Besides, Honor felt the hay was the best thing about the farm; it was there she herself felt safest.

The first runaway she hid there was a boy of twelve or so. Honor found him crouched behind the henhouse when she went out to collect eggs one First Day morning, so cold he could barely move. Handing him a corn cake she had slipped into her apron pocket, she thought quickly. "Wait here until thee sees us leave for Meeting—church," She corrected herself so that he would understand. "Then hide in the straw in the far corner of the barn. Keep still if anyone else comes. I will call out when I come to thee later." Because it was First Day, and a day of rest, she knew Jack would not change the animals' straw, but only feed them.

That evening it rained, a cold drizzle mixed with ice. Honor excused herself to go to the outhouse, where she left the lantern and ran blindly to the barn. "'Tis me," she called softly. She heard the boy emerge but could not see him, only smelling his sweaty fear as he drew close. "Here." She thrust some cold beef and potatoes into the dark.

His hands met hers as he took the food. "Thankee."

"Thee must leave tonight and head for Oberlin, three miles north of here. Go behind the barn and head that way. At Oberlin, look for the candle in the back window of the red house on Mill Street." She left before he could say anything, fearful of being missed inside. She could hear him wolfing down the food as she pulled the door shut.

The next day Honor slipped to the barn while Jack was out delivering cheese and the Haymaker women were stewing apples, taking with her a pail full of peelings to feed to the pigs. She wanted to check that the boy had left no trace, but was astonished to discover he was still there, asleep in a nest of straw. When she woke him, he jumped to his feet, ready to run. "Why is thee here?" Honor cried. "It is dangerous to remain."

The boy shrugged and lay back down in the straw. "Too cold out. I ain't been this warm in a long time. Someone came in this morning to feed the animals and I kep' real still so he didn't find me. You got anything to eat?"

Instead of scolding him, Honor gave him some of the apple peelings and promised to try to bring something else later. Unlike other fugitives she had met, he was talkative, telling her while he ate about his journey from Virginia. Honor learned that he had been traveling with an older man, but the two had become separated in eastern Ohio when they were chased through dense woods. The boy did not know what had happened to the other.

"I didn't want to go up north jes' to Pennsylvania or New York," he explained with the assuredness of a twelve-year-old. "Yankee land still too dangerous. Canada's safer. I had help most the way 'long, especially from the Quakers. You a Quaker?"

Honor nodded. "Thee is almost there," she said. "It will take only a few more days to reach the lake, and then someone will help thee find a boat to Canada."

"Yep." But the boy looked indifferent. He has become so used to the journey, she thought, that he has forgotten about the destination.

Before leaving she covered him so that he looked like an authentic heap of straw. It worked as long as he lay still and did not rustle. The boy could not, though, for his youth made him restless: he jiggled his foot and jerked his legs, and repositioned himself, burrowing deeper into the straw. Honor hoped that if Donovan or another slave hunter came looking, the mantle of fear would silence the boy.

Donovan did not come looking, however, and the boy disappeared that night. She prayed that he reached Canada.

———

A few weeks later she hid another. One morning when she went out to the barn to milk, Honor had the now familiar sense of someone in Wieland Woods, though she was careful not to look that way. The puddles and ruts of mud were frozen; a night outdoors would have been painful. When she went to collect eggs, the feeling was still there. Honor fretted, but could do nothing.

Later that day they had word that a Friend had gone into labor and was asking for Judith's help. Dorcas accompanied her, but Honor stayed behind to help Jack with the evening milking. When his mother was gone, Jack became less serious and more playful. Now he had them milk the same cow, one on each side, and squirted her with milk till Honor laughed and told him to stop.

They worked in silence for a few minutes, Honor leaning her head against the cow's flank and thinking of the runaway in the woods. "A birth," Jack said then. "That will be us soon enough." He grabbed her hand, squeezing it into the cow's wet udder. "We can start now. The hay above makes a good bed."

"After the milking," Honor insisted, smiling into the side of the cow.

But before they had done, Jack was called to ride for the doctor in Oberlin, as the mother was bleeding. When he suggested dropping her at Adam and Abigail's for company, Honor insisted she would be fine alone. "I have Digger with me," she reminded him, "and the milking to finish, and plenty to do." Though the dog remained aloof, he would defend her if needed.

Once Jack had gone, she shut Digger in the house and ran to the edge of the woods with a lantern. Holding it up, she shone it into the dark snarl of trees. "Come out!" she called, her heart racing. "I will hide thee!" Though her sense of urgency made Honor less frightened of the woods than she would normally be, she could not bring herself to enter the trees.

Luckily she did not have to—a woman stepped out from a clump of maples into the circle of light. She was wearing a bonnet and shawl, but still shivering with cold. As Honor led her through the orchard toward the barn, she could hear Digger's furious, muffled barking. Then, beyond that, she caught the sound of Donovan's horse, clattering and thudding along the track from Faithwell.

Honor blew out the lantern and ran, assuming the woman would follow. She did not go to the barn's heavy front door that she and Jack had shut for the night, but headed around the side to a small door built in case fire blocked other exits. If they used the main door, Donovan might hear, and he would certainly spot that it had been left unbolted.

Inside it was so dark Honor could not see her hand in front of her face. She had no time to think, but grabbed the woman's arm and pulled her, bumping along hay bales, to the straw in the corner. Digging down, they covered themselves with handfuls of straw, and waited. They heard Donovan arrive in the yard and jump down, then the sounds of his progress around the various outbuildings: the chickens squawking in the henhouse; the squeak of the wagon-shed door; the slamming of the privy. Finally the sounds stopped. Now they must remain very quiet.

It seemed at last Honor had met someone who could keep as still as she.

She had always taken a secret pride in how still she sat at Meeting. When she settled on a bench, feet firm on the floor, legs pressed together and hands folded in her lap, she could hold her position for two hours without a movement. All around her men and women shifted in their seats to relieve aching legs and buttocks. They shrugged shoulders, scratched heads, coughed, reclasped hands.

Jack was a particular culprit. On the rare occasions when he got up to speak, Honor suspected it was not because he felt moved by the Holy Spirit to do so, but because he needed to stretch. Being a Quaker did not mean you were naturally still.

Huddling in the straw next to her, the woman at her side would not have had Honor's years of experience in not moving. Yet she was still—so still that Honor strained to detect even a single rustle of straw. All she could hear was a nest of mice stirring and squeaking nearby; and, once, the moist click of the woman's blink, a sound that seemed enormous in the silence. It became almost a competition between them to discover who could be quieter.

Then she heard the snap of a stick, the creak of a leather boot, and tensed. Donovan too was playing the quiet game, though less skillfully than the women. The slave did not move except to unstick her tongue from the roof of her mouth with a tiny "tock."

The sound seemed almost a signal. With a painful rasp of metal against metal, Donovan drew back the bolt on the barn doors and swung one open. After the intense darkness his lantern seemed as bright as sunlight. As he stepped inside, the temptation to bolt was almost overwhelming, but Honor knew they could not outrun him. They must remain where they were, and not only keep still, but somehow negate themselves so that he would not sense their presence. This was harder to do than keeping quiet. It meant harnessing and stilling the Inner Light.

Honor closed her eyes, though it went against her instincts. She wanted to be able to watch Donovan, whose outline wavered in the lantern's light as he swung it to light up the corners. However, if she turned off the power of her sight, and in her mind left the barn, she might manage to diminish her self. She tried instead to imagine herself back across the ocean. She was standing with her mother and sister on Colmer's Hill outside Bridport, looking toward the sea.

"Honor Bright." Donovan said her name as if he knew she was there, and his voice brought her right back to the barn. Honor did not open her eyes, but she could feel his gaze on her, even covered in straw. Her spirit was stretching toward him, though he represented everything she opposed.

Inside the barn the air had become thick and tense.

The runaway did not respond to this change, except to blink with another click.

The three of them remained frozen for a long time.

At last Donovan cleared his throat. "I'm gonna let you go this once, Honor. Don't know why. Won't happen again, I guarantee it."

Honor waited for a quarter-hour beyond the last hoofbeat of his horse before easing back into the straw and flexing her cramped legs. "All right," she said. "He has gone."

Still the black woman did not move.

"I have never heard another be so quiet," Honor admitted. "Thee would do well as a Quaker."

At last she heard something: the sound of a smile.

When they were back outside, Honor whispered, "Does thee know where to go?"

Still wordless, the woman pointed up at a star in the northern sky: the pole star. Samuel had explained to her once that everything in the night sky turned around that one unassuming star, and because it did not move, you could follow it. It always astonished her that in a sky full of movement, there could be one fixed point.

Faithwell, Ohio
1st Month 20th 1851

Dearest Biddy,

I was overjoyed today to receive thy letter that accompanied the Star of Bethlehem quilt, along with those from William and my Aunt. It has been a treat to receive the package, with letters from thee and Mother and Aunt Rachel all at once, with so much news and warmth to be found in them. They have truly broken the monotony of these winter days.

When I unwrapped the quilts and spread them on our bed, I cried to see all that familiar fabric and stitching. I am so grateful to thee for giving up the quilt, with such generosity and understanding—in particular since I am beginning to sense from the frequent references in thy recent letters to a certain Sherborne family that thee may soon be in need of quilts thyself! I thank thee, Biddy. My mother-in-law is pleased they have arrived, even if she and Dorcas inspected the quilts with puzzled looks they did not try to conceal. English patchwork is clearly not to their taste.

I had thought that with the coming of winter there would be more time for me to write letters. There is indeed more time, for nothing is growing now, there is snow up to the windows, and apart from milking and feeding the animals and going to Meeting, we rarely go outside. Yet I am disinclined to write, perhaps because there is less to tell thee. Each day is identical to the one before. Like the chickens and the cows, we have been cooped up inside together for a month, and I find I have become weary and dull. I do not recall such a sensation during Dorset winters: it was milder, with less snow, and being in town thee and Grace and I were always going about, with a circulation of people and goods and ideas and sea air to keep us fresh. Here I sit with Dorcas and Judith all day long in the kitchen, where it is warmest, and the air is as stale as our conversation. Then I wonder what I would write to tell thee, and so I put it off. For that I am sorry. But the arrival of thy letter and the quilts has given me a good reason to take up my pen.

I smile now to remember that in my last letter I said I was looking forward to the cold. How I long for summer now! For weeks there has been a thick blanket of snow on the ground, with more added every few days, and no thaw to melt it. Jack has cleared paths to the chickens and well and privy and barn, and regularly takes the horses out to break a path to Faithwell to deliver milk. Yet the snow is hard to get through, and the cold too drives us inside. When I go out in the mornings for the milking, my fingers turn so stiff that I can barely pull at the udders, and I have to warm them against the cows' flanks. At least the beasts are warm, and their breath keeps the barn from freezing. The chickens stay in their house and lay little; occasionally one freezes to death and we have to eat it, which upsets me as that is not what they are meant for.

We are less productive now. It feels strange to be eating through what we worked so hard to store in the summer and autumn, even though of course that is why we stored it. Each day the jars in the pantry lose a member or two. Every week we kill a chicken. We are eating through the ham and bacon of the pig slaughtered last month. The bins of potatoes and carrots in the cellar are diminishing. Out in the barn the hay I thought such a mountain has already become more of a hill. And the corn crib is still full but the horses are eating into it, as well as the oats. When I witness this depletion, and the snow that is trapping us here, and the cold that keeps anything from growing, I get a queer, panicked feeling that we are going to run out of food and starve. Of course the Haymakers have lived through many such winters and are more confident. They are used to making everything we need rather than buying it. I can see Jack and Judith calculating daily, measuring and considering how to make what we have last. Yesterday Judith got out some ham steaks for dinner, then put one back without cooking it. That small gesture troubled me—though as it happened we had plenty to eat. I must trust them to get us through the winter, and assume that one day I will be as content and unconcerned as Dorcas, who maintains a hearty appetite. She did admit to me, though, that when they first moved from North Carolina she found the Ohio winters a trial.

I miss fresh food—all of our vegetables and fruits are pickled or dried, except for a few apples and potatoes and carrots. One food has been a revelation, however: Jack put a shovel heaped with dry corn into the fire so that the kernels popped into white blossoms. 'Popcorn' is the most delicious thing imaginable. Jack was so pleased I liked it that he made it for me three nights in a row, until Judith chided him.

As mentioned previously, I help with the milking each morning and evening, and it has become much easier now that the cows accept me, and I them. I had always thought of them as all alike—dumb beasts who stand in fields eating grass—but I know now that each has her own character, just like people. It took them some weeks to accept a new pair of hands touching them. Like horses and dogs, they are quick to sense uncertainty, and will play upon it, given the chance. I have learned to be firm with them, and they are now docile. Thee would smile at my arms, for they have grown with muscles I had never used before. My forearms are almost as big as my upper arms, and my shoulders are not as sloped as they once were. I should not care about such things, but my body looks peculiar to me—though Jack doesn't mind, being accustomed to dairymaids' arms.

After milking we have breakfast, and while I am clearing up, Judith and Dorcas make cheese and butter from the morning's milk. When I finish in the kitchen I shell half a bushel of corn for the horses. This is the work I hate most, as it hurts my thumbs when I push the dried kernels off the cob. The bases of my thumbs have also grown as a result, and their tips are crisscrossed with scars. Eventually thee will not recognise

me! At times it feels so futile an exercise to shell corn and have it eaten,
then do so again the next morning, and the next. When shut up all
winter in the barn, doing little other than eating and soiling the area
around them, the animals come to seem like machines. I am sure I will
be as glad as the horses and cows when spring comes and they can at last
go out to pasture.

When we have finished our chores for the morning, Judith begins
dinner and Dorcas and I sit by the stove and sew or knit. I am now
working on the second red and white appliqué quilt I am making for
her. I did not manage to convince her to let me make patchwork, but I
do not mind so much now, as I am growing fonder of the simple
cheerfulness of the design, especially during these grey months. It goes
slowly, however: the cold and the stuffy air and the repetition of each
day makes me slow-witted and less inclined to accomplish much. I make
more mistakes, and must unpick them. When we were so busy in the
autumn, I still managed to sew more than I do now. And it is hard to
be so confined together; at times it makes me almost wild with
frustration. I feel trapped here, frozen into a house and a family I still
do not feel I belong to.

I miss the meadows of Dorset, which remained green all winter. I
never appreciated them until faced with the prospect of months of
brown, grey and white. I think now that the stunning show of leaves
in red and yellow and orange in the autumn was one last gift from God
to see us through these colourless winter months.

We rarely see anyone else, for they are shut up in their houses,
waiting out the winter. Only occasionally does someone brave the cold
and snow to come for milk and cheese. And the milliner Belle Mills
came once to visit—in a sleigh! (That is what they call sledges. I have
had to learn many new words.) Does thee recall the parrot a sailor once
had in Bridport? Her arrival was like that parrot landing in
Faithwell—all bright feathers amongst the snow. Judith and Dorcas

didn't say a word. I was so pleased to see her I'm afraid I cried, and Belle teased me, for I cry every time I am with her. She is the only person in Ohio whose friendship approaches what thee and I have— and yet she is as different from thee as American robins are from English ones. Robins here are big and brash, with bright chests, compared to the delicate, more subtle bird thee knows.

Belle brought me some beautiful tan silk I am hoping to use in a quilt when I have finished those for Dorcas. Then I will be able to make what I like, in the spring, when everything will come alive again.

Thy faithful friend,

Honor Haymaker

Sugaring

THE THAW WAS like a fist unclenching, with the world—and Honor in it—expanding in the newly formed palm. It was surprising how little time it took for the cold to lose its dominance. One day Honor woke and the air felt different: still icy but the sharp end of it blunted and less insistent.

She was finishing the quilt for Dorcas, quilting it herself rather than having it done collectively at a frolic, for food stocks were low and it was not the time for such a celebration. As she sat over the small oval frame that held the fabric taut to make piercing with a needle easier, Honor realized she was not holding herself tense to combat the cold. Then Dorcas laughed at something Judith said—a sound Honor had not heard all winter—and she knew others were feeling the shift too.

That night, as she lay against Jack's warm back, monitoring another change that had taken place deep in her body over the past weeks, Honor heard the hopeful sound of dripping outside. Within a day the track to Faithwell had turned into deep, sticky mud, which was almost as hard to get through as snow had been. On her way to Meeting, Honor stepped up to her knees in it, and Jack,

Dorcas and Judith all had to pull to extract her. Even then she left behind a boot, and Jack had to fetch a spade to dig it out.

The next day he put taps into some of the maples in Wieland Woods to drain sap for syrup. After fresh corn, maple syrup was Honor's favorite food in America. She had not thought anything could taste so sweet and earthy and resinous all at the same time. It was not a taste she could easily describe in letters to her family, and she wished she could send them some.

After the dawn milking Jack took her out to Wieland Woods to collect sap for her first sugaring. Boiling it down for syrup took an entire day, so they must start early, bringing back sap that had dripped out during the night. Honor was glad to have a moment alone with her husband—so rare except when they were in bed. Winter had brought the Haymakers into a tight huddle that at times made her want to scream. Now, perhaps, she could enjoy his company without the press of Judith and Dorcas around them. At least there had been no spontaneous visits from Donovan to raise tensions further. As Mrs. Reed had predicted, there were few runaways in the winter; that, combined with the deep snow, had kept him away.

Honor and Jack worked together in the woods, going from tree to tree and transferring sap from the pails hanging on the taps into larger buckets they carried. With its trees bare of leaves and the tangled thicket died back, Wieland Woods had lost some of its wildness during the winter, and Honor felt more comfortable and less threatened there. In the companionable silence, she decided to tell her husband news that would please him. She had held back during the cold, but the thaw shifted something inside her as well. "Jack—" she began.

At that moment a black man stepped out from behind a bur oak, and Jack and Honor jumped.

"Didn't mean to scare you, sir, ma'am," he said, removing his hat and rubbing a scraggly beard. "I heard they was Quakers up this way would look after a man if he asked."

"We are not—"

"Thee is not far from Oberlin," Honor interrupted her husband. "It is just three miles that way." She pointed north. "When thee gets there, go to Mill Street—the second right off Main Street. There is a red house near where the street crosses over Plum Creek. Look for a candle in the back window, and they will help thee."

Jack stared at her in astonishment.

The man nodded. "Thankee." Pulling his hat down over his ears and wrapping his buttonless coat around him, he ran off in the direction she had indicated.

Jack glared at Honor. "How does thee know all of that?"

Honor could not meet his eyes, and instead studied the thin, transparent liquid in the pail. It would only turn brown after hours of boiling.

"We knew thee was leaving out victuals, but didn't know thee was talking to them and giving such detailed instructions—and talking as well to others working on the Underground Railroad, it seems."

Honor looked up. "Thee knew I was hiding food?"

"Of course. It is difficult to hide anything from a farmer. I suppose thee hid runaways as well?"

"A few times."

"I thought so."

In a way it was a relief to have her activities out in the open. "Why did thee not say anything?"

"Mother wanted to, of course. She was furious that thee disobeyed us and was putting us at risk of being fined. And that thee was attracting that slave catcher." Jack picked up the larger bucket and moved to the next tree. "But I asked her to let thee continue."

Honor followed him. "Why?"

Jack took the smaller pail from the tap and poured the sap into the bucket. Then he gave her a sad, sober look. "I wanted to make thee happy, Honor, for I knew that thee was not. I thought if I could let thee act on thy principles, it would make thee more content to be my wife."

Honor stared at him. She had no idea he had been trying so hard to please her. Taking a breath, she reached out a hand, but he had already turned to the next tree. She should speak, tell him what she had been meaning to say, but the words were stuck in her throat. Once the moment had passed, it was impossible to bring up the subject again, especially as Jack was careful to keep his back to her.

When they finished emptying the pails, Honor and Jack took the sap back to the farmyard. Jack had erected a temporary shack there, for boiling down sap created so much steam that it was best not to do it in the house. Judith and Dorcas had built a fire and hung a cast-iron cauldron over it. They would take turns stirring the sap all day, reducing it to a thick, dark syrup.

Honor had wondered if Jack would remain quiet, but he immediately announced that they had seen a runaway in Wieland Woods, and repeated what Honor had told the man.

Judith Haymaker glanced at her son as she took one of the buckets from him, and then at Honor. "Thee must not start that nonsense again," she declared, pouring the sap into the cauldron. "I have deferred to Jack's wishes on this subject long enough. I am sure he will agree with me that not only must thee not put this farm at risk—thee must also think of thy and Jack's child. It would not be fair for him to come into the world with the farm ruined."

Honor turned red. "What?" Jack barked.

Judith widened her half-smile, though it did little to warm her face. "Honor, surely thee did not think thee could hide such a thing from me? It is clear in thy face and in how thee walks." She turned to Jack. "Thee is a man and would not notice such things. I thought to wait for Honor to tell thee herself. I am sorry it has come out in this way, but thee needs to know, to help thy wife understand how much is at stake if she persists in this foolishness."

Jack turned to her. "Is this true? Thee is with child?"

Honor nodded.

Jack's anger at her melted like snow in the sun. He put an arm around her. "I am glad."

"Thee must promise not to get involved again in helping runaways," Judith continued. "It is illegal, it is dangerous, and the Haymakers cannot tolerate it any longer. We have suffered enough already."

"What—what does thee mean?"

The Haymakers exchanged glances. Judith sighed. "Back in North Carolina we lost our farm from having to pay a large fine when we hid a runaway. There have been fines to pay even before this recent Fugitive Slave Law was enacted. The new law is simply more insistent, and harsher."

"Is that why the Haymakers moved to Ohio?"

"Yes," Jack said. "We could not bear to live there after what happened."

"I thought . . ." Honor stopped. Now was not the time to point out that he once said they had moved north because of principles, as most of the southern Quaker families who founded Faithwell had done. Perhaps principles were not as strong a motivation as the reality of losing money and land.

Dorcas was stirring the sap faster and faster, her brow furrowed. "What Mother has not said—" she began, but a shake of Judith's head stopped her. "Am I the only one who has to stir this?" she demanded. "I suppose Honor will have to stay away from it in her condition."

"Nonsense, she is not a fragile vase," Judith said. "We will all take turns. So, Honor, thee must promise not to help slaves if they stop here."

"All right," Honor promised, her heart sinking.

"Good. Now thee can stir the sap. Dorcas, give Honor the spoon."

Faithwell, Ohio
2nd Month 27th 1851

Dear Mother and Father,

I have news for you and the rest of the family: I am with child. I have thought so for some time now, but waited to tell you until the signs seemed certain. I am not sure when the baby will come, but think it may be in 9th or 10th Month. The Haymakers are pleased, of course, though Judith did feel she must point out that I will not be useful at harvest when I am so big or nursing.

The baby has made me a little tired, but otherwise I am well, and not afflicted with the sickness other women have suffered early in their pregnancies—and for some like Abigail, even longer. She still suffers, though the baby is due in a month. (She says two months, but we know it will arrive sooner than that.) I have seen little of her this winter, or Adam Cox—and that is a shame. I had hoped to work in his shop now and then, but the Haymakers said they want me to remain on the farm with them. Though I am glad to have someone from home so close, we are not the friends I had hoped we would be. I expect it will take some time for the awkwardness between us to fade.

I am pleased to report that there is no snow now, and it is a relief not to feel trapped inside. The days are warmer, though the nights are still very cold, and there are snowdrops and even a few early daffodils out. The willows are budding, bringing a welcome green to the grey and brown. In a few weeks we will be able to dig the garden.

It is perhaps foolish of me to hope that one day you may meet your grandchild. That is in God's hands.

Your loving daughter,

Honor Haymaker

Milk

HONOR'S DECISION NOT to help runaways any longer did not stop them coming. As the weather improved, a steady stream passed through from the south. Nor was it easy simply to turn them away as was expected of her.

The first time it was not so hard. A man appeared from behind the outhouse when Honor was coming out. He looked at her expectantly but said nothing. She glanced over at the kitchen garden, where Judith was turning over soil in preparation for planting. Her mother-in-law had stopped and was leaning on the fork, watching them. Honor repeated the words she had been practicing in her head for this moment: "I am sorry but I cannot help thee." Then she added in a low voice, "Go three miles north to Oberlin, to the red house on Mill Street and ask for help. God go with thee." Surely telling him this would not be seen as helping him. Even as she said it, though, she knew that Judith would not approve.

The man nodded, turned on his heel and disappeared into the woods.

That was not so bad, Honor thought, feeling only a little awful.

She waited for Judith to say something, but she simply went back to forking the garden.

The next fugitive was an older woman, surprising Honor: most slaves who ran were younger, for they were stronger and more able to cope with the hardships of the road. She discovered her when Digger began to bark and snarl behind the henhouse, sitting with her arms wrapped around her knees, watching the dog work himself into a frenzy. Her face was covered with deep lines, but her eyes were still clear, and yellow-brown like a cat's. "Quaker lady, you got somethin' to eat?" she asked when Honor had called off Digger. "'Cause I got a hunger."

"I am sorry but I cannot . . ." Honor could not complete the practical phrase she had learned.

"Jes' a piece of bread an' some milk from one o' them cows you got, an' I'll be on my way."

"Wait there." Honor hurried to the kitchen, dragging Digger with her and shutting him inside. Luckily, both Judith and Dorcas were at the general store, and Jack was delivering milk. As she cut a slice of bread and a slab of cheese and poured milk into the tin mug, she tried out in her head the reasoning she would use with Judith: I am not hiding her, I am simply giving her food, as I would any passerby who asked.

She watched the woman eat, keeping an eye on the track for any returning Haymakers. The old woman chewed the bread and cheese slowly, as she had few teeth left. After draining the mug, she smacked her lips. "Good milk. You got some fine cows there." She rose to her feet and adjusted the rags bound around them in place of shoes, then brushed crumbs from her front. "Thankee."

"Does thee know where to go?"

"Oh yes. North." The woman pointed and, following her finger, began to walk.

At dinner Honor waited until there was a pause, quelling her stomach with sips of water. "A fugitive came to the farm today while everyone was out," she announced. "An old woman," she added, hoping to soften the news by making the slave seem particularly needful. "I—I gave her some bread and cheese, and some milk. Then she left."

There was silence. "We have discussed this," Judith said. "Thee has promised not to help runaways."

Honor swallowed. "I know. But it is hard to say no to someone who asks for food as she did. It is only what I would have done for any traveler. I was simply being courteous, not aiding a fugitive." Her rehearsed argument sounded feeble.

Judith pursed her lips. "Thy slave hunter, Donovan, would question that logic. In the future if thee has trouble turning coloreds away, come and get me."

The next time a runaway passed through, Honor could not take up Judith's offer. She felt strangely protective, and did not want to subject any of them to her mother-in-law's smiling mouth and flat eyes. The refusal would sound softer coming from herself. "I am sorry, but I cannot hide thee," she said to a light-skinned man a few days later. Saying "hide" instead of "help" sounded less rigid, as if holding out the hope that she could still help in some small way. She took to carrying a piece of jerky in her apron pocket so that when she next said "I cannot hide you," to two teenage boys, she handed them the food—more to make herself feel less guilty than to give them sustenance.

Eventually, however, her practiced words failed her. One early spring morning, as she and Dorcas were crossing the yard after milking, she heard a cry from Wieland Woods that sounded like a baby. They stopped and listened. The baby's cries came again, though muffled, as if someone were trying to quiet it.

Honor stepped toward the trees, fuzzy with the green buds of leaves about to open. "Surely thee won't go out there and look," Dorcas chided, trailing behind her. "Has thee learned nothing from Mother?"

"It may not be a runaway. It may be someone who has lost her way."

A short, tea-colored woman with round cheeks like pancakes was crouching in the brambles, hugging a child to her breast. She was hardly more than a girl. "You come to turn me in?" she said.

"No," Honor replied.

"I ain't got no milk left for her. That's why she cries."

"Dorcas, go and get some milk, and something to eat," Honor ordered.

Dorcas gave her a look, but turned and went back to the house.

While they waited, Honor tried to smile reassuringly at the baby, though it felt forced. "How old is she?"

"Four months. Don't know why I ran with a little baby. Ain't fair to her. But I jes' couldn't take it no more."

"Where have you two come from?"

"Kentucky. Ain't so far as some has come. But it's close enough my master come after me, him an' a slave catcher from round here."

Honor froze. "Is his name Donovan?"

The girl shrugged.

"Are they close by?"

"They was in Wellington last I knew."

"Not far, then. We cannot hide you both here. But if you stay in these woods, away from the road, you may be as safe as anywhere else." She explained where Mrs. Reed was, but the girl was not listening, her eyes on something behind Honor. Dorcas was returning, and she had brought her mother.

Judith Haymaker held out a mug of milk to the girl, who took it and tried to tip it into the baby's mouth. The child could not gulp, however, and the mother resorted to dipping her finger and letting her suck it off.

"Who has told thee to come here?" Judith demanded.

"A woman in Wellington, ma'am," the girl mumbled, her focus on her child.

"What was her name?"

The girl shook her head.

"What did she look like?"

"White woman. Kinda yaller-looking. Sickly."

"Where did thee see her?"

"It was the back of a shop."

"What kind of shop?" Judith persisted. Honor tried to warn the girl with her eyes.

"Dunno, ma'am." The girl paused, then brightened with a piece of information. "She had feathers in her pockets."

Honor groaned to herself.

"What, she kept poultry?"

"No, ma'am. They was dyed, blue and red."

"The milliner." Judith glanced at Honor before turning back to the girl. "Has the baby finished the milk?"

She had, and was asleep. The girl looked as if she could do with some sleep as well, her head nodding over the baby.

"Then thee must go." Judith stood as solid as her words. The girl's eyes snapped wide. She handed the mug to Dorcas and scrambled to her feet, clearly used to doing so without waking the baby. Laying her in a length of striped cloth, she lifted her up onto her back and tied knots at her chest so that the baby lay like a cocoon against her. "Thankee," she said, gazing at their feet, then trudged off through the woods, disappearing among the maples and beeches.

Judith turned toward the house. "I will go to Wellington to

speak to Belle Mills and put a stop to her sending coloreds this way."

Honor and Dorcas followed. "I would prefer to speak to her myself," Honor said.

"I do not want thee to see her. She is clearly not a good influence."

Tears stung Honor. "Then I will write to her. Please."

Judith grunted. "Tell her not to come visiting here either, for she is not welcome. And show me the letter when thee has written it. I am sorry to say I do not trust thee to do as I ask."

Faithwell, Ohio
4th Month 3rd 1851

Dear Belle,

    I am writing to ask thee not to send fugitives towards Faithwell. I have agreed with my husband and his family that there is too much risk to the farm. Recently a marshal in Greenwich arrested a Friend there for helping a runaway, and he is now imprisoned for six months, with a substantial fine to pay as well. The strengthened Fugitive Slave Law has made such occurrences more common.

    I am very grateful for thy generosity to me, in particular when I was alone and needing help. We think it best, however, if thee does not come to visit us in Faithwell. Our ways are too different from thine. However, I wish thee all happiness, and I will pray that thee will always walk in the Light.

My sincere good wishes,

Honor Haymaker

Onions

HONOR WENT WITH Jack to Oberlin to send her letter to Belle Mills. She had not been to the town in months: first because of the cold and the snow, then because when the thaw came the mud was so bad they could not use the wagon, and Jack would not let her ride a horse for fear of her falling and damaging the baby. Finally, however, the weather improved, and she accompanied him when he went to the college to deliver cheese.

Jack dropped her by Cox's Dry Goods, but rather than go in, Honor waited until her husband had driven on, then hurried south along Main Street. There was someone else she felt she should inform of her decision.

Though she had described her destination often enough to fugitives, Honor had never been there. When she reached the turning, however, and gazed down Mill Street, over the bridge crossing Plum Creek to the little red house on the right, she lost her nerve, and decided to walk on a bit to regain her composure. It was a mild afternoon, full of the breezy sunshine she had missed all winter.

She thought she would continue south to the edge of town where the railroad was being built. Clearance of thousands of trees had begun, though it would be a year before trains would begin to run, eventually connecting Cleveland with Toledo, a hundred miles west. Honor could not imagine ever wanting to go farther west than Faithwell. She never even walked west through Wieland Woods, or west along any of Oberlin's roads. Roads and trains running east were more tempting, though she knew that however far east she traveled, she would always run up against the barrier of the Atlantic.

The planks that made up the walkways along Main Street ran out south of Mill Street, and Honor picked her way through the heavy clay that sucked at her boots and turned the hem of her green dress gray. Toward the junction with Mechanics Street she heard shouts of raucous laughter and paused, trying to look as if she were being held up by mud. She had forgotten about Wack's Hotel.

Oberlin's founding principles of religious fervor, simple living and hard work made it a dry town, but Wack's Hotel was just outside the Corporation line, where the laws did not apply. Run by Chauncey Wack, a pro-slavery Democrat, it was the only place in Oberlin where liquor and tobacco were available, and though most Oberlinites were teetotal, there was always a core of visiting drinkers to keep Wack's in business. Several of them were lounging now on the porch facing the street, taking advantage of the fair weather. Among them was Donovan, leaning back in a chair. Honor caught her breath when she saw him. He was smiling at her, and toasted her with a whiskey bottle. She suspected he had been watching her progress all the way down Main Street.

Though she had not seen him during the winter, with the resumption of runaway traffic he had begun riding again along the track by the farm and lifting his hat at her if she was on the porch or in the yard. Each time she tried and failed to remain unaffected, her pulse beating hard in her throat. It occurred to her now that if she was not going to help runaways, they would stop coming to Faithwell and there would be no need for Donovan to make his visits. Already his reappearance had Judith muttering and Jack angry. I must do the honorable thing, she thought. For the baby; for the family.

She pulled in her stomach, though she knew that, only a few months' pregnant, there was little yet to show. Then she began to walk toward him, clutching her shawl tight. As she approached the hotel, Donovan's porch companions greeted her with jeers and catcalls. Honor stood still and waited for them to die down. "Donovan, I would like to speak with thee," she said, her words renewing the shouts.

"Do you, Honor Bright. That makes a change. I thought you hated the sight of me." Donovan let his chair drop to the ground and stood. "What do you want to talk about?"

Honor gestured toward the road. "Let us walk for a bit."

Donovan looked a little embarrassed—whether from the attention of a woman or the feeling that for once he was not in charge of their encounter, Honor was not sure. However, he came down the steps to join her, shaking off the whistles and coarse comments about what Honor might do to him and he to her. Honor tried not to listen but walked purposefully along the road ahead of him, stopping only to let a wagon pass so that it would not splash her.

When they were far enough from the hotel that the men had lost interest, Honor slowed so that Donovan could walk at her side. By now he had recovered his composure and seemed amused. "What's this all about?" he said. "You never wanted my company before. Haymaker startin' to bore you? That didn't take long. What—"

"I want to speak to thee about my involvement with runaway

slaves," Honor interrupted so that she would not have to hear his remarks descend into the crudeness he was accustomed to.

"Ha! You admit it, then. Course I was always sure you was hiding niggers, but it's nice to hear you say it."

"My husband's family—my family—does not approve, and I do not want to go against their wishes. So thee does not need to come to our farm any more. There will be no one hiding there."

Donovan raised his eyebrows. "Just like that, you're stopping?"

"There have been no runaways over the winter, and only a few since. I will not start again."

"What about your principles? I thought you hated slavery and wanted all niggers to be set free."

"I do. But my family is concerned about the law, and I want to respect their wishes."

"I'll tell you what the Haymakers are concerned about, Honor Bright: keeping you in your place. They don't want a woman who's gonna think for herself."

"That is not true," Honor said, but didn't defend the Haymakers further. She herself felt she was not telling the truth, though she was not exactly lying either.

They had reached the tract of land being cleared for the railroad line, where a narrow strip of trees—mostly ash and elm—had been cut down. Honor studied the stumps still waiting to be extracted, extending as far as she could see. "Why have they done that?" she asked. Around each stump a trench had been dug and filled with water.

"Water softens the wood so it's easier to dig out," Donovan explained. "They've left it like that for a time and gone to work farther along the line, toward Norwalk." He gestured west.

They stood side by side, looking out over the highway of stumps, Honor wondering at the fact that she felt more at ease with Dono-

van than with the Haymakers, even though he was not a Quaker
and his beliefs ran so counter to hers. He accepts me as I am, she
thought. That is why.

Donovan scooped up a handful of pebbles. "Listen, Honor," he
began, throwing them one by one so that they bounced off the
stumps. "You ever want to give it up and come with me, I'd stop
what I was doin'. I could do somethin' else. Work on the railroad,
maybe." His words were halting, as if he were embarrassed to say
them. "We could go west. Bet I'd make you happier than Haymaker."

What surprised her was that she could imagine it, even with a
man like Donovan. There is a good man in there, she thought. "I
do not doubt that thee could change," she said aloud, "but I am
carrying Jack's child."

Donovan grunted and spat in the street. "Was wonderin' when
Haymaker and you would get around to it." His expression remained stiff, but it felt to Honor as if a door had been shut.

She would have liked to stand there for longer with him, looking
at the stumps, but Donovan turned and began to walk back to
town, and she had to follow. For a moment she felt sorry for him.
He was willing to change, but clearly needed someone to change
for. Now it would not happen. She watched his tall broad back
ahead of her, and held back a sob.

At Wack's, Honor insisted he not accompany her farther. "I have
errands," she said. She did not want him to see her going to Mrs.
Reed's.

Donovan removed his hat, held it to his chest and bowed ex-
travagantly. "Fare thee well, Honor Bright. I might come past the
farm now and then anyway for old times' sake, to see you're keepin'
honest. I won't stop, though—promise." He replaced his hat and
hopped onto the porch, catching up a bottle as he did. By the time

she had turned to continue on her way, he was leaning back in his
chair once more, pulling hard at the whiskey.

A dogwood tree was blooming in front of Mrs. Reed's house, its
white, four-petal blossoms tinged with pink. Honor stood admiring
the delicate flowers; it was the one American tree she wished she
had grown up with. The small front garden was brimming with
flowers: the left of the front path was purple with periwinkle, lark-
spur and violets, while on the right there grew yellow daffodils and
primroses. The violets in particular were surprisingly dense, some a
bright blue, others paler and dog-toothed. Honor could imagine
Mrs. Reed reaching down to pick a handful for her hat. Most other
front gardens when planted with flowers looked both formal and
artificial. Judith Haymaker, for instance, had put in daffodil and
hyacinth bulbs so that they came up in rigid rows, a sight English
women would have smiled at. While plentiful, Mrs. Reed's flowers
had a randomness about them that reminded Honor of coming
upon primroses or anemones in the woods. They were just there, as
if they always had been. It took real skill to remove the gardener's
hand from the garden.

   She stood looking at the flowers until she knew she could delay
no longer, then stepped onto the porch and knocked on the front
door, which was peeling with white paint. There was no answer,
though she could smell onions, and heard the distant clank of pots.

   As she stepped back from the porch to look up at the house, a
movement caught her eye, and she turned toward the neighboring
house, similar to Mrs. Reed's but brown, with dirt where her flowers grew. An old black man she had not noticed before was rocking
in a chair on the porch. He was grinning at her, showing all gums
and no teeth, and pointing around the back. It was then Honor

noticed the dirt path scuffed into the crabgrass. Following it, she spied through the open back door a figure moving about inside. When Honor called out, the figure stopped, and after a moment Mrs. Reed appeared. She was not wearing her straw hat, but a red kerchief wrapped around her head. Her spectacles glinted in the light so that Honor could not read the expression in her eyes. "What you doin' here, Honor Bright?" She glanced around. "Git inside 'fore someone see you." She pulled Honor in and shut the door behind her.

It became immediately clear why the door had been left open. Honor's eyes filled with tears from the concentrated sting of a large skillet of frying onions. She pulled out a handkerchief to stanch the stream. "I'm sorry—the onions . . ."

Mrs. Reed did not move to stir the onions, but crossed her arms over her chest. "What you doin' here?" she repeated, her lower lip pushed out by her frown.

Honor finished wiping her eyes, though they soon watered again. She took a deep breath. "I have come to tell thee I will no longer be able to—to help. I am sending word to those directing runaways to me that I cannot hide them or feed them any longer. I felt thee should know as well."

Mrs. Reed did not react except to turn back to her onions, which gave Honor a chance to glance around the kitchen. She had never been in a Negro's house before and did not know what to expect.

Mrs. Reed's kitchen was much smaller than the Haymakers', as was the whole house, which appeared to consist of two rooms downstairs and two up. This was to be expected—farmhouses were generally bigger than houses in towns. Unlike the Haymaker kitchen, which was light and orderly, with clear surfaces and a pantry lined with even rows of jars, this kitchen was dark and cluttered, full of the smell of hot oil and spices and the suggestion that something was just about to catch at the bottom of the pot. The range was old and smoky, its surface spattered with oil and the remnants of past stews. The shelves on either side of the range were full of open jars of pepper and salt and cayenne, scattered bay leaves and sprigs of rosemary, bowls of dried leaves and twigs Honor did not recognize, sacks of cornmeal and flour, and bottles full of dark sauces dripping down the sides. Overhead hung a string of dried chili peppers that could not have come from Ohio. Though the arrangement appeared chaotic, Mrs. Reed herself did not. Indeed, the white apron she wore over her dress was still white and free of splashes, remarkable given the hissing of the onions and the large pot bubbling at the back of the range.

Mrs. Reed picked up the heavy pan of onions. "Get you that wooden spoon," she instructed, jerking her head toward the equally jumbled kitchen table. She held the skillet over the pot, her forearms straining with the weight. Honor fumbled with the spoon and scraped at the onions so that they dropped into the pot to join a stew of stringy chicken and tomatoes.

"Thankee." Mrs. Reed set down the skillet, reached for a handful of chili peppers, and crumbled them into the stew. Then she wiped her hands on her apron before removing her fogged spectacles and wiping them too, a gesture so familiar as to be almost unconscious. She must wipe those spectacles ten times a day, Honor thought.

There was an awkward pause. "Anything else you want to tell me, or you done?" Mrs. Reed said, picking up the sack of cornmeal and two eggs from a basket at her feet. "Git that bowl over there." She nodded at an earthenware bowl on the sideboard. "Jes' dump them walnuts on the side. They too old and bitter to eat now. Don't know why I saved 'em all this time."

Honor did as she was told, wondering if Mrs. Reed would ask

why she had made her decision. The black woman did not seem particularly interested. "I'm carrying a child," she said, to explain further.

Mrs. Reed scooped two handfuls of cornmeal into the bowl, reached for the sack of flour, and added some to the cornmeal. "Are you, now." She glanced sideways at Honor. "Guess you a little bigger than before. Still a little thing, though." She cracked two eggs into the cornmeal and flour, took a small pan off the range, poured the contents into the bowl, and began to beat. "Bring that jug over here. No, not the milk, the buttermilk. Pour some o' that in while I'm stirring. That's enough! Don't want it as wet as that. Git me another handful o' cornmeal, and another egg." Mrs. Reed ordered Honor about with ease, as if used to running a kitchen. "Now, get me three, no, four pinches from that jar. That the sody."

As Honor dropped four pinches of baking soda into the batter, a baby began to cry in the other room. "Damn, baby girl woke early," Mrs. Reed muttered. "That my granddaughter. You go and get her for me, will you? I got to get this in the oven right now or it won't never be ready in time. She in there." She gestured toward the front room.

Honor hesitated. She should get back to Adam's store where she was meeting Jack. And she still had to give Belle's letter to the stage that went to Wellington daily. But the baby's needy wail cut through such thoughts, and it was impossible to say no to Mrs. Reed—so impossible that Honor knew if asked she would have to continue to help runaways. But Mrs. Reed was not asking that.

There was only a ribbon of light from the window to see by as Honor crept in, and before going to the baby she pulled open the curtains. As sunlight flooded the room, the baby turned her head from the pile of bedclothes she was lying on, caged in by a variety of wooden chairs. She caught sight of Honor, widened her glistening eyes, and added a high-pitched scream to her crying. She was a plump baby, with tight black ringlets, fat cheeks and a bow-shaped mouth. As Honor approached her she rolled over in terror and began flailing arms and legs like a turtle caught on a rock. Five or six months old, Honor thought. Old enough to roll over but not to sit up or crawl. She thought back; that meant Mrs. Reed's daughter was pregnant when she had her wedding dress made. Honor hoped there had been enough material.

She moved a chair aside, crouched next to the baby and laid a hand on her back. "There now, my dear. How is it with thee?" She tried to imagine the bump lodged in her womb turning into this squirming, squalling being. It didn't seem possible.

Then she noticed the quilt.

Honor was now familiar with most American quilt styles. She might not like the colors or pattern, but they were designed with care, the cloth chosen from the best fabrics available, even if made from scraps of old clothes. The patterns were deliberate and, whether simple or complex, clearly thought out.

Mrs. Reed's quilt was made up of strips of cloth sewn together to form rough squares, in blue, gray, cream and brown, with the odd yellow strip thrown in. They were of wool or linsey, cut from coats, blankets, shirts, petticoats, and were worn and faded. The cover had not been quilted, but tie knots of brown yarn had been placed at the center of each square—a shortcut method of keeping the batting and backing together. Honor flipped over a corner of the quilt. It was lined with brown linsey cut with thin orange stripes. Running her hand over the squares, she pulled two tight to inspect the stitching: it was even without being overly precise.

What struck her about the quilt was the same thing she had noticed about the front garden. The placement of the colors seemed unplanned, and yet there was something pleasing about them. The gray brought out the clear beauty of the blue. The blue deepened the brown and made the cream rich and clean. The gray and cream should not go together, yet they looked as natural as two rocks side by side. And every now and then a bit of yellow popped out, making the other colors seem uniform. It felt as if there was an overall pattern that tugged at Honor's eyes, yet when she tried to find it, the patchwork fell back into random pieces. Bright, rich, spontaneous, Mrs. Reed's quilt made the red and green appliqué quilts favored by Ohio women look childlike, and Honor's own careful patchwork contrived and overcomplicated.

"That a good sign if a baby quiets without you picking her up. You'll do all right with your own." Mrs. Reed was leaning against the door jamb.

Honor started. The baby was indeed quiet, still lying on her front as if pinned there by Honor's hand on her back. She looked up at Mrs. Reed. "This quilt is"—she searched for the right word— "remarkable."

Mrs. Reed snorted. "That quilt keep me warm, is all." Beneath her gruffness, however, she seemed pleased. She fingered a strip of brown. "That from my husband's old coat. Wore it when my daughter and me ran off. He wouldn't let us go without a coat, an' gave me his 'cause it was warmer."

"Where is he now?" Honor asked, and then wished she hadn't, for Mrs. Reed's face closed.

"In Virginia, if he's still alive. He was goin' to join us later— thought we had more chance just two of us. But he never escaped." Mrs. Reed reached down for her granddaughter. "C'mon, Sukey, let's get you somethin' to eat. Get you some corn mush with a little syrup—you like that." She picked up the baby, who squealed, her tears forgotten. She grabbed at Mrs. Reed's spectacles.

"Stop that, you little monkey. I'm gonna monkey you." Mrs. Reed carried the child into the kitchen.

Honor touched the strip of brown before following Mrs. Reed. The older woman had the baby hooked over her shoulder as she stood by the range, patting her back with one hand and stirring a saucepan of mush with the other. Now she was in a secure place, the baby no longer seemed frightened, but stared hard at the white woman. Honor wondered if it was her skin color that surprised the baby, or simply her strangeness. Perhaps they were one and the same.

Honor cleared her throat. "I must get back." She paused. "I'm sorry."

Mrs. Reed turned slightly toward her, but kept her eyes on the mush. Her spectacles had fogged up again. "Don't say sorry to me," she replied, rhythmically patting the baby's back. "It's them runaways come lookin' for help you got to say sorry to. Good luck with that, Honor Bright."

Belle Mills's Millinery
Main St.
Wellington, Ohio
April 6, 1851

Dear Honor,

I'm going to ignore that letter till you write me another that don't sound like you got your mother-in-law hanging over your shoulder.

Also, you should never put things in writing. In the wrong hands they can be dangerous to people. Tell Mrs. Haymaker that.

You always got a friend in Wellington, whether you want her or not.

Yours ever faithful,

Belle Mills

Straw

FOR A MONTH the flow of runaways dried up. Indeed, Honor had little contact with anyone outside of Faithwell. Though he had threatened to, Donovan did not ride past the farm. There were no letters from her family or Biddy. She did not go to Oberlin, even when Abigail had her baby and Adam could have used an extra pair of hands at the store; nor did Jack offer to take her with him when he delivered cheese. Honor did not complain, but worked hard in the garden, finished Dorcas's quilt and began another, and grew.

Only sometimes she reread Belle Mills's letter and smiled.

She was planting squash in the garden one afternoon when something flickered in the corner of her eye. Honor looked up across the orchard to Wieland Woods and saw a figure ducking from one tree to another. When she went over to the edge of the woods and called softly, a young man emerged, limping, to stand by the brambles where Honor and Dorcas had picked blackberries. He was shaking, from fear or something else Honor did not yet know. As she prepared to explain that he could not stop here, she glanced down at his feet and sucked in her breath.

"Please, ma'am, can you help me?" The man leaned against a maple trunk. "I ain't doin' so good."

"What happened to thee?"

"Got caught in a trap."

Someone had tried to help by dressing the wound with a knot of pine resin, but his foot was swollen, and blood and pus dribbled from it. It smelled of a rotting sweetness that, now she knew what it was, made Honor want to gag. She could not imagine that Belle would have let him go on in this state. "Where has thee come from?"

"Greenwich. They told me to go to Norwalk. This Norwalk?"

Norwalk was twenty miles to the west. "No. I—We cannot keep thee here."

The man stared at her with feverish eyes.

Honor sighed. "Wait here. I will get thee some water." She hurried back to the well. As she drew up the bucket to fill the tin mug, Judith came out onto the back porch. "Thee has promised not to help runaways."

Honor flushed. "I am just giving him water. I will not hide him." The grim line of Judith's mouth made her add, "He has been hurt, his foot caught in a trap. Infection has set in. Can thee look at it? There may be something we can do."

"We are not getting involved in that colored man's troubles."

"But—"

"We have discussed this before, Honor, and thee agreed this family would not help fugitives. Whatever we may feel as Friends, it is against the laws of our government, and we cannot afford to break them. Does thee want thy husband to go to jail? Or thee, for that matter?"

"If thee could just meet the man, thy conscience would tell thee to help him."

"I am not going to meet him."

Honor stood still, trying to tamp down the rage that pushed up through her. "I have promised him water."

"Give him the water, then, and go back to thy work in the garden." Judith turned and went inside.

The hope in the man's face as Honor handed him the mug of water was so painful to see that she dropped her eyes and stepped back. "Leave the mug there when thee has finished. Oberlin is three miles north of here. Go to the red house on Mill Street. They will get thee the doctor thee needs."

She turned away and hurried to the garden, where she continued digging a furrow with the hoe, her back to the man, hot tears streaming down her face. Only when she had finished the row did she dare to turn around. The man was gone, and so was the tin mug.

That night she did not sleep. It was late spring, and warm, though not yet too hot—perhaps the best weather Ohio would ever offer. Honor lay next to Jack, the wedding quilt covering her except for her feet, which she left bare to keep her cool. Jack slept soundly, as he always did after they had coupled. Her growing belly did not seem to put him off, and he never asked if she would rather not. She submitted to his nightly expectation because it was easier to. There had been a window of time when Honor enjoyed what they did in bed, the surprise and novelty and shock of sensation—when their feelings for each other had briefly been like hay. Since the sugaring and her agreement not to help runaways, however, relations between them had become more like straw: dull and gray, the life cut from it. When she lay under Jack, letting him pump away, she no longer found her place in the rhythm of his movement. If he noticed, he said nothing, but fell asleep quickly afterwards.

Honor lay thinking of the man and his foot. She could not sleep, for she could feel he was still nearby, suffering out in Wieland Woods. She must do something to help him, but she did not know what she could do on her own. The Haymakers would not help; nor would Adam Cox, as he would not want to go against her husband's family. She thought of the blacksmith Caleb Wilson, who had recited Whittier and often brought up the issue of slavery at Meeting. He was certainly a man of principle, and might help her—except that his respect for Judith Haymaker was also strong. Indeed, it would be hard to find anyone in Faithwell willing to defy her mother-in-law, even when the cause was just.

The answer hung like a ghost on the edge of her mind for some time before Honor allowed herself to think it. Then she could think of nothing else. Finally she got up and dressed quietly. Jack did not stir. Honor crept downstairs and stepped over Digger, who lay across the doorway. He growled but did not stop her.

Outside she sat for a time on the porch and waited. If Judith or Dorcas heard her and came down to investigate, she could always say she felt ill and needed air. Indeed, as she breathed in the mild night breeze, she felt sharper, fresher and more resolved. I have been obedient, she thought, and it has made no difference.

When she was sure no one had woken, she left the porch and set out across the dewy grass to the track that ran in front of the farm. A half-moon lit it, and she hurried toward Faithwell, through the trees that eventually gave way to the cluster of houses. She passed the general store, the smithy, and Adam and Abigail's house; then she headed toward the main road between Oberlin and Wellington. Honor had never walked on her own at night in Ohio. All around her were the overlapped sawings and chirpings and croakings of thousands of crickets and frogs, the appropriate accompaniment for the multitude of stars spread overhead. It was hard to appreciate them, however, for there were other sounds too, rustlings in the undergrowth that frightened her. The bitter, pungent musk of a nearby skunk made her gulp several times, though she kept walking, wishing she had brought Digger with her. Even after nine months at the farm, she and the dog remained uneasy around each other, but Digger would have reassured her with his serious presence. The only way she could cope with the sounds and the dark was to hurry through them, thinking only of the comparative openness and safety of the larger road.

In the daytime the main road was full of riders and drivers and walkers heading north or south, but now when she got to it, she discovered that at this time of night it was empty of traffic and as dark and still as the Faithwell track. Honor stood in the middle of it, listening to the nightlife around her. What she wanted to hear was the sound of a horse with one thick shoe, coming from either direction—she was not sure which. He would not be asleep: if a runaway was in the area he would be out searching, for most traveled at night and hid during the day. Honor gazed up the road north toward Oberlin, then south to Wellington. She could stand and wait for him, but did not think she could bear to, for her stillness seemed to bring the rustling nearer, and made her fear grow. Better to walk steadily. She turned toward Wellington. If she did not meet Donovan she would go to Belle Mills. She did not dare involve Mrs. Reed. It was not safe for a black woman—particularly an ex-slave—to be out at night, away from her own people. Besides, she could not face Mrs. Reed's flashing spectacles and jutting lower lip.

She walked with shaky steps toward Wellington, fighting her growing terror of the darkness and solitude. She had often felt alone even when sitting among the Haymakers or the Faithwell community at Meeting, but now for the first time in America she really was completely alone, forced to confront the vast indifference of the natural world around her and the stars and moon overhead. This feeling grew so strong that at last it overwhelmed her, the hard cruelty of the world pressing into her like cold metal she could taste in her mouth. Honor had to stop in the road, gulping again and again as if she were drowning. She tried to escape it by turning inward as she did at Meeting to find the warming Inner Light, but she could not shed her overriding desire: that Donovan would come to save her from that metallic taste.

He arrived half an hour later. By then Honor was limp from fighting her fear. She heard the horse with the thick shoe a long way behind her and waited by the side of the road, her cap and the V along her neckline dimly visible in the moonlight. Yet he didn't see her until his horse shied, a side step away from Honor that made Donovan swear and clutch at the animal's mane. When he had calmed the horse, he stared down at her. "Honor Bright," he declared, clearly stunned to find her there.

Honor too could barely speak. "Donovan, I—Someone needs thy help."

"Who?"

"I will show thee."

He reached a hand down to her. "Come up."

Honor hesitated—because of the growing baby, because she had to trust him when she didn't, because she would have to put her arms around his waist and lean against his back and she knew what that would make her feel. But she thought of the man in the woods whom she had failed, and that made her put her foot in the stirrup, take Donovan's hand and swing herself up.

"Where to?"

"Wieland Woods, next to the farm. But . . ." Honor did not want to tell him she was doing this secretly—though it must be apparent, else she wouldn't be out on her own. "Please don't ride through Faithwell or past the farm. I don't want them to hear. We can leave the horse near the village and walk the rest of the way."

Donovan twisted around to look at her. "There a nigger in the woods?"

"Yes."

"You told me a month ago you weren't gonna be tradin' in runaways any more."

"He strayed from Greenwich. I did not intend to get involved, but he is hurt and needs a doctor."

Donovan snorted. "You think I'm gonna take him to a doctor?"

She did not reply. They sat on the horse, Donovan letting it take delicate side steps as it waited for its rider's signal.

"Honor, you know I'll turn him in. That's what I do."

Honor sighed. "I know. But he will die otherwise. It is better that he lives, even in slavery."

"Why you askin' me, anyway?"

She said nothing.

"You live in a town full o' Quakers and you go to *me* for help? You got yourself a problem there, darlin'."

"There is nothing wrong with Friends here. Many would do what they can to help. It is just . . . the Haymakers have had their principles compromised by circumstances. And they are influential in the community." Without meaning to, Honor was leaning against him, the small hard bump of her belly pressing into his back. Donovan felt it and stiffened, then leaned forward so that they were not so close.

"Right," he said at last. "Hold on." He pulled the reins around, clicked his teeth, and set out back up the road.

He was not moving when they found him, but lay propped against a bur oak, his legs stretched out in front of him, the tin mug beside him. Donovan made Honor wait several trees away while he held his lantern briefly to the face with its rictal grimace. Honor closed her eyes but could still see the imprint of the lantern and the man's teeth flashing in the dark.

Donovan came back to Honor and studied her stricken face. When she stepped into his arms, he said nothing, but held her and let her sob into his chest. This time he did not flinch when he felt the baby pressed against him. Honor clung to him long after she had stopped crying. Pressing her cheek against his chest, she breathed in the sharp woodfire smell of him. There was something hard there: the key to her trunk. Donovan was still wearing it around his neck.

If he asked me now, I would go west with him, she thought. For his spirit is with me.

But he did not ask. "Honor, it's getting light," he said at last. "You should get on home before they find out you're gone."

She nodded. Though it hurt to, she let go of him, wiping her face on her sleeve so that she did not have to look at him.

"You want me to bury him?"

"No. Let them see what they have done. What *we* have done."

"You know he probably would have died anyway, even if you got him to a doctor. Smells of gangrene."

Honor's eyes flared. "We should have helped him. At least then he would not have died alone in the dark in the woods."

Donovan said nothing more, but walked her to the edge of the orchard where the apple trees began. He touched her arm briefly, then disappeared back into the trees to circle around the village to his horse.

When Honor emerged from the orchard, Jack and Dorcas were crossing the yard toward the barn, carrying pails for milking. They looked confused. "Where has thee been?" Jack called, taking in her face smeared with dirt and tears, her disheveled cap, the mud on her boots and the meaty smell of horse that lingered on her. "We thought thee was in the outhouse."

Honor ignored him. "Digger!" she called.

The dog came running from the barn, drawn by the novelty of Honor commanding him. "Go." She pointed to the woods. "Find him." Digger followed her finger, sniffed the air, then shot off like a fish snagged on a hook.

"Honor, what is it?"

Honor did not answer. She could not find the words to say it. Instead she turned and headed for the haymow. Little hay was left from the previous year; in a few weeks the first harvest would replenish the much-diminished stacks. There was some straw, however. Though it smelled flat and dull, Honor climbed into the pile, curled up around her belly and slept.

When she woke, her sister-in-law was sitting nearby, plaiting strands of straw. Honor looked at her but did not sit up. Of the three Haymakers, she was glad it was Dorcas who had come to find her: Jack would have upset her and Judith would have made her angry. Over the months Honor had lived at the farm, Dorcas had become more of a benign irritation.

She seemed to understand that now. Setting down the braid, she hugged her knees. "They found him. Some men have come to help bury him." After a pause, she continued. "I do not hate thee, Honor, whatever thee may think of me. Last summer when thee helped me with the yellow jackets, I heard thee speak to the colored man, and I never told Mother or Jack, though I should have." She stopped again. Honor did not speak.

"I want to help thee to understand the Haymakers. There is something we did not tell thee about what happened in North Carolina. I thought we ought to," Dorcas added, for a moment lapsing into her habitual self-defense. "Jack did too, but Mother felt it was old family business that would not be important to thee. But it *is* important, for it may explain some things." She fiddled with the straw plait. "I have not told Mother I am telling thee."

Now Honor did sit up, and brushed the straw from her cap. She still did not speak. Something seemed to have closed her throat.

"Thee knows of the door at the side of the barn, put there in case of fire."

Honor nodded.

"Jack took great care to have it put in." She paused. "Mother told thee that we were fined for helping a runaway slave in North Carolina. But she did not tell thee of a far greater punishment. When Father—when he—" Dorcas pressed her lips together. "I was ten years old, Jack fifteen. Father had helped a few runaways already. One morning one appeared, and Father hid the slave in our barn. When the owner and his men came looking for him, Father said there was no one in the barn. Yes, he lied, but for the greater good. So—so the owner grabbed Father, and had his men set fire to the barn, to see what Father would do. He admitted then that the slave was hidden there. They told him to go and get the slave while they put out the fire. But when he went inside they—they pulled the bolt on the barn door so that neither Father nor the slave could get out that way." Tears were trickling from Dorcas's pale eyes. Honor took up one of her cold hands.

"They would not let us near the barn. Jack even fought them, which thee knows we don't do. We thought Father and the slave might be able to get out through the trapdoor where the hay and straw are dropped down to the animals, but the smoke must have been too thick. We heard—we—we . . ."

Honor squeezed her hand so that Dorcas would not continue.

"The slave owner was not even charged with murder, since Father went willingly into the burning barn," Dorcas began again when she had wiped away her tears. "Instead we were forced to pay a fine for the 'destruction of property'—the death of the slave. Losing Father and the barn and the money was too much, and we came north. So thee can understand now why we do not want to become involved with runaways again."

They sat for a time in silence. For the first time since marrying Jack, Honor felt some warmth toward her sister-in-law; she was just sorry the feeling had to come out of the telling of such a story.

Dorcas left her in the straw, to find her way back when she was ready. Honor did not know if she would ever be ready.

She had begun with a clear principle born of a lifetime of sitting in silent expectation: that all people are equal in God's eyes, and so should not be enslaved to one another. Any system of slavery must be abolished. It had seemed simple in England; yet in Ohio that principle was chipped away at, by economic arguments, by personal circumstances, by deep-seated prejudice that Honor sensed even in Quakers. It was easy for her to picture the Negro pew at the Philadelphia Meeting House and grow indignant; but would she herself feel completely comfortable sitting next to a black person? She helped them, but she did not know them as people. Only Mrs. Reed, a little: the flowers she wore in her hat; the stew so full of onions and chilies; the improvised quilt she had made. These daily details were the things that fleshed out a person.

When an abstract principle became entangled in daily life, it lost its clarity and became compromised and weakened. Honor did not understand how this could happen, and yet it had: the Haymakers had demonstrated how easy it was to justify stepping back from principles and doing nothing. Now that she was a member of this family, she was expected to take on their history and step back as well.

Honor left the barn at dusk to walk across the yard to the house, her eyes wide and dry, her throat stopped with a feeling as if she had swallowed a ball and it had got stuck there. She felt so confused by the gap between what she thought and what was expected of her that she could not speak. Perhaps it was better not to, until she was more sure of what she wanted to say. That way her words could not be twisted and flung back at her. Silence was a powerful tool at Meeting, clearing the way to God. Perhaps now it would allow Honor to be heard.

The Haymakers did not know what to make of her silence. When Honor came back from the barn, Judith and Jack questioned her about being out all night, the smell of horse on her evidence that Donovan must be involved. When she did not speak to confirm or deny this, they took her silence for guilt. Jack raged; Judith threatened to have Honor disowned by the community, though even she knew there were no grounds for doing such a thing. Besides, their anger was intertwined with guilt over the death of the runaway.

Eventually that anger was replaced with defensive embarrassment, for they took her silence to be a judgment on them. Jack and Judith continued to defend their actions, or non-actions, their frustration increasing when they could not tell if their words had any effect on Honor. She gave them her attention whenever they spoke, looked them directly in the eye, then simply did not respond, but went back to her milking or washing or hoeing or sewing.

With her sister-in-law, however, Honor's relationship improved. Perhaps Dorcas felt she did not have to compete any longer. She could talk as much as she liked, and did, often responding on Honor's behalf, and calling her "sister": "I think Honor would like more cherry pie"; "Honor and I will do the milking this evening, won't we, sister?"; "I'm sure Honor is willing to quilt the central panel at the frolic, won't thee, sister?" Honor let Dorcas speak for her; it was easier.

The Haymakers began to treat her as if she could not talk. They stopped asking her questions or expecting her to take part in conversations. When a new family arrived to settle in Faithwell, Jack introduced Honor by saying, "My wife has extended the silence of Meeting into her whole life." She became the mute in the community, smiling and ducking her head when anyone said something that required a response. Jack still turned to her at night, but did not try to give her pleasure, taking only his own. As her belly grew between them, taking on the hard roundness of a pumpkin, he reached for her less and less.

In a way, she *was* mute. Her throat was so tight it was difficult to swallow, though she forced herself to eat, for the baby's sake. She had always been quiet, but never completely silent. Now it became a relief not to speak. Her words could no longer be misunderstood—though now her silence was. And because she did not have to form thoughts into words for others, after a time Honor could stop thinking, and just be. For the first time since she was a girl she could sit in Meeting and not try to harness her impressions into thoughts she might speak aloud. Now she simply watched the sun cross the quiet room, catching dust motes kicked up by shifting Friends. She listened to the insects outside, and learned to distinguish between the chirping of the cricket, the sawing of the grasshopper, the ticking of the beetle, the buzzing of the cicada. She leaned into any breezes that passed from one window to another. She closed her eyes and breathed in the clover in the field next to the Meeting House, the first crop of hay left drying, the honeysuckle that grew around the door. Closing her mouth seemed to heighten her senses. It was a different sensation from the sinking-down feeling she'd had in past Meetings, but she began to think that it was as meaningful. God makes His presence felt in many ways, she thought.

After a time, her silence became less awkward, and Honor could sit at meals or on the porch or at Meeting and feel more content than she had when she spoke. In some profound way she knew that though it was not a conscious decision, she had stopped herself from speaking. She did not ask herself why, but accepted the silence as a gift.

Honor's silence upset not only the Haymakers, but the wider community as well. It seemed even Quakers, with their silent Meetings and tolerance of difference, did not like the judgment of silence.

Adam Cox drew her aside after one First Day Meeting. "I will walk thee back to the farm," he declared, leading her away from the Haymakers as Abigail watched over the head of their baby, a son they had named Elias. "I want to ask why thee has chosen to be silent, but I know thee will not answer," he said as they made their way along the track. The mud had dried into hard, sharp ruts that made walking almost as tricky as when the mud was wet. "Jack said thee was upset by the death of the Negro. So were we all." Caleb Wilson had organized a Meeting of Remembrance for the runaway, but no one had spoken, for no one knew him, not even his name. "But that should not make thee shun thy family and thy community."

Honor of course said nothing.

"Judith has asked me to speak with thee," he continued, "for she thinks perhaps thee will listen to someone from thy past. The Elders see thy silence as an act of aggression. They have asked me to tell thee that it is only because thee carries a child that they have not asked thee to leave the community. But thee must begin to speak after the baby is born or else leave the child with the Haymakers and go from Faithwell."

Honor drew in her breath. Even though she had witnessed the severity of Bridport Friends with Samuel, she had hoped she would not meet with the same treatment.

"I have reminded them that thee has had a difficult year, losing thy sister and Samuel, leaving England when perhaps thee should have stayed. Not everyone is suited to such change, though it is sometimes only after it has happened that this is discovered." Adam paused. "Thee must understand, Honor, that America is a young country. We look forward, not back. We do not dwell on misfortune, but move on—as I have with Abigail and I had hoped thee would with Jack. It is seen as poor form to linger over the bad things that have happened. Thee would do well to accept what thee has with the Haymakers. They are good people."

Adam had not said anything about slavery, or principles being upheld or abandoned. He looked at her, clearly hoping Honor would respond. Instead she studied the wildflowers along the track: Joe-Pye weed, ragged sailors, queen of the prairie. She had been in Ohio a year now, and knew their American names.

The following Sixth Day, with the Haymakers' agreement, Adam asked her to help at the Oberlin store. Perhaps they thought serving customers would force her to speak. Instead Honor demonstrated how little words were needed for a transaction. With smiles and nods and hand signals she could make herself understood. Few customers questioned her muteness. Plenty of people were afflicted in one way or another.

During the afternoon Mrs. Reed came in to have some scissors sharpened. She watched Honor nod and gesture with other customers; then she nodded herself. "Words ain't everything," she commented to the room, taking off her spectacles and polishing them on her sleeve. "Get you in trouble, more likely'n not. Maybe I be quiet one day too." She seemed tickled by the thought.

When Adam had handed back her scissors, she said to Honor in a low voice, "I heard 'bout that man. Sad, but it happens." She paused. "That shouldn't be what's stoppin' you speakin'. You want to keep quiet, that's fine, but leave the runaways out of it." She wrapped the scissors in a rag and tucked them back in her skirt pocket. Then she straightened her hat, which was trimmed with goldenrod. "Good day to you." She nodded at Adam. "And you, Honor Bright." She began to hum as she left, the goldenrod tails bobbing.

East Street
Bridport
Dorset
8th Month 15th 1851

Dear Honor,

Every day now we await a letter from thee, for we have not had one for three months. Thee has always been so careful to write regularly, except when thee was ill, and we are concerned that something has happened. By the time thee receives this thee may have had thy baby, with God's grace, but we hope to hear from thee before then, to say that all is well.

Thy loving parents,

Hannah and Abraham Bright

Water

THERE WAS ALWAYS going to be one last runaway.

It was the last day of the Eighth Month, hot and still, though the heat was chased by the threat of autumn. The sun was just off-center, the leaves dusty rather than vibrant green, an undertone of yellow creeping through them. Honor hurried through a landscape that seemed to be waiting for something to happen, a thunderstorm or the razing of a field or a fire sweeping through. She was late.

The Haymakers were bringing in the hay. It had been a wet summer, and this was only the second crop—a disappointment, as it meant they would be unlikely to add another cow to the herd as planned. Jack, Judith and Dorcas, as well as other Faithwell neighbors, were in the field to the north of Wieland Woods. They would not let Honor help them, however, and she was glad. She had awoken that morning with an uneasy feeling in her belly. Though the baby was not due for another month, it felt large and low, pressing on her bladder so that she had been up several times during the night to use the chamber pot. She sensed its desire to escape from the confines of her womb, and knew it would come early rather than cling inside as so many first babies did.

Judith muttered something about Honor missing this year's harvest as well as last year's, implying she had deliberately timed her pregnancy to do so. Her words did not bother Honor. Now that she did not have to answer back, nothing Judith said bothered her.

She finished milking alone so that Jack and Dorcas and Judith could eat and make a start at the hay with the others. Then she cleared the breakfast things and prepared the meat pies Judith had instructed her to make to take out to the field for dinner. It was a relief to work alone, and she thought of little except when the baby became insistent and she had to sit down. Twice Jack and Dorcas and a neighbor came back with the wagon piled high with hay they transferred to the barn. Honor did not go out to them, and they did not come inside, but drank from the well and refilled a jug for the others.

She even had a little time to spare, and sat out on the porch with a lapful of hexagons she had begun making into rosettes for a grandmother's garden quilt. She had started with green and brown shapes she'd found half-made in her work basket, then gone on to add other colors: yellow and red and green. She had been sewing them for a month now, since finishing Dorcas's final quilt. She had got out the special pieces she'd saved—Grace's dress, Belle's yellow and tan silks, the rust diamonds of Mrs. Reed's daughter's wedding dress—but found no inspiration in them. She wondered if she ever would. But she did not like to have idle hands and so had worked on the hexagons. She now had over a hundred rosettes made, without any idea what she would do with them.

Because she was not working toward a specific quilt, Honor was less focused on her work; the heat too was enervating, and soon she had closed her eyes. It was Digger who woke her. Made to remain behind with her, at midday he stood by her and growled. Honor jumped: she was late to take dinner to the others. Putting the pies, some bread and cheese, a bowl of tomatoes and a jug of milk into a basket, she then hurried up a track along the edge of the woods to the field, the heavy basket bumping against her legs.

They were still working when she arrived; they would have been waiting for her to appear before they stopped. The alfalfa had been cut a few days before and left to dry, then raked up the day before, ready to be brought to the barn. The wagon had been pulled up to one of the many haystacks dotting the field. As Honor set down her basket, Jack and Judith began to dig their pitchforks into the stack.

Suddenly there came a shriek that made Honor's stomach lurch. She froze as a black woman burst from the stack, shielding her eyes from the sun. Before anyone could respond, she ran. Bounding like a deer startled into panicked flight, she headed straight toward Honor, veering away at the last moment. Honor glimpsed wild eyes and lips clamped tight. Then she was gone, crashing into Wieland Woods.

Honor stared after her, catching flashes of arms, a billowing brown skirt, a red kerchief on her head. Eventually she disappeared, though her crackling and crunching in the thicket went on for some time. Finally even that stopped. When Honor turned back, all the Quakers in the field were looking at her.

No, Honor thought. This is not to do with me.

But, apart from Caleb Wilson, who gazed at her with sympathy, she could see in their faces that they were already linking the appearance of the runaway with Honor's arrival. Even if she broke her silence to protest that it was a coincidence, they would not believe her. Judith had already set her mouth in the familiar cold half-smile. She said nothing, but walked over and took the basket of food from Honor.

I cannot bear this any longer, Honor thought. Nothing I say will make any difference to what people think. My words mean nothing to them. It was as if something broke in her head. She could not wait, even for Judith to unpack the food, but turned and walked back along the track toward the farm, ignoring Jack's calls. On one side of her was Wieland Woods: all was still now. Wherever the runaway woman was, she was keeping quiet.

Back at the farm, Honor cleared away the hexagons she had left out on the kitchen table and put them in her work basket. Then she climbed the stairs, pulling herself and the weight of the baby up with the handrail. She stood in the bedroom doorway and looked at the quilt she had smoothed out on their bed earlier. It was the Star of Bethlehem quilt from home—Biddy's quilt, as she always thought of it now. She still felt guilty about having to ask for it back. The signature quilt from Bridport was folded at the bottom of the bed. She could take neither with her.

Honor picked up a shawl, a penknife and a little money she had left from her passage to Ohio, which Jack had never asked for. Then she changed her daily bonnet for the gray and yellow one; if she left it, Judith was likely to give it away out of spite. Back in the kitchen she took a round of hard cheese, a loaf of bread, some beef tack and a sack of plums. She had never packed for such a journey, and had no idea if she was taking the right things. She tried to think what the runaways she had met had with them. Nothing, usually. Often even their feet were bare. Honor changed the light summer slippers she wore for sturdier boots, and added two candles and some matches to the small store, which she tied up in a dishcloth.

She could not take the rosettes, or her grandmother's sewing box, and that almost stopped her. Then she opened the box and took out the porcelain thimble, the needle case and the enameled scissors, as well as the pieces of special cloth she had been saving— the memories in them were irreplaceable.

Digger was lying across the open doorway, catching what little breeze he could. As Honor stepped over him, he did not growl as he would normally have done with her. He knows, she thought. He knows, and is glad.

Crossing the orchard—the apples on the trees reddening, the plums past their best and covered with yellow jackets—Honor entered Wieland Woods and picked her way steadily through maples and beeches, through brambles loaded with blackberries she could not stop for. The trees were thick with leaves in suspension between the ripeness of summer and the decline of autumn. While the oak leaves were still green, the maples' were veined with red, ready to flush.

There was no sign or sound of the Negro. At one point Honor strayed close to the edge bordering the field where the Haymakers were working, and heard their voices, though not what they said. After that she went deep into the middle of the woods, where the woman must be hiding. As she walked she was followed by the song of the bobwhite, named for its distinctive call. Jack had teased her once when she asked what it was, refusing to believe such a common bird did not exist in England. On the road with Thomas over a year ago, she had not even recognized the cardinals and blue jays. There was so much to learn about America, not all of it good.

Eventually, beyond the bobwhite, Honor picked up the chattering of a squirrel, clucking and scolding as if annoyed at a child, or an intruder. Following the sound, she did not try to hide her own presence, but allowed her skirt to brush against the undergrowth and her boots to snap dead branches in the hope that the woman would look out and see who it was, and trust her.

The runaway was perched on the branch of a beech tree six feet above the ground, the squirrel protesting high above her. Honor stepped onto one of the tree's roots, looked up and held out a plum. The woman looked at her. She did not take the plum, but after a moment she climbed down. Taller than Honor, she had long limbs and a yellowish cast to her skin. Indeed, the woman's face was familiar, though it took a moment for Honor to place her. She was the first runaway, who had hidden by the well and left a tin mug of water by her bed—the mug that was now buried with the dead man nearby. Honor remembered that Donovan had caught her; she must have been taken back and was running away again. She looked healthier now: she had filled out somewhat, her skin was clear of pimples, her eyes whiter, and her dress looked newer, if dirty. She was wearing a pair of men's shoes, and carried a bundle similar to Honor's own.

The first time Honor had met the woman she'd held out bread to her. Now she pocketed the plum and untied her bundle to offer some bread and cheese. The runaway shook her head. "She done fed me up at the last place. Don't need nothin' for now. She said to say hello if I saw you—though she told me to go on through to the next stop if I could, an' not to be botherin' you, what with that an' all." She gestured at Honor's belly. "I wouldn't of been in that hay at all but for that slave catcher drivin' me off course. Same one as last time. Caught me in these woods. He persistent, ain't he? Don't think he even knows who I am, but chase me anyway."

The woman stopped. The squirrel had doubled its voice with two women to complain about, but now it went silent, and they could hear a horse in the distance, coming along the track to the south of them, with its uneven hoofbeats. It was the first time Donovan had come out this way since the runaway's death. He did not know about Honor's silence.

And now she was breaking her silence—a sensible, undramatic end to it. "I will go with thee." Honor's first words in over three months came out as a cracked whisper.

"Thankee, but I know where I'm goin'."

Honor cleared her throat to ease the words from it. "We must leave these woods. He will come looking here." As would Jack: in a few hours Dorcas and Judith would go back to the farm for the evening milking, find that Honor was not there, and raise the alarm.

They listened. They could not go north into the hayfield, where even now Honor could hear the distant voices of her family, the jingles of the horses' bridles, the creak of the wagon. Donovan was blocking their escape east along the track past the farm and Faith-well. Honor did not want to go west: the track through Wieland Woods petered out halfway through, and besides would lead them into unknown territory, away from the main road and Oberlin. If they could get close to the main road between Oberlin and Wellington, they could then follow it, keeping in the fields on either side.

"If we cross the track that way"—Honor pointed south—"there is a cornfield that has not yet been cut. We can hide there till dark, then make our way east to the main road."

The other woman nodded. "First I got to drink." She led the way to the creek that bisected the woods, where Honor had rolled Dorcas in the mud to soothe her bee stings. There was little water in it other than a couple of standing puddles scummed over, insects hovering above. The women picked their way along it till they found a small trickle over a rock. The runaway placed her mouth there to suck up the water. After drinking, she stood up and gestured to Honor, who tried to crouch, then went on her hands and knees in an awkward position to accommodate the baby. She hesitated for a moment when she realized she would be putting her mouth where the Negro's had been. But that thought was a mere flicker, and she lowered her mouth to the rock. The water tasted wonderful.

Afterward the woman helped her to her feet, then led the way south toward the track, clearly in charge. Honor did not mind. It was enough for her to be out walking in the woods on a late summer afternoon with a Negro, going . . . she did not know where she was going. She was running away.

The black woman moved through the woods silently, her feet sure, aware of her body in a way that kept her from brushing against branches or crackling leaves. Honor could not imitate her silence: she rustled through the undergrowth and got herself caught in brambles. She was also slowed by the weight she carried, and the pains along her groin and inner thighs. The woman did not slow down, though, and was soon little more than a movement among the trees. At one point Honor stopped and wiped her brow, and listened. She could not hear Donovan's horse. He was probably searching the barn and other farm buildings. Behind her she could hear the wagon with its load of hay bumping down the track that led from the hayfield along the edge of Wieland Woods to the pasture and barn. If Jack came upon Donovan at the barn, what would they say to each other? Would Donovan ask if he'd seen the runaway? Would Jack tell him, or lie? Honor shivered, and hurried to catch up with her companion.

She was leaning against a maple at the wood's edge, the track before them little more than a trickle of crusted mud spreading east and west. Diagonally across it, next to the woods, was the bright green shimmer of the Haymakers' extensive cornfield. Tall and healthy and ripe, it would be left to stand until autumn when the ears had dried in their husks. Seeing it reminded Honor of first lying with Jack Haymaker in a cornfield. She flushed at the memory; only a little over a year ago, yet it felt as far away as England.

"You can go back now," the runaway said. "I be all right from here. I jes' wait in the corn till dark, then go on when no one can see me."

Honor shook her head. "I will go with thee."

The woman glanced at Honor's belly. "You sure you want to go like that?"

"The baby's not due until next month. I'll be fine."

The runaway shrugged and turned to look up and down the track, listening. "Come on, then." She stepped out of the woods. Honor followed, the sunlight blinding her so that she ran without seeing where she was going. In a moment she was crashing into the corn.

"Shh!"

Honor stopped, the stalks banging together around her.

"Go slow or it makes noise," the woman whispered. "And we got to go through without breaking the stalks, so no one know we been here. Get to the middle and wait. Follow me, now."

They stepped carefully along a row, trying not to rattle or break the stalks. Honor kept her eyes on the woman's back, where a patch of sweat was blooming through her brown dress. Several feet in, the woman turned and cut across rows, zigzagging and pushing carefully through the thick corn. Eventually she turned into a row and walked along it, on and on, for far longer than Honor would ever have gone on her own. "Please," she almost said. "Please stop."

She was about to reach out and touch the woman when the runaway did stop, and Honor almost stumbled into her. She was dizzy and the baby was pressing on her bladder.

The woman sat. "Let's wait here."

Honor went a little farther along to squat. It was so hot that the urine dried up just moments after she finished. She came back to sit near the runaway and opened her bundle. This time the woman took one of the plums. Honor savored the fleshy pulp, and sucked for a long time on the stone.

The woman was looking at her sideways. "I like that bonnet," she said. "You think it's jes' gray, then there's that little flash of yellow to give it spice."

"A friend made it for me." Honor felt a pang, thinking of Belle Mills. She had never replied to her letter, and now she would not see her again.

It was uncomfortable sitting in the cornfield. The sun beat down on them, for the stalks did not provide much shade. The leaves caught at her, their surfaces a rough softness. The ears bulged from their husks, but this was feed corn, its kernels too tough for human teeth, and the taste less delicate than the sweet corn Honor had come to love and crave. There was nothing substantial like a tree to lean against, and the corn grew close enough together that it was difficult to find space to lie out. She was exhausted from the sun and the physical exertion, however, and managed to nod off, jerking herself awake.

"You sleep a bit," the runaway said. "I'll keep watch. We'll take turns."

Honor did not argue. She laid her head on her bundle, curled around the baby and, despite the hot sun, the flies and the dull ache in her belly, soon slept.

She woke with a dry mouth, the plum stone tucked in her cheek. The sun was arcing down toward the horizon. Honor had slept a long time. She could hear a horse in the distance, clopping steadily along the track, and sat up, startled. The black woman was sitting on her heels.

"Thee should have woken me," Honor said.

The woman shrugged. "You needed the sleep." Her eyes grazed

over Honor's belly. "I remember wantin' to sleep all the time toward the end."

"Thee has children?" Honor glanced around, as if somehow she could conjure up children in the cornfield.

"Course. That's why I'm here."

Honor shook her head to clear her thoughts. Then she froze: it was Donovan's horse. He rode fast, then slowed, then stopped, then rode slowly again, then turned around and galloped away.

Honor gulped, but the woman seemed unconcerned. She even chuckled. "He been doin' that a while now," she said. "Knows we here somewhere but don't know where."

"Will he come into the corn?"

"I reckon not. They's lots of woods an' fields to search. He gon' wait till we make a move."

Honor did not ask when that would be.

"Remember, he don't know where we are, but we know where he is. We got the advantage."

Honor wished she shared the woman's optimism. Unfortunately, Donovan had the advantage of the law on his side, and a horse, and a gun.

At dusk they heard another horse along the track. As he called her name, Honor recognized Jack's voice. He must have cut short the harvest to look for her: it was good weather and she knew the Haymakers had been planning to work as late as they could to get the hay in before rain came. She could hear anger and impatience in his voice, and winced.

The black woman stared at her. "That your husband?" she whispered when Jack had turned back. "What he callin' you for? Don't he know you out here with me?"

Honor didn't answer.

Then the woman understood. "*You* runnin' away?" she cried, her voice for the first time that day rising above a muffled tone. "What in hell you doin' that for? With a baby comin' an' all? What you got to run away from?"

With each question, Honor shrank further into herself, taking refuge in silence.

When it was clear she would not—or could not—respond, the woman clicked her tongue. "Fool," she muttered.

As it was growing dark, they heard horses again, and Jack and Adam Cox calling this time. The woman reached for her bundle and scrambled to her feet.

Honor grabbed her sleeve. "What is thee doing?"

"I gon' tell them you here."

"Please don't!"

But it was Donovan's voice joining the others'—sarcastic, amused—that stopped the runaway. "Honor Bright, I'm a little surprised you're hidin' out there, after all your promises not to help niggers. Guess I can't trust even a Quaker these days. Time to come out now, darlin'—you're scarin' your husband."

The women remained still, listening to the men shifting about on their horses and talking in low voices. Honor shuddered and took a deep breath.

Then she heard the barking.

"Oh Lord, they got a dog," the black woman whispered. "Oh Lord."

"That's Digger."

"He know you? Well, when he find us least he won't tear you apart. Get ready to run."

"He hates me."

"Your own dog hate you? Oh Lord."

Honor could hear stirring among the corn, and then made out Digger's shadowy form trotting up the row. He did not bark, though, but came to stand at Honor's feet. He gazed up at her, ignoring the runaway, and growled low. Then he turned and ran back down the way he had come. The women stared after him.

"That's him lettin' you go," the black woman murmured. "Good thing he hate you. Thankee, Digger."

"There he is," they heard Jack say. "What has thee found, Digger? Nothing?"

"Thought he was after somethin' there," Donovan said. "Damn dog. That's why I don't like to use 'em—noisy and unreliable. I trust my own senses more than a dog's."

Eventually the men rode away again, and the women began threading their way east across the rows of corn. Honor's legs ached from inactivity, and she shook and stretched them. She could see two stars in the sky. More would soon appear.

At the end of the cornfield they passed through a wood, taking them south of Faithwell. As it grew black Honor kept her eyes on the woman's back again, finally reaching out to touch her so that she could be guided through the dark.

Eventually they reached the familiar main road between Oberlin and Wellington. It was quiet, but Honor suspected Donovan and possibly Jack were somewhere along it, waiting for them.

"We'll go into that corn," the woman said, gesturing across the road. "Stay off the road, but near it so we know where we at, and where the hunter at too. Always better to know that, so you don't get surprised." She spoke with the confidence of someone who had done this often. She hurried across the road, which was a pale river even without a moon. As Honor followed she thought of being in this very spot a few months back, looking for Donovan in the night. Now she was hiding from him. The darkness brought with it the same metallic taste of fear. Honor swallowed but the taste remained, though muted, for this time she was not alone.

In the cornfield the woman turned south. When Honor did not follow, she stopped. "You comin' or what?"

"We should be going that way." Honor pointed at the pole star. "Toward Oberlin."

The woman shook her head. "I jes' come from Oberlin. From the woman in the red house—make one fiery stew. Who said to stay away from you. Now I start to understand why," she added. "Don't you understand? I'm goin' *south*, not north. Already been in the north." She crossed back to Honor. "You don't remember me, do you? I expect we all look alike to you." She clicked her tongue. "Well, I tell you somethin': white folks look the same to us too."

"I do remember thee," Honor whispered. "Thee left water by my bed when I was ill."

The woman's face softened. "I did."

"But I don't understand—why is thee going south?"

"My children. See, after I got caught I ran away again first chance I got. I even stopped at your farm one day, got the victuals you left under the crate. This time I made it to Canada. But once I was there, I couldn't stop thinkin' 'bout my girls, and worryin' 'bout them. It felt good up there, the freedom. Ain't nobody tellin' you what to do. You make your own decisions, where you live, what you do, how you spend the money you earn. You earn money! And livin' with other black folk, it's—well, it's like you livin' with your Quaker kind. It feel right. I want my children to feel that too. So I'm goin' back for them."

"Where are they?"

"Virginia."

"But that is far! What if thee is caught?"

"If I is caught I'll jes' wait till I can run again. That the thing about slavery. They needs you to work, they can't always be lockin' you up. You wait long enough, you always find a time to run. That's why I don't worry if I get caught. They take me back to Virginia, and I'll run again, with my children this time. I done tasted freedom now. I always gon' be wantin' that taste again."

Honor felt as she had done when playing a game with her brothers and sister, where they blindfolded her and spun her round, and when she removed the blindfold, she discovered she was facing a completely different direction from what she thought. It was as if she were standing in the corn, and it had turned around her 180 degrees, so that north was south and south north. She had been expecting to walk to Mrs. Reed's in Oberlin, then make her way northwest to Sandusky, a town on Lake Erie where she could get a boat across to Canada. That was what fugitive slaves did. Now, though, she would have to go the opposite way, or go north without a guide.

"So where *you* goin'?" the black woman asked.

"I . . ." Honor had no idea where she was going. She had only considered what she was running from, not what she was running to. Those were usually two different directions. It was not really a question of her going north or south; she was not a black slave escaping from unjust laws. Hers was more of an east-west decision: known or unknown territory. "I will go with thee to Wellington. From there I will decide." She preferred a companion going south to a night in the woods alone, tasting metal.

"Come on, then, if you really comin'." The woman began crossing the field, weaving through the rows of corn. A breeze had sprung up, rattling the stalks naturally so that the fugitives did not have to worry so much about the noise they made. Still they went slowly, Honor stumbling in the dark.

At the edge of the corn they dropped into a ditch and lay there for a time. Honor was not sure why, and asked. "Waitin' till it feel right," was all the woman would say.

Eventually Donovan rode by, on his own this time, seeming to taunt them by slowing down on the road near to where they lay, then speeding up again.

"He know we 'round here somewhere," the woman said. "He can feel it. But he's confused, 'cause he don't know I—we—headin' south. Thinks it should be north, even though his sense tellin' him otherwise. We jes' got to wait him out."

Donovan returned a few minutes later. Stopping his horse, he called out, "Listen here, Honor Bright. I know you're out there with that nigger. I tell you what, I'll strike a bargain with you. Give yourself up and I'll let you go wherever it is you're goin'. Your husband asked me to find you—even said he'd pay good money—but I don't care 'bout him or his money. You wanna run away from him, I ain't gonna stop you. I always knew you wouldn't take to the Haymakers. He told me you ain't spoken since that nigger died. Well, you don't have to talk to me if you don't want to. Just throw a rock at me so I'll know you're out there, and I'll find you."

The runaway watched Honor, the whites of her eyes flashing in the dark. Honor shook her head to reassure her.

After a minute, Donovan began to laugh. "Listen to me, sittin' out here on my horse talkin' to myself. Guess you've made me crazy, Honor Bright."

He turned and rode north. Honor wondered how many other fields he would stand next to and repeat his offer.

The black woman was glaring at her. "What's with that slave catcher? You friends with him? You leavin' your husband for him?"

"No! No. I'm leaving because—because I don't share the same views as my husband's family."

The woman snorted. "That ridiculous. You don't have to agree 'bout everything with the people you live with."

"They forbade me to help runaways."

"Oh." The woman clicked her tongue.

They remained in the ditch for a long time. The sky was filling with stars.

"All right. We go now," the woman said. "He lookin' for us toward Oberlin, makin' his little speech to you ever' now and then." She chuckled, and led the way into the woods. With every step Honor expected to feel a hand on her shoulder or a shout from behind. But he did not come.

It was much cooler now; not cold, but dew was falling, and Honor pulled her shawl around her. They tramped through the woods, Honor tripping at times, the woman steady and quiet.

The other side of the woods was bounded by a field shorn of its oats. They could not cross it, for they would be easily visible, even without a moon. Instead they went further east, away from the road, to another wood, where they turned south again. Now that they were away from the road and from Donovan, Honor thought they might be able to relax. But the woman hurried on, fearful of cropped fields that could easily be ridden across. "He'll be crisscrossin' every field to the north," she said, "till he realize we not there. Then he'll come this way."

"He may go west," Honor reasoned. "North and west are where runaways go—not south and east."

"Them slave hunters got a sense makes 'em good at guessin' where a runaway is. Otherwise they be out of a job. He'll turn up again tonight—I can guarantee it. But I gots a sense too."

"How does thee do this every night? And all alone?" Honor shivered, thinking of the cold metallic pressure of the night.

"You get used to it. Better to be alone. This"—the woman waved her hand at the woods around them—"this is *safety*. Nature ain't out to enslave me. Might kill me, with the cold or illness or bears, but that ain't likely. No, it's *that*"—she pointed toward the road—"that's the danger. *People*'s the danger."

"Bears?" Honor looked around.

The woman chuckled. "Most bears scared o' *you*. They ain't gon' bother you, 'less you get 'tween them and they children. 'Sides, ain't no bears round here. Got 'em in the mountains, where I'm goin'. Got to scare me some bears to get to *my* children. All right now, we can go." The woman seemed to be obeying some silent signal only she could sense.

They crept and stopped, crept and stopped. At one point they came upon water—the Black River, Honor suspected. The runaway did not hesitate but waded in, holding her bundle above her. Honor had no choice but to follow, emerging cold and sodden on the other side. "You'll dry off soon," the woman said.

In the pre-dawn darkness they reached the edge of Wellington. This would be the hardest part, Honor thought: getting to Belle Mills's in the middle of town without anyone seeing them. Already she could hear dogs barking at farms around them.

The runaway seemed less worried. "You know where the lady's shop is?" she said.

Honor patted her bonnet. "She made this for me."

The woman nodded. "Thought so. Good. All you got to do is go up to her door and knock. You a free woman—can't nobody snatch you off the street. Even that slave hunter can't do that."

"What about thee?"

"I ain't comin' with you." At Honor's panic, the woman gazed at her, holding her eyes. "It's too dangerous right in town with the alarm up. He'd catch me here; I can feel it. Don't you worry now; I got you close enough you don't have to be scared no more. You can walk right on up the road—don't have to hide in the woods with the bears. See, it ain't so dark now."

Honor looked around. There was a dimness in the east that made the darkness less heavy. Soon she would be able to see to walk more easily. "But where will thee go?"

"I'll hide myself away. Ain't gon' tell you. Better you don't know so the slave hunter can't get it out of you. You go on now, 'fore some o' these dogs come out an' find us. Got to get me to some water—break the trail so they don't come after me."

Honor knew she was right. "Wait." She opened her bundle and handed over all of her food, the penknife, and most of the money. Then she took off her gray and yellow bonnet and held it out.

"Oh." The woman touched the yellow lining. "This too nice for me."

"Please. I would like thee to have it."

"All right." She started to put it on over her red kerchief.

"Wait—thee should have my cap too. Let me have thy kerchief." I will use it for the quilt, she thought.

With the cap on and the bonnet tied tight under her chin, the woman looked from the side like a white woman. "Thankee," she said. "Now, you best go."

Honor hesitated. Her eyes filled with tears.

"Go on, find your way."

"God go with thee."

"And thee." The woman smiled. "Look at me, wearin' a bonnet an' talkin' like a Quaker." She turned and walked into the woods, the darkness taking her away.

———

He was waiting for her outside Belle Mills's shop, leaning so still against the corner of the building that Honor didn't notice him until she had raised her hand to knock on the door.

"What you doin' with your head uncovered, Honor Bright? And where's that nigger?"

"I do not know," Honor could honestly respond when she recovered from her fright.

"Why are you wet? You been wadin' in the river? She showed you all her nigger tricks, did she?"

Honor glanced down at her skirt in the dawn light. She thought it had dried, but saw now that it was once again sopping.

"Oh," she breathed. "Oh."

My dear parents,

Do not be alarmed by a stranger's hand: Belle Mills is writing this letter for me, as I am too weak to sit up for long. I wanted you to know immediately that you are grandparents now, to Comfort Grace Haymaker. She was born three days ago with Belle and an able Wellington doctor in attendance. She is beautiful. I am tired but joyful.

For the moment it is best to write to me in Wellington.

Your loving daughter,

Honor

This part I write from myself, though Honor don't know it because she and the baby are asleep now. I don't know if she's written to tell you she's broken with her family. First she gave them the silent treatment, which I guess is the kind of punishment a Quaker would come up with. Then she ran away and is staying with me.

She can be silent all day long like no one else I ever met. I'll tell you one thing, though: birthing that baby made her yell loud as any other woman, so loud her throat is sore now. Even Dr. Johns was surprised, and he's heard some yelling in his time. But it was good to hear her voice loud, even if it came from pain.

You're her family, so maybe you can talk sense to her. She needs to figure out what to do. She can stay with me for a time, but I'm dying. Liver. It's slow but it's happening. She don't know that, and don't need to. She's got enough on her plate. Eventually, though, I'll be gone and

*this store will be turned over to my brother, and you don't want her
staying here then. That would be a disaster.*

*I'll tell you another thing for free: Honor won't do no better than
Jack Haymaker—not in Ohio, anyway. She wants the perfect man she's
going to have to go back to England to find him. Maybe he's not even
there.*

Baby's crying—time for me to stop.

Yours ever faithful,

Belle Mills

Comfort

 HONOR WAS FINALLY beginning to appreciate rocking chairs. They were everywhere in America: on the front porches of almost every house, in corners of kitchens, in the parlors of travelers' inns, outside of saloons, in shops by the stove. Only Friends Meeting Houses—and churches, Honor suspected, though she had not been inside one—did not have them.

Before Comfort's arrival, she had always been suspicious of them: the rocking seemed to her an aggressive sign of leisureliness. The constant rhythm set by someone else bothered her when she was sitting near an occupied rocker. Americans demonstrated their own rhythm in a much more public way than the English, and it did not seem to occur to them that others might not care for it. Indeed, Americans often went their own way with little consideration for how others felt: proud of their individuality, they liked to flaunt it.

When Honor visited other Faithwell families, she had always chosen a straight-backed chair, saying it was better for the sewing she brought with her. Really, though, she did not want to rock in front of others and impose her internal rhythm on them.

Once Comfort was born, however, Honor discovered how soothing rocking could be, for baby and mother. She often sat with her daughter in the rocker by the stove in Belle's shop, nursing or letting her sleep in her arms. Customers smiled and nodded at her, and seemed not to mind.

Perhaps, Honor thought one day, it is not that Americans are so wedded to individual expression, but that we British are too judgmental.

Given the violence with which she entered the world—the lengthy pain, the blood, the pushing and screaming that turned Honor briefly into an animal—it was perhaps not surprising that Comfort Haymaker was a vocal baby. She had corn-flax hair and her father's blue eyes, but was small like her mother, and her tiny stomach filled and emptied quickly. She cried, was fed, slept for an hour, and then cried again to be fed, cycling through this infant rhythm all day and all night. Honor had never had such an insistent demand made on her, not even when nursing Grace through her final illness. For a time she was so exhausted she could do little more than doze with Comfort between feeds.

If she had been at the Haymakers', Honor would have felt no guilt, for new mothers were expected to convalesce for several weeks. But at Belle's she felt conspicuously idle, especially when she came down to sit in the shop rather than lie in the bedroom that had been given over to her. Belle seemed unbothered by either the crying or the idleness, but Honor insisted on doing what sewing she could when Comfort slept, though in her fatigue she kept unthreading her needle and sewing crooked seams.

Comfort soon grew used to her mother rocking her in the chair, and would wake and cry when Honor tried to transfer her to the quilt-lined basket Belle had lent her. Honor herself became tearful from exhausted frustration. Mother would know what to do to get her to sleep, she thought. Or Judith Haymaker.

Belle watched her struggle with the crying baby. "She needs a cradle," she remarked pointedly.

Honor pressed her lips together and said nothing. The day after Comfort was born Belle had sent word to the Haymakers, and Jack had come to visit.

Honor was surprised by how glad she was to see him. When he held his daughter in his arms, gazing proudly on her sleeping face, Honor got that feeling she had when she was sewing together patchwork pieces, and saw that they fit. "She has thy hair, and thy eyes," she said. They were the first words she had spoken to her husband in months.

Jack smiled, looking relieved. "It is good to hear thy voice."

Honor smiled back. "And thine. I have missed thee." At this moment, she meant it.

"I have made the baby a cradle. Mother says—" Jack stopped. "She can sleep in it when thee comes back to the farm."

Honor felt her shoulders rise, and as if in response, Comfort began to cry. Jack had to hand her back, and the feeling of being a family was broken.

"Honor, why did thee run off?" he said. "I was so worried. We all were."

Honor was positioning Comfort so that she would latch on to her breast. The initial sucking was so painful she caught her breath.

"It was irresponsible," Jack continued. "What if the baby had come when thee was out in the woods, alone and far from anyone? You both could have died."

"I was not alone."

Jack frowned at the reminder of the runaway.

Though tempted to retreat back into the silence of the past months, Honor resisted. "I would like to name her Comfort," she said. "Comfort Grace Haymaker."

"Why didn't you tell Jack to bring the cradle here?" Belle demanded when he had left. She must have been listening.

"It is his mother's bargain. The cradle is ready for her, but only if I return to them."

Belle looked as if she wanted to say something, but didn't.

Various customers mentioned cradles as they watched Honor struggle to get Comfort to sleep. "Pretty baby. Where's her cradle?" "Don't that baby have a cradle to sleep in?" "You need to get yourself a cradle, young lady." Then one morning a customer's son brought in an old cradle carved from hickory, with faded cherries painted on the tiny bedboard. "I slept in this when I was a baby," he said. "Now Ma's holdin' on to it for her grandchildren. But I'm headin' west and don't need no cradle yet. Can make one out there. So you can have it." He left before Honor could even thank him.

The cradle was old and rickety, but it rocked, and Comfort immediately fell asleep in it. Then Honor could move it with her foot and still sew.

When Judith and Dorcas Haymaker visited, bringing with them a basket each of cheese and apples, Judith frowned at the old cradle. But her face softened and her smile was genuine as she took her first grandchild into her arms. Fighting the urge to snatch Comfort back, Honor sat very straight and clutched her hands in her lap. The baby flailed her tiny arms and moved her head from side to side, searching for her mother's breast, blue eyes blurred and unable yet to focus.

Honor was more at ease when Dorcas took the baby. Rocking Comfort in her arms, Dorcas appeared more content than Honor had ever seen her. "A new family has moved to Faithwell," she remarked. "From Pennsylvania. They're dairy farmers too."

Judith grunted. "They are restless at Meeting. The father speaks as if preaching."

They were sitting in the tiny back kitchen, and Honor caught the amused looks of customers at the three Quaker women in their sober dress, contrasting with the bright feathers and flowers of the shop.

Then Comfort began to cry, and Honor reached for her daughter.

That evening, when the Haymaker women had left and the baby was sleeping, the two women worked, Honor sewing white rabbit fur around a green bonnet for winter, Belle lining a gray bonnet with light blue silk.

"How old is Dorcas?" Belle asked, holding up the bonnet and frowning at the rim. "Is this lopsided?"

"No. She is the same age as me."

"It *is* lopsided. Damn." Belle began to unpick the seam. "Why'd she mention the new family in Faithwell, do you think?"

Honor did not pause in her rhythmic stitching. "People often fill silence with words."

"No, honey, these were pointing at something. You just didn't notice 'cause you were fussing over the baby, but Dorcas was smiling to herself after she talked about 'em. And it made your mother-in-law look like she'd eaten a sour apple."

Honor stopped sewing, looked at Belle, and waited for her to explain what she had clearly already thought through.

"There'll be a husband in there somewhere for her," Belle declared.

Honor began stitching again. She did not want to indulge in speculation. She was glad, though, that she had finished the quilts she owed Dorcas. She had five more quilts to make for her marriage, but before that she thought she would sew a quick cot quilt for Comfort. She did not yet know what the design would be; she would need to get to know her daughter first.

Once she was stronger she took Comfort out for short walks around Wellington. Since most of the townswomen bought their bonnets and hats at Belle's, and went there often to browse if not to buy, Honor found she was already acquainted with many of them, and they nodded and said hello as she passed. She suspected they spoke about her afterward, for a Quaker with a quarrel with her husband's family was gossip few could resist. However, Honor would not let herself turn around to witness the heads leaning toward each other, the lowered voices, the gleeful, horrified looks. To her face the women of Wellington remained pleasant, and that was the best she could hope for.

Often she took Comfort down to see the train pass through Wellington on its way to Columbus or Cleveland. At first she could not bear the size and noise of the metal monster puffing and panting into the depot, and it made Comfort scream. However, she could not deny that it was thrilling to see all the different people getting on and off, the goods being unloaded, the simple possibility of movement and change, of going away and of coming back. Eventually both mother and daughter grew used to the disruption, and looked forward to it.

Occasionally Honor ran into Donovan, coming from the town stables or talking to other men in the street. He tipped his hat at her but did not speak. The sight of Comfort clearly made him uneasy.

"Thy brother does not like babies," she remarked to Belle as they passed him one day, sitting outside Wadsworth Hotel.

Belle chuckled. "Most men don't—babies scare 'em, and take all the mother's attention they don't get. It's more than that with Donovan, though: that baby reminds him you're married. He's been havin' fun this past year pretending you don't have any attachments. Now he's got a real live reminder that a man's already been where he wanted to be."

Honor flushed.

"Got yourself a family now, honey, not just one you married into. Donovan knows he can't compete. He don't like that much. Notice how he's stayed away since you've been here?"

It was true that, when her waters had broken, after Donovan had roused Belle and helped to get Honor inside, he'd backed off and left her alone. He did not ride up and down the street in front of the millinery shop as he had when she'd last stayed—though one evening when he was drunk, he sat at the Wadsworth Hotel bar across the street and stared through the window at Honor while she was rocking Comfort. Then he spat out his plug of tobacco, an action he knew Honor did not like. She closed her eyes, and when she opened them, he was gone.

But Honor herself had changed. Her mind was on her baby, the responsibility for another pushing away everything that was not essential to Comfort's survival. When she saw Donovan, she felt as if she were looking on a distant shore of a place she had once loved but no longer felt such an urgency to get to. Donovan had become like England.

She was still concerned for him, however. Later, as she sat up with Belle, Honor brought him up again. "Does thee think thy brother could change?"

Belle was stretching a hat of chocolate brown felt, dampening it and then putting it over a wooden block cut in half and bisected by a metal screw with a handle on the end. Turning the handle expanded the block so that it stretched the felt. "My brother is a bad man," she said. "He ain't got your ways, and never will. He thinks Negroes are barely more than animals. It's how we was brought up to think in Kentucky, and nothin' you say or do is gonna change that, whatever you think with your forgiving Quaker ways."

"But thee changed thy thinking. Why can't he?"

"Some people are born bad." Belle turned the handle till the felt would stretch no further. "I think deep down, most southerners have always known slavery ain't right, but they built up layers of ideas to justify what they were doin'. Those layers just solidified over the years. Hard to break out of that thinking, to find the guts to say, 'This is wrong.' I had to come to Ohio before I could do that. You can, in Ohio—it's that sort of place. I'm kinda fond of it now." She patted the felt hat as if she were patting the whole state. "But Donovan . . . he's too hard to shift. I help runaways in part to balance out the bad in him—and to punish him for running off my husband. But listen, honey, you shouldn't be wasting your thoughts on lost causes. Everything you do should be what's best for *her*." She nodded at the cradle where Comfort lay asleep, her arms thrown above her head like the victor in a race.

Belle Mills's Millinery
Main St
Wellington, Ohio
10th Month 1st 1851

Dearest Biddy,

It has been so long since I have written, thee must wonder what has happened to thy friend to be so neglectful. I am sorry. Silence took me over completely for several months, so that I could not speak to anyone, nor write. I hope that thee can forgive me. I am now speaking again, though sparingly.

First thee must note the address from which I am writing, and where I have been staying for the last month. I have told thee in the past of Belle Mills the milliner, who was so kind to me when I first arrived in Ohio. It was Belle's kindness that has drawn me back to her when I could have gone another way.

My parents will have given thee the news that I now have a daughter, Comfort, born just as I arrived at Belle's. She is a beautiful baby, with a head of light hair and wide blue eyes and an intent expression, as if she knows her mind and will make herself heard. She cries often, for she is small yet—she arrived earlier than expected—and hungry, but she is also growing quickly. Already I cannot imagine my life without her in it.

Of course thee must be surprised that I am not in Faithwell with my husband and his family. It is hard to explain why, but I could not go on living there. They were not unkind to me, but we do not see the world in the same way. I left the farm, helped by a runaway slave who was going south, back to get her children and bring them north. I know I had little cause to, but I envied her the certainty of what she was doing. I have not felt certainty since Samuel released me from our engagement. It is hard to live untethered for so long.

Jack has been to see Comfort and me several times, and each time asks when I am coming back. I do not know what to answer.

Judith Haymaker has come twice, and that was harder, as she is so much more rigid than Jack, and less loving or forgiving. She sees me as an embarrassment to the Haymakers, and said unkind things one would not expect from a Friend—out of frustration, I expect. 'I should not have allowed Jack to marry thee,' she said the other day. 'Thee brings nothing to this family but English ways that are not our ways.' Then she told me the Elders of the Meeting have decided that I must return to Faithwell by the 1st of the 11th Month or they will disown me, and take Comfort away. It made me reluctant to allow Judith to hold Comfort, for I feared she might not give her back. Comfort herself did not take to her grandmother—though she did not cry, she lay stiff in her arms, frowning the whole while. It was altogether an upsetting visit, though, like my daughter, I did not cry.

The most helpful visit has been from Dorcas Haymaker, who managed to come once on her own, with the help of a willing Faithwell farmer who gave her a lift. It was surprising as she and I did not always get on well. She at least was practical, bringing me clothes and my sewing box and work basket, and the signature quilt thee and others made for me. She also brought baby clothes I had made, asking me not to let Jack or Judith know about them, as giving them to me implies she believes I am not coming back. She asked this with great reluctance, for it is dishonest of us both to conceal the purpose of her visit.

Best of all, Dorcas brought thy letter, which I was delighted to receive, especially with its news that thee will be married at the beginning of next year. Truly I wish I were there to share thy happiness and meet the Friend from Sherborne who has captured thy heart. I feel very guilty to have still the Star of Bethlehem quilt thee sent to me for my marriage. I promise that when I can get it, I will send it back—though perhaps the Sherborne family is not so exacting as the

Haymakers about the number of quilts thee should have when thee marries.

Belle has been very good to me. She does not ask many questions, but lets me speak when I will. And she does not judge, nor ask how long I intend to stay. She simply gives me work. She is very pleased with my sewing, as are many of the ladies in Wellington. Belle does not normally make dresses, but I have begun doing alterations and repairs when customers bring them in. She has also taught me much about hat making during this month, though of course they are not for me to wear, being too fancy for a Friend. I do admire them, however, though I know I should not, as the feathers and flowers are so frivolous.

I try to help with household chores, when Comfort lets me. Belle hardly cooks, for she eats little. She says she likes the smell of my cooking but then she only has a bite or two. Clothes hang off her. Her skin and eyes have a yellow cast, and I suspect jaundice, though she has said nothing about it.

Biddy, I feel very confused now. I am in a part of the country where there is much movement, and yet I do not know where to move myself. And America is such a peculiar country. It is young and untested, its foundations uncertain. I think back to the Bridport Friends Meeting House, which has stood for almost two hundred years. When I sat in silence there I felt the strength of that history, the thousands of people who have also sat there over the years, shoring me up and making me feel part of a greater whole. There was an easiness—though some might call it a complacency, I suppose—of knowing where one comes from.

The Meeting at Faithwell does not have that permanence. It is not just that the building is new, and made of wood rather than stone. There is also a flimsiness of community, a feeling that no one has been there long, and no one may remain long. Many talk of moving west. That is always an option in America. If crops fail, or there is a dispute with neighbours, or one feels hemmed in, one can always simply pick up and move on. It means that family is even more important. But my family here is not strong; I do not feel I belong. So I must choose whether to move—but I do not know in which direction.

It is best for now, then, if thee writes to me at Belle's. I do not know where I will be in four months by the time this letter reaches thee and thee writes back. But Belle will know where I am.

Be patient with me, Biddy. With God's will may we meet again.

Thy faithful friend,

Honor

Ohio Star

 ONE MORNING AN older woman Honor had not seen before came into the shop. "Thomas is making a delivery tomorrow afternoon," she told Belle. "Big one. Make sure you got the space."

Belle nodded. "Thankee, Mary," she said around the pins in her mouth, for she was attaching ruffles to a burgundy bonnet.

"Got both logs and kindling for you. That all right?"

"Course. How's that li'l granddaughter o' yours? Go on, take one o' them ribbons for her hair. Girl always likes a new ribbon."

"Thankee. You mind if I take two?" The woman chose two red ribbons from a basket on the counter. She hesitated at the door. "You all right, Belle? You're mighty thin these days."

"Tapeworm. It'll pass."

Honor looked up from her usual position, in the rocker feeding Comfort. The bones in Belle's triangular face were even more pronounced, so that her hazel eyes blazed above the balls of her cheekbones.

"Belle—" she began when the woman had left.

"No questions," Belle interrupted. "Usually I can count on you to keep quiet. Stick to that now. You done there?"

Honor nodded.

"Good. You mind the shop a little while—I got to make room for the wood coming." She disappeared before Honor could be sure Comfort would not wake when she transferred her from her arms to the cradle. Perhaps Comfort sensed Belle's no-nonsense attitude, for she remained asleep. Honor was able to serve the string of customers who appeared over the next hour while Belle was rearranging the wood still left in the lean-to. She also made several trips upstairs, which surprised Honor, though she knew better than to ask why.

Late the next afternoon, as it was growing dark and Belle was lighting lamps, a man appeared with a wagon full of wood. When he came in to greet Belle, he nodded at Honor, and she recognized him as the old man who had brought her from Hudson over a year ago. "Got yourself a little one, I hear," Thomas said. "That's good."

Honor smiled. "Yes, it is."

Belle took Thomas out back while Honor remained with the two customers in the store: a young woman and her mother dithering over wool linings for their winter bonnets. Finally they chose and paid. The moment they left, Thomas came back out and went to run his wagon around the back.

"I'll just be helping with the wood," Belle said. "Any customers come, you look after them. Keep 'em occupied." She held Honor's gaze a moment, then turned and hurried through the kitchen and out of the back door.

She had hardly gone before Donovan's horse was heard trotting up the street. Then Honor understood. She closed her eyes and prayed that he would not stop.

He did. She watched from the window as he threw his reins over the hitching post. "Where's Belle?" he demanded as he entered, his eyes flicking over Comfort in her cradle before they settled on Honor.

"She is out back, seeing to a delivery of wood."

A woman passed along the boards outside, slowing to study the bonnets in the window. Please come in, Honor thought. Please. But she moved on; darkness was not the time for a woman to be out.

"Is she, now? Well, darlin', if you'll excuse me, I'll just have a look, make sure she ain't gettin' a load o' green wood." Donovan stepped around her and strode toward the kitchen.

"Donovan—"

He stopped. "What?"

She had to keep him with her somehow, so that he would not go back to the lean-to.

"I have always—I have always wanted to thank thee for helping me that night. In the woods, with the black man."

Donovan snorted. "Didn't help none—nigger was dead, wasn't he? Not much use to you *or* me."

"But thee found me when I was on the road, in the dark. I do not know what I would have done if thee had not come." Though she did not speak of it, she was making herself remember the feeling she'd had with him that night, that brief moment when they'd shared a closeness. By recalling it she hoped he would too, and break off his focus on what was happening at the back of the house. "I wish," she added, "thee would change thy ways."

"Would that make any difference?"

Before Honor could answer, Comfort let out the little cry that signaled she would soon wake.

Donovan grimaced. "It wouldn't, would it? Not now." He turned and headed back to Belle.

Honor rocked the cradle, hoping the movement might send Comfort back to sleep. It did not, however, and she picked up the baby and put her over her shoulder, walking around the room and patting her back. At the same time she listened out for what might be taking place by the wood.

A few minutes later Belle reappeared, her arms full of logs, which she dropped in the box by the stove. Donovan was following her. "Donovan, no brother should let his sister bring in wood without carrying some himself. What the hell's the matter with you? People like Honor here got a low enough opinion of you without you makin' it worse by bein' so ungentlemanly." She squatted and began arranging the wood. "You gonna bring in another load or do I have to do all the work myself?"

Donovan frowned, then went back the way he'd come. He must be younger than Belle, Honor thought, reminded of the natural authority her older brothers had held over her and Grace.

Belle opened the stove and added another log, though the fire didn't need it: there would be no more customers for the day and they would move to the kitchen fire. It was this unnecessary action that told Honor Belle was nervous.

Donovan came back with a stack of wood, Thomas behind him.

"That should see you up to Christmas, Belle," Thomas said. "Though I'll top it up when I'm in town, if you like."

"Thankee, Thomas. What do I owe you?" While Belle and Thomas went over to the counter to settle up, Donovan began stacking the wood on top of what his sister had brought in. Comfort's eyes had begun to focus and she followed his movements over Honor's shoulder. This seemed to bother Donovan, and he hurried to finish. As Thomas was leaving through the kitchen to go back to his wagon, Donovan stood up and made a move toward the front door.

"You want some coffee before you go, Donovan?" Belle said, sounding amused.

"I'll just scare off your customers. You watch yourself, Belle, Honor. I ain't through here." He banged the door behind him.

Belle chuckled. "That baby sure spooks him more'n anything else can. She should stay here all the time. That would keep him away, like a lucky charm." She kissed the top of Comfort's head, dusted with wispy white-blond hair. It was rare for her to show the baby affection.

They listened to Donovan's horse clop away. "Honor, go to the window and check he's ridin' it," Belle said. "He's tried that one before."

Honor looked, and recognized his tall silhouette slumped in the saddle. She watched till he was out of sight. "He's gone."

"Good. Now, you stay there, and make sure he don't come back." Belle hurried to the back of the house. A few minutes later Honor saw Thomas's wagon go past, rattling now it was empty of its load of wood.

She and Comfort stood on in the window, the baby quiet, balanced on her mother's shoulder and reaching her hand out toward the darkness. In the last few days she had stopped flailing so much, her movements more controlled.

Soon Belle was back. "All right. I'm gonna fix supper." When Honor opened her mouth to speak, Belle interrupted her. "Don't ask. If you don't know, then you won't have nothin' to tell Donovan when he comes back. 'Cause he will come back tonight. He'll be back for another look." She was talking as if Honor knew what was happening. She did know. She just did not let herself think openly about it. Some things should remain hidden.

But they did not remain hidden. Honor and Belle were eating in the kitchen, the baby asleep in the cradle at Honor's feet, when she heard a whimper. It was not Comfort—Honor was so attuned to her child's noises that she did not even glance down at the cradle. She froze, her knife stopped in the groove it was carving into a pork chop, and listened.

Belle, however, clattered her cutlery onto her plate and stood up, pushing her chair back so that the legs scraped along the wood floor. "You know what I feel like with supper?" she said. "Tea. The English drink tea anytime, don't they? I'm gonna boil some water." She picked up a jug of water and filled the kettle. "Makes a change from coffee or whiskey, don't it?" Belle banged the kettle on the range. "You ain't never touched a drop o' liquor, though, have you? No whiskey or beer or nothin'. Poor Quaker."

Even under Belle's valiant effort to make noise, Honor heard another whimper, then the low murmur of a woman's voice. Not just any voice: it was a mother's, shushing her child. Now that Honor herself was a mother, she was much more sensitive to the sorts of tones a mother needed to use.

"Where are they?" she said in a pause among Belle's clatter.

Belle looked almost relieved, and smiled as if to apologize for thinking Honor would be fooled by her clumsy attempt at conceal-ment. "If I show you," she said, "you gotta think about what you'll say if Donovan asks you 'bout 'em. I know you Quakers ain't sup-posed to lie, but ain't a small lie that helps a bigger truth all right? God ain't gonna judge you for lying to my brother, is He? And if the Haymakers judge you for it, well . . ." She did not bother to fill in her thoughts about Honor's in-laws.

Honor thought. "I have heard of Friends blindfolding them-selves so that they do not see those they're helping. That way they can honestly answer no if asked whether they have seen them."

Belle snorted. "That's just a game that God's gonna see right through anyway. Ain't playin' with the truth like that worse than lyin' outright for the greater good?"

"Perhaps." The child was no longer whimpering, but crying out-right, the sound coming from the hole by the range that led into the lean-to. Belle could reach in through the hole for wood without having to go outside. Though covered with a thick cloth to keep out drafts, it did not completely muffle the sounds. Honor could not bear the crying. She let out a deep breath she did not realize she had been holding. "Please bring in the child," she said. "I would not have it freeze because of me. I will lie to Donovan if I must."

Belle nodded. Pulling aside the cloth, she called through the hole. "It's all right, Virginie, bring 'em in for a little while."

After a moment a pair of brown hands pushed first one, then a second girl through the hole and into Belle's arms. She set them on their feet, side by side. They were twins, identical, about five years old, with wide dark eyes, their hair plaited and tied with the red ribbons Thomas's wife had taken the day before. They stood solemn and mute in front of Belle and Honor, the only difference between them being the runny nose and wheezy cough of the one who had been crying.

Belle pulled them aside as a gray bonnet pushed through the hole. Honor caught a flash of its pale yellow lining and started.

Belle smiled. "So that's where that bonnet got to. Didn't recognize it in the dark before. I thought you'd left it with the Haymakers—though Lord knows what they would do with it. Make it into a milk bucket, maybe." She gave a hand to the runaway woman so that she could stand. Honor recalled her slender height, her sallow skin, her steady gaze.

The woman looked back at Honor and nodded. "I see you still here. Got your baby now. Well, I got my babies too." She put her arms around the girls. Now that she was out in the open, her mother beside her, the girl with the cold felt confident enough to begin crying freely.

"Honor, get her some raspberry jam in hot water," Belle commanded. "Kettle's boiled. Add a drop o' whiskey to it. Don't you frown at me—it'll do her good. I'll make up a poultice for her chest." She glanced at the window, which had a heavy curtain pulled across it, and at the door between the kitchen and shop, which she had pulled shut. "Can't be out like this for long—Donovan'll be back. We fooled him once—he thinks you ain't here yet. But he'll come round again soon enough."

"When did they get in?" Honor asked.

"Right at the end, just when Donovan was leaving. That's always the best time, when they're still here but not suspicious any more. Old Thomas moved 'em. He hid 'em in his wagon, in a compartment under the bottom of the wagon. You lay out flat an' they put the false bottom over you. It ain't comfortable, is it, Virginie?"

"Is that how Thomas brought the runaway from Hudson when he drove me here?" Honor thought of Thomas stamping his feet now and then, and his talking while she was in the woods, and the feeling she had had that someone was with them.

"Yep. And Donovan still don't know about it. He looks under the front seat."

Now that she knew Honor wouldn't give away her secrets, Belle became chatty, proud of the ruses she and Thomas and others working on the Underground Railroad had developed to keep runaways hidden. Once they'd dosed the sick child with raspberry jam and whiskey, and spread a mustard paste on her chest, Belle had Honor crawl through the hole into the lean-to, which was deeper along the side of the house than she'd realized from seeing it from the outside. Belle and Thomas had stacked the wood so that it seemed to be up against the back wall, but actually there was a gap between the woodpile and the wall, making a small chamber barely bigger than a cupboard, which you got to by squeezing around the stack. Inside the chamber were three stumps the runaways must use as stools, though turned on their sides they would look innocuous enough. Indeed, if you pushed the back stack of wood into the space it would turn into a messy pile waiting to be burned. As she gazed on it, Honor wondered how many runaways had hidden here. Dozens? Hundreds?

Belle had lived in Wellington for fifteen years, and there had been runaways probably for as long as there had been slavery.

Honor heard Comfort crying then, and hurried to get back to her, struggling through the hole so clumsily that Belle chuckled. By the time she was on her feet, Comfort was quiet in the black woman's arms. Though Honor reached out, the woman did not hand Comfort back. "I looked after a string o' little white babies for the mistress," she said, swinging Comfort in the crook of her arm with ease. "Feels good to hold a baby again. Look at her, girls," she said to her daughters seated at the table. "She ain't smilin' yet. She only a month old. Too young to smile at us yet. We got to *earn* her smile."

Honor struggled not to snatch her daughter back, even though rationally she knew that Comfort could come to no harm.

The woman's name was Virginie. The whole night Honor had been with her in the woods and fields, she had not thought to ask her name. Indeed, she had never asked any of the runaways their names. Now she wondered why. Perhaps she had not wanted to personalize them in that way. Without names it was easier for them to disappear from her life. And they did—all except the nameless man buried in Wieland Woods.

Look for the measure of Light in her, she counseled herself, for it is there, as it is in every person. Never forget that.

Comfort was too young to make any judgment other than whether she felt secure in the arms that held her. And she did. She looked up at the black woman, who began to sing:

> I'm wading deep waters
> Trying to get home
> Lord, I'm wading deep waters
> Trying to get home
> Well, I'm wading deep waters

Wading deep waters

Yes, I'm wading deep waters

Trying to get home.

"She is smiling!" Honor cried.

Virginie chuckled. "Jes' wind. But nice to see anyway. Go on back to your mama, li'l girl, an' give *her* a smile."

Belle fed the runaways chipped beef and corn bread, spreading the latter with apple butter Honor had made the day before. One twin gobbled it down, but the other picked at the food, then laid her head on her arms. Belle studied her when she came down from the bedrooms, her arms full of quilts. "Y'all best get back there now." She stuffed the quilts through the hole, but went outside to look around before entering the lean-to.

Honor and Virginie nodded good night and then the runaways crawled through the hole to their hiding place. After a few minutes Belle returned via the back door. "Hope that little one's gonna be all right." She shook her head. "It's snug enough in there, but we don't want her gettin' worse. And they're so close to Canada. Even at a little girl's pace they can't be more'n a week away from Lake Erie. Plus if they get to Oberlin they can hide in the black community a while till she improves."

"Belle, is thee a—a station master?"

Belle snorted. "You know, I never use those silly phrases: *station master*, *depot*, *conductor*. Even *Underground Railroad* tries my patience. Makes it sound like children playin' a game, when this surely ain't no game."

The girl's coughing began again. Honor listened as she washed dishes. "The cold air is getting to her chest," she remarked.

Belle sighed. "Donovan'll hear her when he comes snoopin' 'round in the middle of the night. She needs to sleep inside in a bed where it's warm. That'll quiet her—that and some paregoric. Can't bring 'em all in, though—we couldn't hide 'em all from Donovan." She drew aside the cloth and whispered into the hole. A few minutes later the sick girl was passed through to Belle. She gave her a spoonful of thick brown liquid from a bottle, then said, "C'mon, honey, I'll put you in my bed. You be real quiet now."

Honor went to bed herself soon after, exhausted from nights of broken sleep and from the tension of the day. Leaving the door ajar so that she could hear and see a little from the light downstairs, she lay in bed, baby at her side where she could easily feed her in the night without getting up. Belle was still down in the kitchen, making flowers out of straw for her hats, waiting.

Honor was not yet asleep when she felt a tiny presence next to the bed. In the glow from downstairs she could just make out the girl's outline. Without saying anything the girl climbed into bed, careful around the baby, and slid under the quilt to press up against Honor's back, like a little animal looking for warmth. She coughed a bit and then fell asleep.

Honor lay very still, listening to the girl's snuffling breath and her daughter's almost imperceptible sigh, marveling that a black girl was snuggling up to her, as Grace had done when they were girls and it was cold. The barrier between them was dissolving in the warm bed; here there was no separate bench. Whatever the uncertainty downstairs, outside, in the world at large, in this bed with the children close by and reliant on her, Honor felt calm, and part of a family. With that clarity she too was able to sleep.

Donovan was never going to enter quietly. Honor jerked awake with the banging on the front door. Her movement, or the noise, woke the girl, who whimpered.

"Shhh," Honor whispered. "Be as quiet as thee can, and don't move." Luckily she was on her side facing the doorway, and with the girl huddled against her back under the quilt, Donovan might not see her. Honor pulled the quilt over the child's head, hiding her plaits tied with red ribbons.

She heard voices, steady, not raised, then the methodical searching of first the shop, then the kitchen. Donovan was not deliberately destructive. He did not break glass counterpanes or tear up cloth or stamp on hats. He did not throw down crockery or upend furniture. Honor even heard Belle laugh as if sharing a familial joke. Doubtless he had searched her house many times. Perhaps he was simply going through the motions. Or he suspected she was smarter than him and one day he would work out how she hid her runaways.

Then the girl coughed, juddering against her. It was not loud but it was distinct. Honor felt a spike of ice in her stomach. She heard Donovan's voice, and Belle answering him. She thought she heard her name.

The girl coughed again, and when she stopped, Honor coughed too, trying to imitate a small girl's breathy chest. She heard footsteps on the stairs, felt the girl's quivering fear at her back, joined it with her own.

Then Belle's voice came, telling her what to do. "Donovan, you gonna interrupt her feeding her baby. You really wanna do that?"

Honor reached for Comfort, shaking her gently as she gathered the warm round body to her. Unbuttoning the neck of her nightgown, she pulled out a full, swollen breast that began to leak milk even before Comfort stirred and, half-asleep, opened her mouth and latched on. Gumming the nipple, she sucked hard, so that Honor took in a deep breath of pain and release.

Donovan searched the small bedroom where Belle slept first;

then the lantern light swung into the larger bedroom, arcing over her and Comfort. Honor prayed the girl would not cough or move. He stared down at her, trying not to let his eyes slip to the baby and the breast, but failing. Though he fought it, a kind of longing spread across his face. It had the effect Honor had hoped for: he did not come further into the room to ransack the piles of material Belle stored there, or look under the bed.

"Sorry," he said. But he did not leave immediately. His eyes wandered over the quilt. "That's Ma's quilt," he said. "What'd you call that design? You told me once, when we first met."

"Star of Bethlehem."

"That's it." Donovan looked at her for a moment, then nodded and backed out.

Honor and the girl remained still and silent. Only Comfort squirmed and sucked, her tiny hand grasping at Honor's nightgown. They could hear Donovan go out of the back door. Now he would find the others or not. What would they do with this girl if Donovan took them away? Perhaps that was what she herself was thinking about, for suddenly the girl began to sob.

"Oh no, not that. Thee mustn't. Not now." With difficulty, Honor detached Comfort and sat up. Leaning against the headboard, she put the baby back on her breast and her free arm around the girl. "Don't cry, now. We must pray that God will keep them safe." She closed her eyes, and listened.

He did not find them. Half an hour later Belle came up and sat on the edge of Honor's bed, careful not to disturb the sleeping baby. "He's gone. You can go to sleep now. You too, little one," she added for the benefit of the girl pressed against Honor.

"Belle, how will we get them safely away from the house?"

"Honey, don't you worry 'bout that. I always got tricks up my sleeve."

———————

Comfort woke twice more that night to feed, and each time the girl was asleep. When the rising sun at last woke Honor, the girl had gone.

Down in the kitchen, Belle was frying griddle cakes and bacon—far more than the two of them could eat. She nodded toward the hole. "Little girl's doing better. She almost smiled at me." She piled the griddle cakes and bacon onto a plate and pushed it through the hole.

After breakfast Belle went out without saying where she was going, leaving Honor to mind the shop. On her return she handed Honor a wine-colored dress. "Customer wants the hem and sleeves let out."

All day, as Honor sewed—first the dress, then a child's skirt—she thought about the three runaways crammed into the small space behind the woodpile. It would be dark and uncomfortable, the wood offering little other than splinters and mice. Yet perhaps it was better than hiding in the cold woods.

Belle was in an overbright mood, displaying a nervous energy as she helped customers try on bonnets, removed flowers that were too summery for the growing cold, added tartan ribbons or feathers, measured for winter linings. When it was quiet, she worked at the table in the corner, sewing yellow netting onto the brown felt hat she had been stretching. Now and then she went to the window to glance out.

When Honor handed her the altered clothes, she noticed Belle was holding a familiar gray bonnet: she had replaced the worn yellow ribbons with a much wider gray ribbon that went round the crown and when tied pulled the brim close around the face. She had also added a row of white lace to the brim, hiding the yellow lining.

It was now far too fancy for Honor to wear—or indeed Virginie. No black woman wore something so decorative.

Honor widened her eyes. Belle shrugged and hummed under her breath; Honor recognized it as the tune Virginie had sung to Comfort the night before. "Is that a hymn?"

"No, just a song you hear in the fields in the South. Negroes sing it to keep themselves goin'."

Late in the day, when Belle was lighting lamps, three women came into the shop, accompanied by several young girls. "Look after 'em, Honor," Belle said, heading to the kitchen. "I'll be back."

Honor stared after her, surprised that she would hurry away from such a large group. The women and girls were lively, trying on so many different hats and bonnets that she could not keep up with replacing them. In the middle of it, Comfort began to cry in her cradle. Before Honor could get to her one of the older girls had picked her up and went jigging around the shop. Comfort stopped crying with the novelty of it all, and the other girls gathered around the baby. There seemed to be more of them now, and they clattered and laughed and played around Honor's daughter.

In the distance the train whistle sounded, cutting through the noise. "C'mon, girls, time to go," one of the women called. Immediately the girl handed Comfort over and grabbed the hand of one of the younger ones. The others found partners and linked arms. As they passed through the door one of the smaller girls wearing a wide-brimmed bonnet and a shawl around her neck and chin turned to peek at Honor. It was one of Virginie's twins, though only a strip of her dark skin was showing. In the dusk outside, her arm linked through another's, she would be indistinguishable. Honor smiled at her, but the girl looked too terrified to speak.

The other twin left as well, bundled along with the rest of the group, and suddenly it was quiet. Only a woman remained behind.

Then Belle was back in the room, pulling Virginie behind her. The runaway was transformed by the burgundy dress and a shawl, the gray and yellow bonnet tied tight under her chin so that from the side her face was hidden. You could only see her if you looked head-on.

"No time to wait," Belle said. "Town's out to meet the train. Go out and cry, 'Wait up, ladies!' and run after 'em. Act like you goin' to see the train. He's across the street, watchin', so you got to be bold."

Virginie squeezed Belle's arm. "Thankee."

Belle laughed. "All in a day's work, honey. Off you go, now. If you're lucky I won't see you again!"

"God go with thee, Virginie," Honor added. "And thy girls."

Virginie nodded, then ducked out of the door after the other woman.

"Come back away from the window," Belle commanded. "Can't have Donovan see us takin' an interest or he'll get suspicious."

The door opened then and another Wellington woman entered. "I ain't too late, am I?" she asked. "I just need a new ribbon for my bonnet."

"We'll stay open for you," Belle said. "Honor, you put all these bonnets back, will you? Those girls just now made the biggest mess."

Honor stacked bonnets one-handed, bouncing Comfort with the other. Her heart was pounding. She ached to look out and see whether Donovan had followed the women, but knew she could not.

Ten minutes later Belle showed the customer to the door, then she turned the lock and began shuttering the windows. "He's gone," she announced, "though whether he's gone after the women I just don't know. Could've gone inside the bar for an evening whiskey. God knows I could use one. In fact . . ." Belle made her way to the kitchen, where she poured out a fingerful of whiskey and drank it in one gulp.

Honor watched from the doorway. "Is it always this difficult?"

"Naw." Belle slammed down the glass. "Lot of times he don't even know they're passin' through. And he prefers to catch 'em in the open. He's more at home out in the woods or on the roads than in a hat shop. But now you're here he's sniffin' 'round more, even if he ain't ridin' up and down the street in front of the shop like he did before. Can't hide people so easily with all that happenin'."

"I am putting the runaways in more danger." Honor stated what was now so obvious she should have realized it weeks ago.

Belle shrugged. "I sent word they shouldn't come this way for a time, so we ain't had any while you've been here, 'cept Virginie, and she been here before."

Honor shuddered. Virginie and her daughters could have been caught because she remained at Belle's, frozen with indecision. Indeed, other runaways could be caught because they were taking other routes to avoid Wellington. Belle had not complained about Honor staying with her, but clearly it had consequences.

The next day a boy came by to say that the runaways had left town safely, and were on their way to Oberlin. Belle celebrated with another whiskey.

It was the last First Day before Honor must return to the Haymakers or be disowned by Faithwell Friends. The shop was closed, and Belle was sleeping in, having stayed up much of the night with a whiskey bottle. In that way she resembled her brother. Like the first time Honor stayed with her, Belle was not going to church. "God and I gonna have a long talk when I meet Him," she said. "Set things right then." She made it sound as if such a meeting would not be long in coming. Honor's stomach tightened at the thought.

She looked in on Belle now. Her friend was sleeping on her back, her bony frame outlined under a ragged quilt in an Ohio Star pattern, with squares and triangles making up eight-pointed stars in red and brown. Honor had offered to repair the tears in the seams, but Belle had shrugged. "Waste of time," she'd said, without explaining further. In sleep her face was sunken even more, leaving her cheekbones exposed, the skin pulled over bone that seemed almost visible. Her yellow skin had gone gray. She could be lying in a coffin. Honor caught back a sob, and backed out of the room.

She went down to the kitchen and stood at the range, staring into the corn mush she had made for their breakfast. She had been up three hours already, roused by Comfort, and was waiting for Belle to wake and eat. Though Belle ate even less these days, Honor liked to have the company. Now, though, having seen the state of her companion, she was no longer hungry. She pushed the pot to the back of the range and placed a plate over it to keep it warm.

Comfort was asleep in her cradle. For once Honor wished her daughter were awake so that she could hold her. Instead she sat down on one of the straight chairs in the middle of the quiet kitchen and closed her eyes. Since staying with Belle she had not often had the opportunity to sit in silence. It was always harder to do so without the strength and focus of a community. Collective silence contained a purposeful anticipation. Now, alone, her silence felt empty, as if she were not searching hard enough or in the right place.

She sat for a long time, taken out of the sinking feeling she sought by the interruption of sounds she would not normally notice: the crumbling of embers in the stove; the tapping of wood drying somewhere in the house; the clopping of a horse and turning of wagon wheels in the street in front of the shop. Honor found herself thinking about the cot quilt she was going to start and whether the rosettes she had made all summer would really suit Comfort. They seemed very English, and Comfort was not.

Then she heard scratching at the back door and opened her eyes. Through the small window in the upper half of the door she could see the crown of a brown felt hat trimmed with red and orange maple leaves.

Honor hurried to open the door. "Quick, now, let me in," Mrs. Reed said. "Don't want people to see." She stepped past Honor into the kitchen. "Shut the door," she instructed, for Honor was so surprised she was standing still with her hand on the latch.

Mrs. Reed was wearing a man's coat with a brown shawl over it. Her mouth was set in its habitual downturn, her lower lip protruding. She wiped her glasses with the end of her shawl, then looked around the kitchen. Spotting the cradle, she brightened, as she had with her own granddaughter when Honor had visited her. This was a woman who liked babies. She might be grim and suspicious with others, but babies got her unconditional smile. She leaned over and put her face right in Comfort's. "Hello, baby girl, sleepin' like a li'l angel. Bet you don't always. I done heard 'bout you. Expect I'll hear those lungs soon. Comfort to your mama, that's what you are."

"Will thee sit?" Honor offered the rocking chair, hoping Mrs. Reed would not wake her daughter. It was always harder to talk when Comfort was awake.

Mrs. Reed sat in one of the straight-backed chairs rather than the rocker. Clearly she was here on business instead of a leisurely visit; a rocking chair would muddle the two. However, she did accept a cup of coffee, sweetened with brown sugar.

"What in the name of our good Lord are you doin' here, Honor Bright?" Mrs. Reed demanded after she'd tasted the coffee, grimaced, and reached for more sugar. "Apart from burning the coffee, that is. I didn't even know you was here till Virginie told me. I asked Adam Cox 'bout the baby and he told me you'd had it, but didn't say nothin' 'bout you bein' in Wellington."

"How is Virginie's little girl?" Honor deflected the subject from herself.

"The one who was ill? She fine now. A little chili pepper chased away that cold. They stayed with me a few days, then was off to Sandusky. Should be there by now, waitin' for a boat, with any luck. But don't change the subject. This visit ain't about them, it about you. Why are you here and not with your husband?" Mrs. Reed watched Honor steadily, her eyes now clear through the glasses. It was a straight look: not angry, or sad, or frustrated, or any of the other things Honor had seen in others' eyes while she had been at Belle's. That straightforwardness made her feel she too should be direct.

"I don't agree with the Haymakers about not helping runaways," she said. "That makes me feel I am not a part of the family and never will be."

Mrs. Reed nodded. "Virginie done told me that part. That the only reason? 'Cause if it is, it ain't enough."

Honor stared at her visitor.

"Honor, you think you singlehandedly savin' all the runaways? You think that one meal you give 'em or the sleep they get in your barn is goin' to make all the difference? They already come hundreds o' miles by the time they get to you. They been through some terrible times. You jes' one small link in a big chain. Sure, we grateful for what you done, but we managed before you come along last year, and we'll manage without you. Someone will step into the gap, or the Railroad will shift, is all. We been doin' this a long time,

and will be a long time more. You know how many slaves there are
in the South?"

Honor shook her head, lowering her eyes to her hands in her lap
so that Mrs. Reed would not see the tears welling.

"Millions! Millions. And how many you helped in the last
year—maybe twenty? We got us a long way to go. It surely ain't
somethin' you need to break your marriage over. That's jes' foolishness. Any runaway would tell you that. All they want is the freedom to make the kind of life you got. You go and throw that away
for their sake, you jes' mockin' they own dreams."

Honor gave up trying to hide her tears and let them roll freely
down her face.

"I don't know what Belle here been sayin' to you, but someone
got to say somethin', 'cause you ain't thinkin' straight."

"It ain't so easy sayin' those things to 'em when they're livin' with
you, 'cause you got to go on livin' with 'em." Belle was leaning in the
doorway, startling the women. Now that she was up, her face had
regained some of its color, though the gray had not entirely disappeared. "Glad to hear you talkin' some sense to her." She gazed at
Mrs. Reed, who stared back. The women nodded simultaneously.
Their interest in each other gave Honor the chance to wipe her eyes
and take a shaky breath.

"Good to meet you at last, Belle," Mrs. Reed said.

"And you, Elsie."

"You have never met?" Honor was astonished.

"Better not to—don't want to draw attention," Belle replied.
"But we know 'bout each other." She turned back to Mrs. Reed.
"Anybody see you come in?"

"Not that I saw. I got a man waitin' with a horse in the woods
out o' town, took me that far. Then I walked in. Really I shouldn't

be down here—ain't safe for me these days. I've stayed closer to home ever since the new law come in last year. But I made an exception for this one." Mrs. Reed nodded at Honor. "Ask myself why, though."

Belle chuckled. "She sure has that effect on people, don't she?"

Honor looked from one woman to the other, her eyes wide.

"Guess I got to help a runaway when I see one, whatever they color. It's in my nature." Mrs. Reed shifted her gaze onto Honor. "Now, I don't want you usin' the runaways as the excuse for *you* to run away. You got a problem with your husband's family, you stay and sort it out. Or do you have a problem with *him*?"

Honor considered the question.

Belle joined in. "Does he provide for you? Does he hit you? Is he gentle in bed?"

Honor nodded or shook her head with answers the women already knew.

"Course he's a Quaker, so he don't smoke or drink or spit," Belle continued. "That's something. What in hell's name is the matter with him, then? Apart from his mother." She and Mrs. Reed waited for an answer.

For once Honor wished Comfort would wake to distract them. "There is nothing wrong with Jack," she said at last. "It is with me. I don't belong in this country."

As Belle and Mrs. Reed smiled the same skeptical smile, Honor knew she sounded ridiculous to a woman facing death and a woman whose freedom was precarious. "I am of course grateful to have been taken in by the Haymakers," she continued, "but I do not feel settled. It is as if—as if I am floating just above the ground, with my feet not touching. Back in England I knew where I was, and felt tied to my place."

To her surprise—for Honor did not expect them to understand—

both women nodded. "That jes' Ohio," Mrs. Reed said. "Lots o' people say that."

"Everyone's just passin' through Ohio to get to somewhere else," Belle added. "Runaways goin' north; settlers headin' west. You meet someone, you never can be sure you'll see 'em the next day. Next day or next month or next year they may be off. Elsie and I are the veterans. How long you been in Oberlin?" she asked Mrs. Reed.

"Twelve years."

"I been here fifteen. That's ancient for most. Wellington was only settled in 1818, and it ain't even been officially incorporated yet. And Oberlin's newer than that."

"The town I am from is a thousand years old," Honor said.

Mrs. Reed and Belle chuckled. "Well then, honey, we're just little children to you," Belle said.

"That what you want, Honor Bright?" Mrs. Reed said. "A town with a thousand-year history, and people who live there all they lives? You in the wrong state for that."

"You want that rooted-down feeling, you go to Boston or Philadelphia," Belle added. "But they're only a couple hundred years old. Really you're in the wrong country. Maybe you should go back to England. What's stoppin' you?"

Honor thought of the penetrating nausea on board the *Adventurer*, of the weeks with no solid footing. But had she ever found her feet in America? Her stomach might be settled, but her legs still felt unsteady.

"Why you leave England in the first place?" Mrs. Reed asked. If she closed her eyes, Honor could not always tell who was asking the questions.

"My sister came here to marry, but died on the way."

"I didn't ask about your sister, I asked about *you*. You got family back in England?"

Honor nodded.

"Why didn't you stay with them? You didn't have to come with your sister."

Honor's mouth filled with a bitter taste, but she knew she must answer. "I was meant to marry, but he met another. He left the Society of Friends to be with her." Thinking of Samuel reminded Honor that soon she too would no longer be a Friend.

"So? That don't mean you couldn't stay."

Honor took a breath and forced herself to voice what she had never said aloud, or even allowed herself to think clearly. "Back home there was a slot in which my life was meant to fit. Then it was taken away and it felt as if there was no place for me. I thought it better to go and start somewhere new. So I thought."

"That's a very American notion, leaving problems behind and movin' on," Belle said. "If you thought that, maybe you're not so English after all. Maybe you got it in you to start over. Now, name me some things you *like* about Ohio."

When Honor did not immediately answer, Belle added, "I can tell you one thing." She nodded at Mrs. Reed's hat. "Maple leaves. You're always pointing out that red they change to in the fall, saying that don't happen with English trees."

Honor nodded. "Yes, they are beautiful. And the cardinals, and the red-bellied woodpeckers. I did not think birds could be so red. I also like hummingbirds." She paused. "Fresh corn. Popcorn. Maple syrup. Peaches. Fireflies. Chipmunks. Dogwood trees. Some of the quilts." She glanced at Mrs. Reed, thinking of the quilt in her front room.

"Listen to you. Not so bad, is it? You keep lookin', with an open mind, and you'll find more."

A sound came then from the cradle: Comfort was not crying, but simply announcing, in her baby way, I am here.

"Ah, baby girl." Before Honor could move, Mrs. Reed had lifted

Comfort from the cradle and was holding her against her chest and patting her back. Comfort did not cry, but lay in the stranger's arms, accepting where she was. "Love the feeling o' babies' weight," Mrs. Reed said. "They like a sack o' cornmeal, just settin' there all solid and waitin' to be eaten up." She smacked her lips against the baby's ear. "I love me some babies."

Honor looked at her daughter and had for a moment that patchwork feeling of being locked into place, and fitting. This time it was not with Jack, but with two women, alike in ways that made their skin color irrelevant. But she knew it could not last: Mrs. Reed had her own community, and Belle—sitting now, already drained of whatever energy she had stored during the night—would not last long. Honor could not remain here; she saw that. The question was whether she could find that settled feeling elsewhere.

The sound was so loud that Belle and Mrs. Reed shouted. It made Honor go silent, though, and so did Comfort, though after a second she began to scream.

Donovan had broken down the back door, kicking it in so that the hinges twisted and the glass shattered. The women jumped up and swung to face him, Mrs. Reed holding tight to Comfort.

"Jesus Christ Almighty, Donovan, what are you doing?" Belle cried. "God damn you, breakin' down my door! You're gonna pay to have that fixed. Hell, I'll make *you* fix it."

"Havin' yourselves a little tea party, are you, ladies?" Donovan said. "Sorry to interrupt, but I'm lookin' for someone."

"She ain't here—you missed her by a week."

"I ain't missed her—she's right here." He grinned at Mrs. Reed.

"What you want with me?" Mrs. Reed looked grim. Comfort was no longer screaming, but had settled into a steady wail.

"Stop that goddamned baby crying," Donovan growled.

Mrs. Reed handed Comfort to Honor, who wrapped the baby in her shawl to protect her from the cold air coming in through the gap where the door had been.

"What you want with me?" Mrs. Reed repeated.

"Got a little business to take care of. Your old master in Virginia will be mighty pleased to see you back after all these years. Even if you an old woman now, he might still get some work out o' you."

"What the hell are you talkin' about?" Belle interjected. "She's a free woman, lives in Oberlin."

"Oh, I know where Mrs. Reed lives, dear sister," Donovan answered. "In that little red house on Mill Street, got all the interesting activity goin' on. I know all about her—ran away from her master twelve years ago, her and her daughter. Don't worry, I'll be lookin' for her too, and your granddaughter. Take you back all together. It'll be worth it for the baby, grow up to make a fine slave, if she ain't been spoiled yet by freedom." He pronounced the last word as if it were a disease.

"You can't do that," Belle protested. "She's protected by the law. And the baby was born free."

"You know very well the Fugitive Slave Law gives me the power to take her back even if she ran away years ago." He turned to Mrs. Reed. "Tell me, what are you doin' down here having coffee with my sister and Honor Bright? That was a risk, wasn't it, strayin' so far from home, for what—her?" He jerked his head at Honor.

Mrs. Reed did not answer except with the tight line of her mouth.

Comfort had stopped crying and was now hiccuping. "Donovan, please leave Mrs. Reed alone," Honor said in a low voice. She knew why he was doing this: to punish her for having a child with Jack. "Comfort and I will leave Wellington tomorrow and thee will never have to see us again. Please."

"Too late for that." Donovan gazed at her and Comfort as if from a distance, his eyes flat, and Honor understood that something had clicked back into place, a way of thinking that was easier for him. The moment when they had stood together looking at the stumps outside Oberlin and he had offered to change for her now seemed a very long time ago.

He took from his pocket a length of rope. Grabbing Mrs. Reed's wrists, he twisted them behind her back and tied them together, all in a quick motion, as if expecting her to fight. Mrs. Reed did not fight, however. She simply looked at him over her shoulder, the spectacles blanking out her eyes.

Then Belle ran at him and was on his back like a cat, beating at him and trying to choke him. Though her action surprised him, Belle was so weak that her blows had little effect, and Donovan threw her off easily. Honor stumbled over and crouched by her where she fell. Belle moved her hand a little. "Don't mind me. Help Elsie." For a moment Honor did not know whom she meant, then remembered: it was Mrs. Reed's first name. Honor had never asked her.

Donovan was already dragging his prize out of the back door and down the porch steps. Mrs. Reed did not resist so much as simply let her weight slump; in that way she seemed to maintain her dignity. He dragged her through the frosty crabgrass at the side of the house to the front and into Public Square. It was a cold, gray morning, and very still. Honor followed, still holding Comfort, who gasped in the chilly air, but otherwise remained silent. "Please stop, Donovan," Honor called, knowing that it would have no effect. She looked around the square, hoping a neighbor would be out who might help. But it was deserted—everyone was at church. Even the hotel bar was empty.

Everyone except her husband: Jack Haymaker was walking down Main Street from the north in his broad-brimmed black hat

and his black coat, his suspenders flashing against his white shirt as
he moved. He was carrying a bunch of late asters from his mother's
front garden. Moving steadily, he smiled as he caught sight of
Honor and Comfort. Honor had never thought she would be so
relieved to see him. "Jack!" she cried, and ran to him.

Jack's smile vanished, however, as he recognized Donovan, now
struggling to get Mrs. Reed onto his horse.

"Thee must help us!" Honor urged as she reached her husband.

Jack stared at Donovan. He cleared his throat. "Friend, what is
thee doing?"

Donovan turned. Taking in the family triangle before him, he
smiled. "Jack Haymaker," he drawled. "Just the man I need. I been
meanin' to get you to help me with another runaway, but out of
respect for your wife, I ain't asked till now. Help me get this nigger
up on my horse. She and I got a little trip to take."

"I don't need his help to get up on this here horse," Mrs. Reed
interjected. "You jes' give me a leg up and I'll get on. Don't need to
involve them Quakers in this."

"Oh yes, I *do* need to involve 'em. So, Haymaker, you gonna help
me and upset your wife, or break the law and ruin your farm and
family? You chose the law last time I asked. You gonna do the same
this time too? I hope so. You got a daughter now."

Jack turned pale. He glanced at Honor, and she felt a familiar
sickening twist in her stomach. "Jack—" she began.

"Don't you do it, Jack Haymaker," Mrs. Reed interrupted. "This
man jes' tryin' to set your wife against you. Don't you dare help
him."

Jack looked around wildly. "Honor, I—" He took a step toward
Donovan.

Honor heard the click first. Somehow it seemed louder than the
explosion that followed.

She screamed. Longer and louder than ever in her life, she screamed as Donovan's chest burst like a red flower blooming; as his horse whinnied and bucked with the sound and broke free to run off down the street; as Mrs. Reed went, "Huh," as if someone had punched her in the gut, and reeled into the walkway in front of the shop; as Comfort stiffened with fright and matched her mother's scream with her own. Then Jack was gathering her and Comfort in his arms and squeezing them so tight that Honor could not breathe. She freed her face to draw in a breath, and saw over his shoulder Belle Mills, still standing by the side of the house, holding the shotgun she had once used to kill a copperhead. The gunpowder had sprayed into her face so that her yellowish skin was peppered with black. As Honor watched, Belle sank to her knees, her dress billowing around her, and laid the shotgun down in front of her.

The blast had seemed so loud that Honor thought it would bring people running. It was surprising how long it took for anyone to reach them. The owner appeared in the doorway of Wadsworth Hotel, wiping his hands on a towel, but did not come over. The group of men who emerged from the Methodist Church made slow progress down the center of the street, as if in a dream.

Honor was at Belle's side, holding Comfort.

"Don't worry 'bout me, honey," Belle said. "You know I'm dyin'. That's been clear since we first met. Noose'll make it go a little faster, is all."

Jack had cut loose Mrs. Reed's hands. She approached Belle. "I'm sorry you had to do that," she said, "but I thank you."

Belle nodded. "It ain't so hard choosin' between good and bad."

"I got to disappear now." Mrs. Reed glanced at the distant group of men. "Ain't never good for a Negro to be 'round a shooting."

"Go round the back down to the railroad tracks, then follow 'em out of town," Belle said. "They're less likely to go that way. I'm real glad to have met you, Elsie."

"Me too." Mrs. Reed removed her glasses and wiped her eyes. There had been no change in her face, but Honor saw now that she was crying.

She put her spectacles back on and wrapped her shawl tight around her. "I gon' pray for you." Mrs. Reed glanced at Honor and Jack. "All of you. If I ride fast enough I might jes' get to church before the service end." She headed around the shop toward the backyard, then looked back. "Bye bye, baby girl," she said to Comfort. "Get those parents to look after you good."

As if on cue, Comfort began to cry. Mrs. Reed smiled; then she turned and disappeared behind the shop.

"Honor," Belle whispered. "You see that bonnet in the window? Gray one I was workin' on?"

Honor glanced up at the gray bonnet with its sky-blue lining.

"That's yours. Time you had a change of color. But you knew that."

She did know it.

"Honor," Belle said again. "He dead?"

No one had gone to Donovan, who lay on his back, blood pooling in the road under him. His brown vest was shredded and turning a dark red. Next to him were his hat and the bunch of flowers Jack had dropped.

"He has not passed yet." Honor could feel his presence still, like a runaway in the woods.

"Nobody should have to die alone, not even a bastard like Donovan," Belle murmured. "Somebody needs to see him out. He's my brother."

The group of townsmen had arrived in Public Square, but stood back. They had taken in Belle and her shotgun, and were waiting for the drama to run its course.

Honor bit her lip. Then she got to her feet and went up to her husband. They gazed at each other. "We cannot continue as we were before," she said. "We must find a new way, different from thy family's."

Jack nodded.

"Now I have to do this."

Jack nodded again.

Honor handed their daughter to him and walked over to Donovan. Kneeling beside him, she saw, amid the meaty, metallic blood and torn cloth on his chest, the glistening key to her trunk. His brown vest was broken up with tiny yellow stripes. I will use some of it for the next quilt, she thought, for he should be a part of it.

Honor looked into his face. His eyes were closed, his mouth a grimace that told her death was waiting.

Then Donovan opened his eyes. Honor could just make out the black flecks in them, suspended in the brown.

"Hold my hand, Honor Bright," he said.

And she did, squeezing until she felt the Light fade.

Dearest Biddy,

This is the last letter I shall write from Faithwell. When I finish it I must pack away my writing things, to go in the wagon with our other belongings. Tomorrow Jack and Comfort and I are going west. All winter we have been debating where to go. For the moment we will head to Wisconsin, which Friends from Faithwell have gone to and written well of. There are prospects for dairy farms there. I have heard too that parts of the west have what they call prairie, with few trees and a great open space. I look forward to that.

We have been waiting for the winter to pass, and for Dorcas to marry. She did, last week, to a dairy farmer who has moved here. He is taking on the farm—and Judith Haymaker as well. We gave her the choice to come with us or remain in Faithwell, and I am relieved to report she has decided to stay. She says she has moved enough. I am content to accept that as her reason.

We are leaving most things behind, for we can buy or make them where we are going. We are taking four quilts, however. (I am very glad now that I sent thy quilt back to thee!) The signature quilt from Bridport, of course, whose names will remain dear to me always, wherever I go. Our marriage quilt, made so quickly by the Faithwell women. It is not the finest stitching, but it is warm—sometimes that is the most one should expect of a quilt. I have also made a small cot quilt for Comfort out of scraps of material from both Dorset and Ohio. It is in a patchwork pattern called Ohio Star, made up of triangles and squares in brown and yellow, red, cream and rust. Comfort sleeps well under it. Finally, a Negro woman called Mrs Reed has given me a quilt I once admired, made up of blue, cream, grey, brown and yellow strips of cloth. It is very different from any quilt thee will have seen, for *there is a pleasing randomness to it that defies description. I would like to learn to make such a quilt. Perhaps in the west I shall.*

Thee will be pleased to hear that for the first time I spoke at Meeting, the last I attended in Faithwell. I have always felt that words cannot truly capture what I feel inside. But I found the urgency of the Spirit pushing me to open my mouth to explain, even imperfectly, what I feel about helping runaways until that day arrives when slavery is finally ended in this country. For I do believe it will end. It must. When I sat down, the air felt thick with thoughts, and afterwards the blacksmith commended me for finding my voice.

I am not sorry to leave Ohio and go west, except that it is taking me farther from thee, Biddy. I will write again once we have found a place to settle. Because thee remains there, it is easier for me to go, for thee can be the shore I look back on, the star that remains fixed. After the voyage across the ocean, I had not thought I would ever have the spirit to move again, but now that I have chosen to go, I am glad.

I am anxious, of course. I expect I shall not sleep tonight for thinking about what lies ahead. But I feel different from when I left Bridport with Grace. Then I was running away, and it was as if my eyes were shut and there was nothing to hold on to. Now my eyes are open, and I can walk forward, holding on to Jack and Comfort. It is what Americans do. Perhaps that is what I am becoming, at last. I am learning the difference between running from and running towards.

Always with thee in spirit,

Thy faithful friend,

Honor Haymaker

Acknowledgments

I have used many resources to create this book, but here are a few for those who want to pursue some of its subjects.

On the Underground Railroad and abolition: *The Underground Railroad from Slavery to Freedom* by Wilbur H. Siebert (1898) is the classic from which all the others draw their material; *Let My People Go: The Story of the Underground Railroad and the Growth of the Abolition Movement* by Henrietta Buckmaster (1941); *Freedom's Struggle: A Response to Slavery from the Ohio Borderlands* by Gary L. Knepp (2008).

On Quakers: *The Quaker Reader*, edited by Jessamyn West (1962); *An Introduction to Quakerism* by Pink Dandelion (2007); *Reminiscences of Levi Coffin, the Reputed President of the Underground Railroad*, edited by Ben Richmond (1991); *Slavery and the Meetinghouse: The Quakers and the Abolitionist Dilemma, 1820–1865* by Ryan P. Jordan (2007); *A Fine Meeting There Is There: 300 Years of Bridport's Quaker History* by Suzanne Finch (2000; thank you, Marian Vincent, for finding this for me).

On Oberlin and its surrounds: *Oberlin: The Colony and the College* by James H. Fairchild (1883); *The Town that Started the Civil War* by

Nat Brandt (1990); *A Place on the Glacial Till: Time, Land, and Nature Within an American Town* by Thomas Fairchild Sherman (1997).

Quilts: There are many books on quilts and their fascinating history, but those most useful to Honor's quilting were *Quilts in Community: Ohio's Traditions*, edited by Ricky Clark (1991), *Classic Quilts from the American Museum in Britain* by Laura Beresford and Katherine Hebert (2009), and *Philena's Friendship Quilt: A Quaker Farewell to Ohio* by Lynda Salter Chenoweth (2009).

Writing from the period: *Buckeye Cookery and Practical Housekeeping* (1877; thanks to Carole DeSanti for lending me this treasure); *Our Cousins in Ohio* by Mary Botham Howitt (1849)—less a novel, more a year in the life of an Ohio farm; and, of course, *Uncle Tom's Cabin* by Harriet Beecher Stowe (1852). For nineteenth-century English views on Americans, you can't do better than *Domestic Manners of the Americans* by Frances Trollope (1832) and *American Notes* by Charles Dickens (1842); although both were highly critical of the United States, many of their observations still hold true today.

I am grateful to many people for their help with this book.

In Ohio: Gwen Mayer, Hudson's most passionate archivist, and Sue Flechner, for her generous hospitality. I am sorry that Hudson did not figure larger; however, it did provide me with a name and profession: Belle Mills the milliner, for which I owe Hudson a great debt. Tim Simonson on Wellington history; Bob Gordon on farming; and a special thank-you to Maddie Shetler for twice showing me around her family farm. Various unsung helpers at the Oberlin Heritage Center and Oberlin College Archives. Finally, my biggest thanks are to Kathie Linehan and Glenn Loafmann for many and varied services on the ground (and, with Glenn, up in the air!), from sending maps to finding answers to big and small questions, connecting me with knowledgeable people, flying me over the landscape of the novel, putting me up and up with me, and taking such an active interest in my Ohio research that they became a part of the process itself. Oberlin is a special place, and Kathie and Glenn are head of the class of its finest inhabitants.

Hats: Rose Cory and her millinery class in Woolwich, and Shelley Zetuni for introducing me; Oriole Cullen at the Victoria and Albert Museum, London.

Quilts: Of course I had to learn to make them myself. Thanks to Fiona Fletcher for teaching me the basics; and to the Flying Geese quilting group in north London, who have been so helpful and supportive through every step of making my first quilt. May your stitches always be even.

Quakers: Christopher Densmore at Swarthmore College for answering my varied queries; Hampstead Meeting for shared hours of waiting in expectation.

I would like to thank John Wieland for buying the privilege of having a wood named after him, in an auction to raise funds for the Woodland Trust, a UK charity devoted to woodland conservation.

For wordsmithery, thanks to Richenda Todd and Rick Ball.

Finally, thanks as ever to my handholders: Clare Ferraro and Denise Roy at Dutton, Katie Espiner at HarperCollins, Jonny Geller at Curtis Brown and Deborah Schneider at Gelfman Schneider.

About the Author

Tracy Chevalier is the *New York Times* bestselling author of six previous novels, including *Girl with a Pearl Earring*, which has been translated into thirty-nine languages and made into an Oscar-nominated film. Born and raised in Washington, D.C., she lives in London with her husband and son.